A Matter of Trust

BlackThorpe Security

Book 3

Kimberly Rae Jordan

THREE**STRAND**
P R E S S

A CORD OF THREE STRANDS IS NOT EASILY BROKEN.

A man, a woman & their God.

Three Strand Press publishes Christian Romance stories

that intertwine love, faith and family.

Always clean. Always heartwarming. Always uplifting.

1

MELANIE THORPE watched Justin Morrell and his girlfriend, Alana Jensen, make their way across the crowded room. The muscled man had his arm around Alana's shoulders, his expression softening as he looked down at her. Justin was not a man known for adoring looks and blatant affection. That he indulged in both with Alana—without a care for who saw them—was a true indication of the love he had for the woman. A knot tightened in Melanie's stomach as her gaze followed them to where they stopped to congratulate Than Miller and Lindsay Hamilton on their engagement.

She had thought that Justin was a die-hard bachelor. Married to the job. Devoted to BlackThorpe. Instead, Alana had walked into his life, and suddenly, the intense focus he'd had on his job had faded away to a more normal one. It hadn't taken long for him to start walking around with the same look that Eric McKinley, Trent Hause, and Than had had on their faces as they'd fallen in love.

Justin was a good man. If Melanie had been interested in having a man in her life, he would have been one she'd consider. But things had worked out as they should. Alana was good for him. She'd pulled emotion from him that no one else had, and her friend was happier than she'd ever seen him in the years they'd known each other.

For a brief moment—as she studied the two couples standing together—Melanie wondered what it would be like to fall in love. Truly fall in love with a person you could trust with your heart. Your life. Someone whose love brought happiness, not fear.

"What did Justin do to tick you off?"

Melanie turned to look at the woman sitting next to her at the round table. Her sister's blue eyes were narrowed as she waited for an answer to her question.

Leaning back in her chair, Melanie crossed her legs and rested her hands in her lap. "He didn't do anything."

"Then why are you scowling at him and Alana?"

"I wasn't scowling *at* them." Melanie let out a sigh. "I was thinking about something else."

"Were you thinking about the changes you're going to make when you turn thirty?" Adrianne asked, a grin lifting the corners of her mouth.

"Changes?" Melanie had actually been trying to avoid thinking about the birthday that was just around the corner. "What kind of changes?"

Adrianne reached out to tug a short strand of her hair. "Well, for starters, you could lose the goth look."

"It's not goth." Melanie lifted her chin. "Besides, I like this look and don't see any reason to change."

"I kinda—sorta—get the hair. I mean, the dark brown hair is beautiful, but why do you keep wearing those colored contacts? It's like you don't want to look anything like Alex or me."

"Not looking like you guys has nothing to do with it. I just...it's a personal preference." And after fourteen years of sporting the short dark brown hair and brown eyes, Melanie had almost forgotten what she used to look like.

Almost.

"Well, then the next thing you need to change is your approach to dating."

That made Melanie laugh. "You're one to talk, Annie."

Adrianne's eyebrows drew together at the use of the nickname. "At least I go out on dates. You just flat out turn down any guy brave enough to ask."

Melanie's gaze moved from Adrianne to Alex, their brother, Adrianne's twin. He currently sat with his head bent, listening to something Marcus Black was saying. Of the three of them, Adrianne was the one who dated the most, but even she hadn't found someone that she wanted to date for more than a month or two.

Alex was more like her than his twin. He didn't date, period. Melanie had no clue why he never asked anyone out, but she didn't press him about it as she had her own reasons for avoiding dating.

She hoped that Adrianne would find someone to marry soon. It would be great if she could give their parents the wedding and the grandchildren they kept pestering for because Melanie sure wasn't going to be the one to give them either of those things.

"Maybe for your birthday I'll set up a profile for you on one of those online dating sites," Adrianne said.

"Go for it," Melanie challenged her. "I'll just change my profile to your picture and all your details. *Loves long walks on the beach, sitting in front of a blazing fire and knitting socks for all my family.*"

"Only if you can crack the password."

"I know people who can do that for me," Melanie said with a smirk.

Adrianne rolled her eyes. "And for the record, I only gave you guys socks for *one* Christmas."

"It's not a talent that should be overlooked when searching for a mate," Melanie told her. "I mean, we do live in Minnesota after all. You never know when you'll need to keep your feet warm during a snowstorm."

Adrianne gave her a frustrated look before turning her attention to the other side of the room. "They sure do look happy, don't they?"

Melanie had to agree with her sister. Than and Lindsay looked deliriously happy, and she was glad for them. But now with them engaged, and Justin and Alana looking like they were on their way to that point as well, half the BlackThorpe management team was off the market. That left her, Adrianne, Alex and Marcus. If she had to put her money on one of them, she'd put it on Adrianne. After all, a person had to actually date in order to find someone to marry.

All she knew for certain was that that person wouldn't be her.

Tyler Harris propped his elbows on the desk and pressed the heels of his hands against his eyes. He'd been staring at the computer screen for way too long without a break.

Pushing away from his desk, Tyler stood. He steadied himself on one foot before carefully shifting his weight to the other. For the next couple of minutes, he stretched his body side to side to ease the tightness in his back.

Deciding that a fresh cup of coffee would help his focus, Tyler leaned over his desk to snag his travel mug, grimacing when a muscle spasmed in his back. Hopefully, the walk to the lunch room would help to work out any remaining kinks in his body.

As he straightened, he heard a rap on his door. Swinging around, Tyler spotted Melanie Thorpe standing in the doorway and smiled.

"Hey. Long time no see." It had been a couple of weeks since he'd last seen her. Busy work schedules had kept their paths from crossing lately. "What are you doing in my neck of the woods?"

She returned his smile, her expression warm albeit a bit reserved. "Do you have a minute to chat?"

"For you? Always."

Tyler waited until she'd seated herself in the chair on the other side of his desk before he settled back in the one he'd been so relieved to get out of just moments earlier. Melanie's dark eyes regarded him as he waited for her to begin their conversation.

As he had ever since they'd first met and he'd realized who she was, Tyler had tried to figure out why Melanie looked so different from her siblings. With her short dark brown hair and piercing nearly-black eyes, she presented a striking picture that was pretty much the opposite of Alex and Adrianne. He'd commented on it once, but she'd just brushed it aside as looking like different sides of the family.

"I hope I'm not interrupting you," she said, waving her hand at the piles of paper on his desk.

"Nope." Tyler leaned back in his chair, interlacing his fingers behind his head. "I was getting ready to take a break anyway."

"I won't keep you too long." She paused. "I'm here to ask a favor."

"What's that?" Tyler asked even though he had a feeling he knew what the favor would be. It was one she'd asked of him before, and one he never refused.

"We've had a new guy at the Wellness Center for a week or so, but he's resisting any type of rehabilitation."

Frowning, Tyler lowered his arms and sat forward. "If he doesn't want the help, why is he there?"

BlackThorpe's program to help soldiers wounded overseas usually took in men and women who wanted to make use of the resources that the company had for them. To have someone taking a spot in the program who didn't want to be there was a shame.

"We took him in as a favor. His older brother is a friend of Alex and Marcus. Unfortunately, it seems that he wants his sibling there more than his brother wants to be there."

Tyler dragged a hand through his hair, wincing as his fingers caught in a tangle of curls. "Let me guess. He needs prosthetics."

Melanie nodded. "Just one actually. Left leg."

"You want me to talk to him?" Tyler asked.

"If you have some time to stop by." Melanie smiled at him—a smile, that as usual, didn't quite reach her eyes. "You're our best success story."

Tyler shifted in his seat. It was true that he'd accomplished quite a bit with BlackThorpe's help. Not only had they assisted him with rehabilitation after his accident in Afghanistan, but Marcus had given him a job. He'd been working at the company for over five years now.

"What's the best time to drop by?" Tyler asked, his mind already flipping through his schedule for the next few days.

"He has therapy—not that he makes use of it—at nine and again at three, so sometime around then would be great."

"Okay. I'll try to stop by tomorrow."

Melanie got to her feet in one fluid movement. "Thanks so much, Tyler."

"You're welcome," Tyler said and stood as well, though not quite as smoothly as she had.

"Good to see you again." She gave him one last smile as she headed for the door. "See you tomorrow."

Tyler watched as she disappeared into the hallway, a bit perplexed at the quick visit. Usually, she'd spend a few minutes shooting the breeze with him, so the fact that she'd warmed the chair in his office for not even five minutes told him something was up with her. However, unless she offered up the information, he wouldn't learn anything. Neither of them pried into things the other person didn't choose willingly to share. No doubt some would say that made their friendship a little weird, but so far it had worked for them.

When they'd first met over six years ago, she'd been a student who worked part-time at the BlackThorpe Wellness Center while attending college. He'd been a wounded former soldier who was determined to get his life back to normal...or as close to normal as possible, with two prosthetic legs.

When he'd left the military hospital to return stateside, Tyler had decided he wanted to go someplace that would offer him well-rounded and intensive therapy as he worked to get his life back. That's when his stepfather, Hank, had given him information on the BlackThorpe Wellness Center.

At the time, his main source of support had come from his wife. *Kelly*. She'd come from Texas to be with him in Minnesota. But that hadn't lasted much beyond a couple of months. It wasn't long before she'd decided she needed to be home in Texas, to go back to her job. Her phone calls and visits gradually dropped off as she carried on with the life they'd once shared together...without him. Friends had been hinting that she'd found someone new not long after his accident, so the divorce papers hadn't been a huge surprise when they'd arrived six months after his accident.

Though she'd never said anything about the way Kelly had faded from his life, Melanie seemed to be around more once she'd gone. As a student, Melanie hadn't been in charge of his therapy or even involved in it really, but she'd taken the time each day to stop and chat if she saw him. Their conversations were rarely related to his recovery. Once she discovered he enjoyed basketball, she'd ask him how his team was doing. Sometimes she'd talk to him about something significant in the news.

He'd found himself enjoying their chats, grateful for a friendly face. She'd never flirted with him, and he'd appreciated that. It would have taken them to an awkward place because he had absolutely zero interest in any kind of relationship beyond friends. And he still felt that way— although to a somewhat lesser degree. Once burned was definitely twice shy in his situation. Eventually, she'd graduated and after a year working as a psychologist, counseling the men and women who came through the doors, Melanie had stepped into the role of director of the Wellness Center.

When he'd gotten to the point where he was able to do most of what he wanted on his prosthetics, Marcus had approached him about working for BlackThorpe. With no other direction in his life, Tyler hadn't hesitated to accept the job offer. And while he really wasn't thrilled about the winters in Minnesota, everything else in his life was good so he wouldn't complain. Much.

Tyler and Melanie had kept up their casual friendship over the years since, chatting at least once a week. They'd go out for dinner with a group of people from BlackThorpe once in a while and occasionally had coffee when they had the time. They were in contact enough that when two weeks had gone by without seeing or hearing from her, Tyler had started to worry.

He still wasn't convinced that everything was okay with her, but he wasn't sure he had the right to pry. It was somewhat perplexing to him why he suddenly seemed to *want* to.

Snagging his mug, Tyler made his way out of the office and down the hall to where the lunchroom for their floor was situated. There was a small deli on the main floor, but each floor also had its own lunchroom. As he walked into the brightly lit room, he spotted one of his good friends sitting at a table near one of the large windows looking out over the skyline of the Twin Cities.

"Hey, Ryan," Tyler called out as he approached the coffee machine.

"Yo!" His friend twisted to give him a salute. "How's it going?"

"It's going." Tyler finished doctoring his coffee and joined Ryan at his table. "Melanie stopped by to see if I'd meet with a vet who's having a hard time with the rehab."

Ryan McFadden arched a dark brow over the mug he held. "I think she's just using that as an excuse to talk to you."

"Get real." Tyler let out a huff at his friend's observation. "She doesn't need an excuse to talk to me. We're friends."

"Maybe you should consider becoming more," Ryan said as he tilted his mug to his lips, a grin teasing the corners of his mouth. This wasn't the first time he'd offered this particular piece of advice, but Tyler wasn't any more inclined to take it this time than he had been on previous occasions.

"Not a chance." Tyler stretched out his legs, glad for the break from his computer. "Just following your lead, my friend. You seem to have no interest in taking any of your female friendships to the next level."

Tyler still hadn't figured out why the man didn't date. It certainly had nothing to do with his looks since Tyler had inside knowledge that the ladies found Ryan attractive. He got asked on a regular basis if his friend was available. Even after leaving the military, Ryan had kept up his exercise regime and that combined with his black hair and green eyes apparently kept the women interested.

"We still on for Friday night?"

Tyler nodded, grateful for the change of subject. "Have to be at the church by six. We'll have pizza and then chaperone for the night."

"Can't believe I'm a chaperone." Ryan scowled. "Guess I really have to accept that I've grown up."

"Nah. We just have to make *other* people think that."

"Max came to talk to me last week about how to approach a girl he liked." Ryan shook his head. "It made me feel old...like I was his dad or something."

"Well, better he went to you than me. I'm obviously a fail in that department." He bent his head and stared at the liquid in his mug, thoughts of the divorce he'd never wanted churning through his mind. He would have stuck by Kelly if their roles had been reversed. But clearly, she'd viewed him as less of a man because he'd lost the lower portion of both his legs.

"Tyler?"

"Hmmm?" He looked up and saw a big grin had replaced the scowl on Ryan's face just before the guy turned to face the window. Slowly, Tyler swung around to see Melanie standing a few feet from the table. When he made a move to get to his feet, she motioned for him to stay seated.

He had to tilt his head back to meet her gaze. "What's up?"

"I just remembered that Simon has a doctor's appointment in the morning, so the afternoon would be better if you planned to come out tomorrow."

"Okay. I'll keep that in mind."

"Thanks." Her gaze flicked to Ryan and a smile curved her lips. "Good to see you again, Ryan."

"You too, Melanie."

Tyler looked at his friend and then to Melanie. Was she interested in him? He watched her leave the room then turned to Ryan.

"Maybe there's something between *you* two?" The idea felt all kinds of wrong to him, but he wouldn't begrudge his friends any happiness they might find together.

"No." Ryan frowned as he crossed his arms over his chest. "I would never do that to you, man. Besides, I have no interest in her."

Do *what* to him? "Why not? She's beautiful, smart and has a great sense of humor."

"Sorry. Not interested," Ryan said again. "Still think maybe you should be the one."

Tyler rolled his eyes and shook his head again. They were quite a pair, the two of them. They were neighbors, sharing a side-by-side duplex that his stepfather had bought to give him a place to stay once he'd left the Center. He'd managed the rental on the other side for several years, but when his previous neighbors had left earlier in the year, he'd offered the place to Ryan, who'd moved to the Twin Cities and started working at BlackThorpe.

They'd quickly become best friends as they bonded over their jobs, sports, video games and their involvement at the church they both attended. The only disagreement they'd ever really had was over Ryan's insistence that he should ask Melanie out on a date. Unfortunately, it was an ongoing one.

Melanie sighed as she walked down the hallway to the elevators. It was time to leave the fortress—as she liked to call the BlackThorpe compound in the Twin Cities—and return to the place she loved. If it weren't for the Tuesday morning meetings, she'd never come to the company headquarters. She'd tried to get out of the meetings, but it never worked.

Today's meeting had included a little bit of fun news. Justin had announced that he and Alana had gotten engaged. Though she was happy for them, Melanie had felt a pang of...something at the joy on Justin's face when he'd shared the announcement.

She punched the button on the elevator with a little more force than necessary. If only her mom would just back off and leave well enough alone. It was the constant pressure on the three of them to get married that had begun to put unwanted thoughts in her mind. Relationships made one vulnerable, and she wasn't going to be that way ever again.

The doors of the elevator slid open, and Melanie was relieved to see it was empty. She stepped inside and pressed the button for the basement parking garage. She relaxed against the wall, tilting her head back and closing her eyes.

There was just too much love-induced happiness floating around lately. And she should be happy for them. She *was* happy for them. It was just that never had her decision to not trust love been so tested.

Melanie thought of what she knew about Alana, the abusive background she'd come from, and yet she was choosing to trust Justin's love for her. Lindsay chose to trust the love Than said he had for her even though up until that point he'd been more interested in serial dating than a serious committed relationship.

She wanted so badly to believe it would be okay for her too. That if she took a chance on loving someone, they wouldn't betray her.

"You're beautiful, Lanie." The emotion in his dark chocolate brown eyes pulled her in. "You take my breath away."

Melanie ducked her head, her cheeks heating beneath the warmth of his gaze. She'd just turned sixteen and was falling in love for the first time. It was so wonderful. Everything she'd ever dreamed it would be. "You're not so bad yourself."

She wanted to smack herself in the head. That wasn't what she should have said.

He slid his hand over hers, entwining their fingers. "Want to go somewhere special tonight?"

She glanced at him through her lashes. "Special?"

He'd been the ultimate gentleman. They'd shared kisses, but he'd never pressured for anything more. Was that about to change?

"Yes. I'd like to take you for a nice dinner."

A meal together? Something besides McDonalds after youth group or hot dogs at a football game? "That would be lovely."

There had been just one dinner before things had gone horribly wrong. What followed that dinner had been two weeks of unending horror. All because she'd believed a guy when he'd said he loved her.

The elevator stopped with a bounce and jarred her from the past. Melanie took a deep breath and let it out, willing the images to fade from her memory.

She was safe.

But if she wanted to stay that way, she could never trust herself to love again.

2

IT ENDED UP being Thursday before Tyler was able to make it to the Center. Marcus had wanted to meet with him Wednesday afternoon and by the time they were done, it was too late to head out.

As he pulled through the security gate of the Center, Tyler had to admit he was looking forward to a change of scenery for a couple of hours. The latest project Marcus had given him required a lot of computer time, and his body was starting to rebel. It was normal for him to spend a lot of time at the computer, but this was on top of his normal workload.

Once he found a parking spot, he got out of his SUV and made his way through the parking lot to the front doors of the large BlackThorpe Wellness Center. They had expanded it a lot since he'd been there to try to regain his life after his injury. He knew that while BlackThorpe financially supported the Center, it was also sustained by the contributions of many families and other corporations. It was through those donations that BlackThorpe had been able to bring the place to its present level.

Two sets of large glass doors slid open as Tyler approached them, and he stepped into the foyer of the building. A curved desk sat directly in front of the door, and he lifted a hand in greeting to the woman who sat behind it.

"Afternoon, Molly," he said as he neared the desk. "How are you doing?"

The middle age woman smiled. "I'm doing great, Tyler. And you?"

"Can't complain." He waved his hand to the second floor. "I'm here to see Melanie."

Molly nodded. "She's in her office. You can go on up."

"Thanks," Tyler said as he turned and headed for the stairs that would take him to the floor where Melanie had her office.

The staircase curved slightly, and as he climbed, Tyler could look out the floor to ceiling windows that ran the whole front of the building. Though part of the view was of the parking lot, the rest of it was of the acreage that lay beyond the building. Trees and grass created a park-like setting that had paths and trails for residents and their visitors to use.

When he reached the second floor, Tyler walked to the railing that ran around the edge of part of the second floor. To his right were the offices of the people who worked at the Center and to the left were some of the rooms used by the people who were there for long-term rehabilitation.

Gripping the metal rail, he leaned forward and looked down. The space was all open from the main floor up to the third floor. The roof was all glass so that natural light spilled over the space below. There were lots of plants and flowers and places for people to sit and relax. Even in the dead of winter, they could enjoy the beauty of nature and sunlight. Soothing instrumental music played softly in the background, adding to the ambiance along with gentle sounds from a waterfall that stood in the middle of the room.

Pushing back from the railing, Tyler turned and headed down the hallway. Just briefly observing the area below had been soothing for him. Hopefully, his meeting with Melanie and the vet didn't disrupt that too much.

"Hey, Tyler."

Tyler smiled at Heather, Melanie's assistant, where she sat at a desk just outside Melanie's office. "Is Melanie available? She asked me to come talk with one of the vets."

Heather nodded. "She said you might be stopping by. Go on in."

Tyler approached the door that was open a couple of inches and grasped the handle. As he pushed it open, he spotted Melanie behind her desk, phone receiver pressed to her ear. When she saw him, she waved for him to come in.

As usual, she looked striking with her short dark hair artfully styled—short in some places, long in others—and makeup accenting her dark eyes. As he watched her, Tyler had to admit she was something of an enigma to him. At first glance, one would assume she was dainty and delicate given her slender build and lack of height, but there was an air of strength that surrounded her. She was definitely capable and confident, but it was more than that.

"I'll give you a call back once I have more information," Melanie said to whoever was on the other end. "Talk to you soon."

Tyler wasn't sure if he should sit, but as soon as she hung up the phone, Melanie got up. "Thanks for coming, Tyler. Simon is in physical therapy right now, so why don't we head over there."

"Sounds good," Tyler said as he stepped back so she could precede him from the office. He noticed she wore her usual work attire which consisted of a pantsuit and high heels that brought the top of her head an inch or so above his shoulder.

"I'm just taking Tyler to meet Simon," Melanie told Heather. "I have my phone if anyone is looking for me."

Once out of the office, Tyler fell into step with Melanie as they headed further down the hallway. They passed several offices before reaching a set of large doors. Tyler pushed one of them open and held it for Melanie, catching a whiff of her familiar perfume as she walked by him.

The atmosphere beyond the doors was different from where they'd just left. This was the more practical area of the building. The main floor housed a couple of pools and a sauna, but on the floor they were on, there were several areas with machines to help people regain strength or to learn to walk again. Basically anything that was necessary to help a vet physically get to where they wanted to be was available here.

"How long has it been since Simon's accident?" Tyler asked as they continued to walk along the hallway. This section didn't have the openness of the previous one.

"Fifteen months."

"That's quite a while. Why is he here now?"

"His family brought him after he refused any further care at the military hospital and then went on to drink himself into oblivion and tried to numb his pain with addictive painkillers. They see this as a last resort. They know he needs the psychological help we offer as well as the physical."

"The physical will never come until he gets the mental sorted out," Tyler commented, remembering those early days after the incident when he'd lost his legs. Waking up in the hospital with no memory of what had happened had been hard enough, but then he'd looked down to see where the blankets had flattened just beyond his knees and knew his life had changed forever.

"Yes, you're absolutely right. Some of the other guys who are here have tried to help Simon. You know we encourage them to be there for each other since they're all at different places on a similar journey. It just hasn't gotten through to him."

Tyler laid a hand on Melanie's arm, bringing her to a halt. When she turned to look at him, he said, "Why do you think I'll be able to?"

She stared at him for a moment, her dark gaze unreadable. "You've gone on to lead a full life. You're further along than the guys here so you can show him that life does go on, and it doesn't end just because he's missing part of his leg."

Tyler nodded and let his hand slide from her arm. He wasn't so sure he'd call his life full, but he was basically happy with it. "I'll do my best."

Melanie pushed open the door to a large room. In keeping with the natural light theme, this room also had floor to ceiling windows facing out the back of the building to the trees and grass that made up the view. She paused for a moment then headed in the direction of a man seated in a wheelchair looking out the window.

"Hi, Simon," Melanie said as she came to stand beside the wheelchair. "How are you doing today?"

The man shot her a look and then turned his attention back to the view, though Tyler would bet his last buck that the guy wasn't actually seeing it. If he had to guess, he'd say that Simon was seeing the sand of a desert on the other side of the globe.

"Same as yesterday." The man's voice was tight and low.

"I have someone I want you to meet." Melanie waved for Tyler to move to her side. "This is Tyler Harris. He works for BlackThorpe."

"Shrink or physio?" the man asked without even looking their way.

"Neither," Tyler said. "I work in security intelligence for BlackThorpe."

That got a look from Simon. "Intelligence? What do you want with me?"

Tyler looked at Melanie and gave her a nod as he snagged a nearby chair and swung it around. He straddled the seat and rested his hands on the back of it. "I'm not here because of my job."

Out of the corner of his eye, he saw Melanie move a little ways away, but she didn't leave the room.

"Then why are you here?"

"I've been where you are."

The man looked at him then, skepticism written all over his face. He had light blue eyes and his blond hair had long since passed the nape of his neck. Despite the dark circles and the haunted look in the guy's eyes, his youth was unmistakeable. "How's that? If you were in intelligence?"

"I was LRS." He didn't bother to use the longer name of Long Range Surveillance, the guy would know what he had been. "We ran into a bad situation."

Tyler really couldn't give him many more details from his own memory. He just knew what he'd been told by the medical personnel who were obviously reporting what they'd heard from the other members of his team who *did* remember. He'd been hurt the worst when the mine had gone off.

Simon looked at Tyler starting from the top of his head to his feet. "You look like you came out unscathed."

Tyler returned the favor, taking in the left leg where it ended just above the guy's knee. "Looks can be deceiving." He lowered his arms and hitched up his pant legs so Simon could see his two prosthetic limbs.

Simon's gaze met his briefly before sliding away. "You lost both?"

Tyler nodded. "Double amputation below the knee."

"So, I suppose you're here to show me that life goes on."

Tyler released his pant legs and rested his arms on the back of the chair again. "Actually, I'm not. You already know that life goes on. You even know that life can be better. Maybe not what you'd thought it would be, but still good. I'm sure the guys here have already shown and told you that. I'm here to try to help you decide that you're worth having that life."

When Simon's shoulders stiffened and his head bent forward, Tyler had a pretty good idea what the guy's mindset was. Simon didn't say anything and in the silence, Tyler prayed that God would give him the words to reach this man.

Melanie stood several feet away, arms crossed, observing Tyler with Simon. She had no idea how Simon would react to his presence and didn't want to leave them alone until she was sure he didn't outright reject Tyler.

Though there had been other people she could have asked to meet with Simon, for some reason she'd known that Tyler would be the best person for the job. And watching them together so far, it seemed she was right.

He sat there so casually, his tanned arms resting on the back of the chair and his white dress shirt—with sleeves haphazardly rolled up to his elbows—stretched across his shoulders. Given his curly somewhat out-of-control hair, Tyler wasn't a conventionally handsome man when compared to someone like Than Miller or Justin Morrell, but the compassionate way he dealt with people was something that Melanie admired.

Even when Tyler had first come to the Center, she'd figured he'd be frustrated and angry—like most the people who came to them tended to be initially—but he hadn't been. He'd been focused and determined, but he'd still taken the time to try to encourage the others there with him.

That was the main reason she was glad to be able to call him a friend, and why—when she had someone who needed encouragement, compassion, and hope—she went to him.

She couldn't hear what Tyler was saying to Simon, but the man slouched in the wheelchair didn't seem to be ignoring him, so that was a step in the right direction. Melanie glanced over to where Derrick, the physical therapist who had been trying to work with Simon, stood, his gaze on the two men.

Moving to Derrick's side, Melanie said in a low voice, "I'm going to head back to my office. If something happens, let me know. And could you ask Tyler to come by and see me when he's done here?"

When Derrick nodded, Melanie sent one more look toward Tyler and Simon before leaving the room. Once back in her office, she dove right into the files on her desk. Though she wasn't completely sure why, she felt the need to be distracted.

Melanie had been working for about half an hour when there was a knock on her door. Expecting to see Tyler, she was surprised when Adrianne walked in and made herself comfortable in one of the chairs across the desk from her.

"What brings you out this way?" Melanie asked as she settled back in her chair.

Adrianne grinned. "Do I need a reason to come see you?"

"Usually." Melanie looked at her older sister, wondering how different their relationship might have been if she'd made it through her teen years without incident like Adrianne had. People looking at them might assume they were close, which in some ways, they were, but Melanie knew the truth. If she considered herself close to anyone, it would be Adrianne, but it was hard to feel that they were super close when she kept so much of what she felt hidden.

"Actually, I come bearing some good news."

Melanie arched an eyebrow. "You got a date?"

"No," Adrianne said as she rolled her eyes. "This is business related. Me having a date isn't newsworthy. That would be the case if *you* had a date."

"Be nice or next time you're going out, I'll tell Mom."

This time, Adrianne glared at her. "Do you want to hear what I came to tell you or not?"

Almost five years separated them, but Melanie had learned young how to yank her older sister's chain. "I have a feeling you'll explode if you don't spill it."

Adrianne moved like she was going to get up out of her chair and leave, but then she flopped back into the chair and let out a heavy sigh. "Yeah. Okay. Fine. I do *have* to tell you this."

"So what's the news?" For all her teasing, Melanie was curious. Adrianne didn't come out to the Center very often.

"We got a large donation to the Center." Adrianne was BlackThorpe's Public Relations person and was responsible for events to connect with security clients as well as organizing fundraising. The way the Wellness Center had grown over the past several years was a testament to her skill at the job. "They've donated before but never this large."

"Who was it?" Melanie asked.

"It was given by Henry and Shauna Wakeford with thanks for helping someone special to them in honor of their birthday. It was for two million dollars."

"Wow." Melanie knew her eyes widened at the amount. "That's terrific, but the name doesn't ring any bells for me. How about you?"

"I did a quick search, and we don't have anyone in our files with that last name. Of course, they didn't say it was a son or daughter so it could be another relation."

Melanie scooted forward in her chair to rest her arms on the desk. "I suppose if they wanted us to know, they would have attached a name to the donation, right?"

Adrianne nodded. "Yep, that's true. I just wanted you to know because donations like that speak to the good work you're doing here with your team."

A knock on the door drew Melanie's attention from Adrianne. This time, it *was* Tyler who stood in the doorway.

"Hey, Tyler," Adrianne said with a smile at the man. "I didn't know you were over here."

Melanie waved her hand at the chair beside Adrianne. "Do you have a few minutes?"

Tyler nodded and sat down, stretching out his legs. "How're you doing, Adrianne?"

"Can't complain. How about you?"

"Pretty much the same."

"Tyler is here helping with a vet who's struggling," Melanie said. "How did it go with Simon?"

"About what you'd expect. I did most the talking this time around, telling him about my experiences. He seemed open to interaction with me, so maybe next time he'll do a little more talking."

"Thanks, Tyler. I think his family is at their wit's end and scared. Between the depression, the alcohol, and the pain meds, I think they're afraid they're losing him."

"Unfortunately, their concerns are valid. Some do slip away, but I think we can pull Simon back from the edge."

Melanie watched as Adrianne laid a hand on Tyler's arm and said, "BlackThorpe is fortunate to have you, not just as an employee, but as someone who can help others because of your own experiences."

Tyler looked at Adrianne, his expression serious. "I'm the one who's fortunate. I doubt I'd be where I am now without the help offered by BlackThorpe."

The two exchanged a smile before Adrianne moved her hand back to her lap. The urge to tell her sister to back off shocked Melanie. She had no claim on Tyler and didn't want to give him any ideas to the contrary. But man, it rubbed her the wrong way to see Adrianne being so friendly with him.

"Well, I'll leave you two to chat," Adrianne said as she got up. "I just wanted to share the good news."

"See you at home," Melanie called out as her sister walked out of the office. When it was just the two of them, she turned back to Tyler. "Thanks again for being willing to come by and meet with Simon."

"His outlook seems to be that he doesn't deserve to have his life any better than it is right now." Tyler dragged a hand through his curls, which only served to make them even more unruly. "Do you know the circumstances around the loss of his leg?"

Melanie thought back to the information in his file. "I believe his convoy was attacked and when the vehicle he was in flipped over, his leg was pinned underneath, crushing it. The resulting damage was too much to repair."

"Were there casualties?" Tyler sat forward, bracing his elbows on his knees. His deep blue eyes looked straight at her, so direct she fought the urge to look away. For the first time, she was afraid he could see right into her soul and the secrets she held so tightly there. "I just seem to be getting a feeling of survivor's guilt from the little he said."

"Yes, there were, but I don't know exactly how many or how they died." She dropped her gaze to a pile of folders on her desk. "I could get you the information from his file if you think it would help you to work with him."

"It would."

When he didn't say anything more, she looked up to find him watching her intently. Swallowing, she said, "Uh, I'll have to talk with Sharon—she's his counselor—to get the file. I can't give you the file itself and will have to make sure that I'm not giving you confidential information since technically you don't work for the Center."

"That's fine. If you give me dates, I can probably even find the information online."

"Once I've talked to Sharon, I'll give you a call with that info." Melanie shifted in her chair. "How do *you* find life now?"

Though they talked about a lot of other things when they were together, they didn't often speak of what had brought him to the Center in the first place.

Tyler stared at her for a moment, one eyebrow lifting slightly. "Are you asking as a shrink or my employer?"

Melanie's eyes widened at the question. "Neither. And I'm not your employer."

"Your name is part of the company."

"Well, that makes *Alex* your boss, not me."

Tyler grinned. "Okay, so then you're asking as a shrink?"

What was that flutter in her stomach from? Trying to ignore it, she asked, "How about as a friend?"

He tilted his head. "After leaving here, living with the prosthetics became my new normal, but after so many years with them, it's just...normal. It has its inconveniences, of course, but it's easier to adapt now than it used to be. Probably the hardest part is dealing with people who seem to feel I need sympathy." He paused, his jaw tightening. "I don't."

"You're a good role model, Tyler," Melanie said, wishing things were different for her because if they had been, she might have been able to love a man like him. But sadly, he deserved better than her. After all he'd dealt with, he deserved someone who didn't come with a ton of baggage.

"I hope I'm a good role model for more than just learning to live my life without my lower legs. There are people out there who have it much worse than me." Tyler crossed his arms. "The bottom line is that God gave me a second chance at life. I've been trying my best to make it count."

Melanie thought over his words. She'd been given a second chance as well, but she hadn't embraced it quite the way Tyler had. "Well, I appreciate you taking the time to help Simon. Hopefully, your outlook will rub off on him."

"I'm praying to that end," Tyler said as he pushed to his feet. "I'd better be going. I'll probably come back around on Monday. Is that okay?"

Melanie got to her feet as well. "That would be great."

"Have a good weekend," Tyler said with a smile then walked out of her office.

Melanie placed her hands flat on her desk and bent her head. What was happening to her? It was as if that night at Than and Lindsay's engagement party had created a crack in the walls she kept around her heart and emotions. And now a man she'd long considered her friend was starting to mean more to her than she wanted.

When they were just hanging out as friends, she could enjoy his presence because he was a fun person to be around. But it was at times like this when she saw exactly how deep his goodness went.

Was it possible that she could take another chance? For a moment, she allowed herself to consider it. But then memories swamped her, and her shoulders curved forward as she fought off the fear and pain that raced through her body with every rapid beat of her heart. Even if she convinced herself Tyler could be trusted, she was too messed up to be able to handle a relationship with someone like him.

While the counseling sessions she'd had and her own education hadn't been able to free her from the chains that bound her to the events of fourteen years ago, they did give her the tools to deal with moments like this.

Taking deep breaths, Melanie closed her eyes and sought the peaceful place in her mind.

The cabin. The crackle of the fire in the fireplace as it spreads its warmth into the room. The comfortable chair with a lamp next to it. The soft blanket covering my legs.

There's a storm raging outside but inside I'm safe. It's peaceful. Secure.

I am safe.

Deep breath in. Slow exhale.

I am safe.

Deep breath in. Slow exhale.

Melanie stayed there until her heartbeat calmed. She took several more deep breaths before straightening. When she opened her eyes, she wasn't surprised to find them damp. It had been awhile since her last attack, and even though she hated the moments of weakness with a passion, this time it had served as a clear reminder of why she couldn't have what other people had...even if her heart was beginning to awaken and long for it.

3

TYLER SETTLED onto the couch, phone in hand, wincing as his hip protested the movement. A game of basketball had gotten a little too competitive with a bunch of the guys on Saturday night. While most of the time he was fairly agile, he and a couple others had crashed to the floor as they tried to get their hands on a loose ball. His hip had taken the brunt of his fall, and it had already started to turn a delightful shade of purple.

When his phone rang as it did every Sunday afternoon at four o'clock, he tapped the screen to accept the call and then pressed it to his ear. "Hello, Momma."

"Hi, darling!" His mother's voice floated over the telephone line. "How are you doing?"

"I'm doing really well. How about you?" Knowing that question would open up a five-minute monologue by his mom on everything she'd done that week, Tyler leaned his head back against the couch.

He responded appropriately throughout her report then braced himself for the next question. "So have you met a nice young lady yet?"

This had started about six months ago. Every. Single. Week. The same question. "I've met several, actually, Momma, but none that I'm dating. I don't have time for that right now. Marcus just dumped a huge project into my lap, so between work and church, I don't have time for dating."

"You need to *make* time, sweetheart. You're going to be turning thirty-one soon. It's time you settled down."

Tyler almost laughed at that. He really couldn't be any more settled than he was. "Well, I'll keep that in mind."

"On the subject of your birthday, we'll be arriving the day before so we can spend some time with you. Hope that's okay."

Of course, it was okay. They'd spent every birthday together except the two when he was overseas. "It's fine, Momma. Perfect, in fact."

"And it's okay I'm not coming alone?"

Tyler rubbed a hand over his face, wondering why they were still having this discussion after almost twelve years. "Again, it's fine, Momma. You know I don't have a problem with Hank. He's a great guy."

"He is, isn't he?" His mom's voice went soft, and Tyler had to smile. Yeah, his mom was head over heels in love with her husband, and thankfully, the man returned the affection as much, if not more. Tyler truly was happy that after raising him as a single mom—a young single mom—she'd found love.

"I'll have a room ready for you guys. Looking forward to seeing you."

"Me, too, sweetheart. It's been too long this time."

After a few more minutes, their weekly call ended, but Tyler stayed sprawled out on the couch. Tonight was going to have to be an early night if he didn't want to fall asleep at his desk the next day. Between the youth event Friday night, doing work around the house and yard on Saturday and the game where he'd bruised his hip, he was wiped out.

He took a deep breath, sank lower on the couch and closed his eyes. Tyler let his thoughts drifted lazily to the week ahead. The big project for Marcus. Visit Simon. See Melanie.

His eyes popped open, and he stared at the ceiling. *See Melanie?* He gave his head a shake. Ryan needed to stop putting thoughts into his mind. Thoughts he could do nothing about.

One would think that Melanie would be the ideal person to have a relationship with. After all, she understood more than most women could what his injury and life with prosthetics was all about.

His eyes slid shut again. However, there had been an awkwardness—a stiltedness—to their last few interactions. Had she heard Ryan teasing him about her in the lunchroom? If the teasing had made her uncomfortable around him, it was no doubt because she didn't view him in that light.

Which was for the best. He couldn't allow himself to think of her that way either, and Tyler wasn't prepared to lose a perfectly good friendship to the possibility of some sort of romantic relationship. So how did he go about reassuring her that what Ryan was suggesting wasn't something she had to worry about?

Even if he *was* interested in her, while BlackThorpe didn't prohibit dating among its employees, it wasn't really encouraged and something told him that as a member of the Thorpe family, Melanie wouldn't cross that line.

So, the sooner he could get her to relax back into their friendship, the better.

"Yo! Harris!"

The yell dragged Tyler from sleep, and he reluctantly cracked his eyes open. Ryan stood in front of him with a large flat box in one hand and a six-pack of pop in the other. He squinted at him for a moment then sat up, rubbing a hand along the back of his neck. "Did we have plans?"

"Nope. But I'm hungry and figured you would be too." Ryan placed the pizza and drinks on the coffee table and dropped down on the couch next to him. "Maybe we could play some video games or watch a movie."

Tyler turned to stare at the man. "Something wrong?"

It wasn't that they didn't spend time together just like this—Ryan lived in the other side of the duplex and they shared a weight room in the basement—but there was something about his friend's demeanor that made him think this was more than just a desire to hang out.

Ryan didn't look at him as he freed one of the pop cans from the plastic rings and popped it open. He took a long drink then leaned back, resting the can on his stomach. "Nope. Just felt like hanging out."

Tyler was unconvinced but before he could say anything, his phone rang. With a final look at his friend, he grabbed his phone from where it had slid between the cushions during his nap. *Melanie.* He pushed up from the couch as he tapped the screen to accept the call.

"Hello?" He found the remote on the coffee table and tossed it to Ryan before making his way to the kitchen to get some plates and napkins.

"Hi, Tyler. It's Melanie. Sorry to disturb you on the weekend, but I just realized I forgot to phone you with the information on Simon."

Tyler kept one hand on the phone as he reached into the cupboard for two plates. He didn't bother to tell her that he'd managed to find out what he needed by doing a little investigative research. Who was he to cut short their conversation? "No problem. What've you got?"

As she rattled off some dates and places, Tyler grabbed a roll of paper towels and headed back to the living room. Ryan had the television on and was surfing through the channels. The lid of the pizza box was open, but he hadn't taken a piece out yet. Tyler handed him a plate and the roll of paper towels.

"You're making me use a plate, man?" Ryan griped as he took the stuff from Tyler.

Tyler waved his hand at him, but Melanie had already heard his voice. "I'm so sorry. You've got company. I'll let you go."

"It's not company," Tyler told her. "It's just Ryan."

"You guys don't get enough of each other at work?" she asked, a hint of humor in her voice.

"Actually, he showed up with pizza and pop. That was just too much temptation to turn down."

Melanie laughed, and Tyler found himself smiling at the sound.

"Well, I won't keep you from pizza. I just wanted to make sure I got you that information. I'll see you tomorrow."

"Sure thing. Do you want me to come by your office first?"

"It's not necessary, but I wouldn't mind if you stopped by afterward to let me know how it went."

"Will do."

"Enjoy your evening," she said.

"You too." Tyler ended the call and set his phone on the coffee table as he sat back down beside Ryan. "So? Movie or video games?"

Melanie turned her playlist back on then set her phone in the holder on the treadmill. She had only been halfway through her run when she'd realized she needed to phone Tyler. Normally, she didn't interrupt her workout for anything, but in this case, she hadn't wanted to forget again.

At least that's what she told herself.

She hit the button to restart the treadmill and began to work back up to her normal pace for the ten miles she ran each day. Her arms pumped as her feet pounded a matching rhythm to the beat of the music coming from her phone.

Slowly, the burn built in her legs. It was familiar and necessary.

She pushed through the scream of her muscles. *Left. Right. Left. Right.*

With her conversation with Tyler so fresh in her mind, Melanie found her thoughts centered on him even though she normally tried to clear her mind when she ran, focusing on nothing but the *thud, thud, thud* as her running shoes hit the surface of the treadmill.

But tonight, her mind drifted to Thursday and watching Tyler with Simon. The compassion on his face as he'd talked to the man. The understanding. The way he'd spoken to him. Not pushing. Not lecturing. Just...sharing. Encouraging.

Left. Right. Left. Right.

Dragging her thoughts away from Tyler, she tried to find something else to occupy her mind. The usual blank focus wasn't going to work. Thoughts of Tyler were just waiting to grab her attention.

After church, she'd gone with Adrianne and Alex to their parents' large home for Sunday dinner. The meal had gone much the same as previous ones. A little business discussion and then moving right along to questions on their relationship statuses.

Alex brushed aside his mother's queries. He did it so well now. The questions from his mother didn't even seem to faze him. She had no problem ignoring them either. Her position on relationships had been set for years, and she was resolute in her decision. That made it much easier to ignore her mother's repeated attempts to set her up or coerce her into dating one of her friends' sons.

Unfortunately, Adrianne wasn't immune to their mother's manipulations. That was probably because she actually did want to be in a relationship. She wanted marriage and kids. She just hadn't found the right man yet. Sadly, that made her way too vulnerable to their mother. And it seemed that with her last child hitting the big 3-0, Pamela Thorpe was getting a bit more desperate.

As the ten-mile mark edged closer on the display, Melanie made the decision to push past it. *Go for eleven. Just one more*. She knew she could do it.

When the display showed she'd reached the eleventh mile, Melanie pressed the button to slow the treadmill while she cooled down. After a few minutes of walking, she hit the off button and slid backwards until she stepped onto the floor.

She bent over and braced her hands on her knees as she breathed deeply. Once her heart began to slow, Melanie did a few stretches before moving to her weight machine. It had never been her goal to look like she pumped iron so she didn't do heavy weights, she just did a lot of reps of lower weights. She wanted to be strong without looking like a bodybuilder.

When she was finally finished with her workout, Melanie grabbed the towel she'd dropped on the weight bench earlier and mopped up the sweat on her face. Her short hair was now plastered to her head. Her body ached with that feeling of having been well-used. She loved that feeling. It meant her body was strong and able to move quickly, that it would be able to respond to whatever she needed it to do.

Draping the towel around her neck, Melanie left the exercise room, shutting the door behind her. She walked to her ensuite bathroom and turned on the Jacuzzi taps. While water flowed into the large tub, she took a quick shower to wash away the sweat in her hair and on her body.

Even as she loved the ache in her body after a workout, she loved the heat of the water as she sank beneath it, the jets pulsing against sore muscles. As the warmth soothed the ache in her limbs, the ritual of her evening soothed her mind.

She was ready. She was prepared.

Next time around, her body would not betray her.

Adrianne shot Melanie a dark look when she walked into the kitchen the next morning and muttered a terse, "Morning."

Melanie set her briefcase on a chair and laid her jacket over the back of it. As she walked to the large refrigerator, she asked, "What's got your panties in a twist so early in the day?"

Her sister lifted a mug to her lips and took a sip before lowering it back down to the counter. "What do you think?"

As she pulled out the fruits and vegetables she used to make her morning smoothie, Melanie glanced over at Adrianne again. "Mom?"

Adrianne's eyelashes fluttered as she gave a single nod. A knot formed in Melanie's stomach. She hated it when Adrianne got like this...or rather, she hated it when their mom pushed the buttons that turned Adrianne into this angry, insecure woman.

"You need to just ignore her comments, Annie," Melanie said as she placed her stuff on the counter. She gave her sister a quick side hug before pulling out the machine to mix her smoothie.

"How exactly do I ignore comments like *you have such a pretty face, darling. You just need to lose a little weight and you'd have no problem getting a boyfriend*?" Anger and hurt rang loud and clear in Adrianne's voice. "And you're no help."

"What do you mean?" Melanie frowned as she put her fruit, yogurt and kale into the blender. Her mother must have made those comments when she and Alex weren't around because the two of them would have stood up for Adrianne in a heartbeat.

"Look at you!" Adrianne waved a hand at her. "Not an extra ounce of fat on you. Always eating healthy. No wonder Mom keeps harping on me."

As she punched the button to mix everything together, Melanie mulled over Adrianne's words. She didn't do this in order to be attractive to the opposite sex. Frankly, she really couldn't care less if a man found her attractive. Okay, so lately that wasn't *entirely* true.

"I don't have a boyfriend either," Melanie pointed out when she shut off the blender. "So looking like this doesn't really matter."

The derision in Adrianne's snort of laughter was unmistakable. "That's because you don't seem to *want* a boyfriend. Do you know how many times a guy has asked me if you're available? Like I'm your DUFF or something?"

Melanie picked up the cup she'd poured her smoothie into and turned toward Adrianne. "My DUFF? What on earth is that?"

"Your Designated Ugly Fat Friend." Adrianne kept her gaze on the mug in her hands. "Why does it matter that I'm not a perfect size 2?"

"It doesn't," Melanie said. "And for the record, you're far from my DUFF. You're beautiful. And I mean that without a word of a lie. You need to just let Mom's comments roll off you. You have dates, but you're just picky. There's nothing wrong with that. Don't settle for some guy just to make Mom happy. You wait for the guy that makes *you* happy."

Adrianne took a deep breath and let it out. "Sorry to vent at you. Just not a great start to a Monday when Mom calls first thing to find out how my date went last night. When I said that I didn't think it would lead to anything further, she automatically assumed it was the guy shutting it down."

"And it wasn't," Melanie stated.

"Nope." She took another sip of her coffee. "He was a nice enough guy, but just not what I'm looking for."

"Did you tell her that?"

"Yeah, like she'd believe me," Adrianne scoffed. "She'd just figure I was lying."

"Mom does love you," Melanie told her. "I think she's just getting so desperate for one of us to settle down, she isn't thinking about what she's saying. You're the only one actively dating, so I guess you're the one with the target on your back."

"Why does Adrianne have a target on her back?" Alex asked as he walked into the kitchen and headed straight for the coffee machine.

Adrianne drained her mug and stuck it in the dishwasher as she muttered, "Same old, same old."

"Just ignore her, sis." Alex poured himself a cup of coffee and immediately took a big gulp.

Melanie wasn't surprised that Alex picked up on what was bothering Adrianne. Even though they were twins, they weren't any more genetically alike to each other than they were to her, yet they had this uncanny ability to know what the other was thinking. It had made Melanie feel left out a lot when she was younger. Now she just accepted it as part of the complexity of the relationships in their family.

"Well, see, that's the thing," Adrianne said as she picked up her briefcase. "I shouldn't *have* to ignore things my mother says. She should love me enough to not say them in the first place."

With that, she spun on her heel and stomped—as much as she could in heels—out of the kitchen into the hallway that led to the three car garage that was attached to the large house. Melanie hoped her sister's day improved once she got to the office where there was no doubt she was a star at her job.

"So I hear you've been spending time with Tyler."

Melanie knew enough not to rise to her brother's bait. She turned toward him and took a swallow of her smoothie. "Yes. I asked him to come by the Center and spend some time with Simon. He's still resisting any type of therapy."

"Why did you choose Tyler to meet with him?" Alex leaned a hip against the counter and pinned her with his piercing blue gaze as his hand slid down the blue paisley tie he wore. "We have other people who have volunteered to come and talk with people like Simon."

"Yes, we do, but I felt that in addition to the experience that Tyler could share with him, he'd do it with a lot more compassion and understanding than some of the other guys."

Alex's eyebrows lifted at that. "How would you know that?"

Melanie arched one of her brows back at him. "You forget that I was around him back when he was in the Center. Even back then he showed that side of himself."

"And that's the only reason you sought him out for this?" Alex asked as he topped up his coffee.

Melanie picked up the lid for her smoothie cup and twisted it into place. She gave Alex her best quizzical look. "Should there have been another reason?"

He stared at her for so long that Melanie was certain he would see past the façade she was trying to keep in place. Finally, he gave a shake of his head and sighed.

"Just know that if you were to show an interest in a guy, Tyler is one that I wouldn't mind you having in your life. He's a good guy."

"Yes, he is. That's why I contacted him." She set her cup down on the counter while she shrugged into her jacket. "But it was for Simon's sake. No other reason. We're just friends."

Then she grabbed her cup and briefcase and followed the direction Adrianne had taken a few minutes earlier. By the time she was backing her SUV out of the garage, Alex had climbed into his truck. With a toot of her horn, she headed down the winding driveway to the gate that slid open as she approached. She didn't bother to close it knowing that Alex was right behind her.

As she drove, Melanie tried to keep her thoughts from going to Tyler's visit to the Center later that day. First, she had to get through a meeting with her own staff and that was where her attention needed to be.

Tyler watched as the macro he'd written worked its way through the list of numbers on his screen. A year's worth of telephone calls on four different numbers. This was probably going to take a little bit. In the meantime, he brought up the files that the research department had sent to him earlier.

Though Marcus hadn't given him specifics, Tyler was pretty sure that this project was tied to the issues they'd been having at the company lately. The shooting earlier in the year had been the latest in a series of attacks on BlackThorpe. The first had been the thwarted kidnapping of Eric McKinley, which had been followed by an unsuccessful attempt to hack into the company network. Unfortunately, the shooting had been more successful with injuries to four people including Marcus and Alex. Marcus had still not completely recovered from the injury to his leg.

Though there had been no lives lost, it wasn't hard to see that the attacks were escalating. It was possible that the next one would result in the death of someone. As Tyler looked at the four files that he'd been sent, he wondered if Marcus had an idea of who it was that was targeting BlackThorpe. Rumors were floating around with the most common one being it had something to do with the two guys who had initially started the company with Marcus and Alex, but then left.

Tyler could have done research to get their names, but he preferred to go into this with no prejudices. The four names on his screen belonged to four faceless people. He didn't know their connections to each other or to Marcus and Alex. However, if there was a link somewhere, he'd find it.

But not right then.

Leaving the macro running, Tyler locked his screen so no one could come into his office and see what his computer was doing. With a groan, he got to his feet and stretched. The bruise on his hip was still giving him grief and almost had him walking with a limp. Was he really too old to be playing basketball at just thirty years of age? He didn't remember injuries bothering him this much in past years.

He grabbed his jacket from the back of his chair and shrugged into it, checking to make sure his phone and keys were in the pocket. Before heading to the elevator, he let the receptionist for their floor know that he was gone, likely for the day. It was only three o'clock, but anticipating that he might go directly home from the Center, he'd come in around seven o'clock instead of his usual nine.

During his drive out to the Center, Tyler mulled over his visit with Simon. And Melanie. Yeah, he was looking forward to that a little bit more than he should be. As tempting as it was to consider breaking his "no relationship" vow to himself, he really didn't like the idea of losing her as a friend if things went south.

Keeping in mind that Melanie had said she didn't need to see him before he went to talk with Simon, Tyler walked passed the door to her office without knocking. He even managed to keep from looking into the office, but just barely.

4

MELANIE CHECKED the time in the corner of her monitor and then glanced at her office door. She'd happened to be standing next to Heather's desk when Tyler had walked by earlier. He hadn't paused or even looked into her office. Just strode right on past, his gait easy and sure. No one watching him would ever guess he was a double amputee with two prosthetic legs.

It had been about forty-five minutes since she'd seen him, so she figured any time now he could show up. She tried to curb the flutter of excitement that thought brought to life within her but then let out a sigh. Maybe it was time to take a vacation. Get away from all the happy relationships that were blossoming around her. Of course, there were at least two more weddings in the not-so-distant future, and it was highly probable that she would be invited to at least one, if not both, of them.

Was love contagious? It sure seemed like it was.

Though she'd justified asking for Tyler's help to Alex—and it had all been true—it was getting harder to deny to herself that there was something more. And having Tyler around was the worst thing she could do for herself.

They were friends, just like she'd told Alex, but now... She couldn't have Tyler in her life the way those feelings and emotions demanded. That didn't fit with her relationship resolution. Would she need to step back?

Letting out a long sigh, Melanie tried to rein in her emotions. It was that blasted birthday/engagement party that Than had put on for Lindsay. Seeing them together had stirred something in her. Then seeing Justin and Alana had just intensified that feeling. She'd been able to brush it aside when it had first flared up when she'd attended Eric's wedding, but then there had been Lucas and Brook, Trent and Victoria. Too much love was floating around to be healthy for her. It was impairing her judgment.

Which had led to the spontaneous decision last week to go by Tyler's office after the meeting. She'd had another name and number scribbled on her notepad in her office, but in the end it had been Tyler she'd gone to.

"Knock. Knock."

Melanie jerked her gaze to the door and felt her breath catch when she saw Tyler standing there. Hoping the tumult of emotions she'd been feeling wasn't visible on her face, she stood up and smiled.

"Hey, Tyler. Come in."

He returned her smile with an easy one of his own. It was rare to see him without a smile when he was interacting with someone.

Once he was seated across from her, Melanie said, "So? How did the visit with Simon go?"

Her question dimmed his smile slightly. "Still about the same. He talked a bit more today. Asked questions about my accident and injuries. I suppose that, all things considered, it's progress."

"But not enough to make you happy?" Melanie asked.

"It pains me to see someone so unhappy." Tyler leaned forward, bracing his elbows on his knees. "I certainly don't expect people to just get over traumatic events. What saddens me, though, is to see someone *choosing* to not take advantage of the help that's available to them. *Choosing* to not take the steps to move themselves forward.

"Simon is more than willing to talk about my experiences, but I get the feeling it's because he wants to avoid his own, not because he hopes to learn something from what I've gone through."

Melanie watched as Tyler straightened and ran a hand through his hair. "So do you think it's a waste of your time to come see him?"

Tyler's eyebrows rose above his blue eyes. "Not at all. Helping people is never a waste of my time, even if they don't seem to want my help."

Warmth unfurled within Melanie, and she pressed a hand to her stomach, grateful that the height of her desk hid the movement. "If anyone can help Simon, I'm sure it's you."

The smile reappeared on Tyler's face, his eyes sparkling. "I appreciate your vote of confidence. I can only pray that you're right."

At Tyler's mention of prayer, Melanie found herself thinking about his faith. She went to church...sometimes...like this last weekend. Usually, it was precipitated by a call from her mother to remind her that they hadn't seen her there for a couple of weeks. She'd been more interested in church and the youth group before everything had gone wrong.

Maybe experiencing tragedy as an adult allowed one to view God differently than someone who experienced it as a young teenager. Tyler had always clung to his faith even when he'd first showed up at the Center, seemingly confident that God still had a plan for him. She, on the other hand, had spent her teen and adult years wondering where God had been when things had gone so very wrong for her.

"I hope that coming to see Simon won't take you away from other things you need to do," Melanie said.

"It won't." Tyler leaned back in his chair. "Would it be possible to take him out once in a while?"

"Like for coffee?"

"Maybe, but I was thinking more like having him come with me to my Saturday night basketball games. You know the ones I go to with a group of guys from work and church. It's *usually* just a friendly game." He paused as he rubbed his hand against his hip. "There are people with prosthetics like me. A couple in wheelchairs and some like Ryan, who have no disability."

"If you think it might be something he'd like, for sure you can invite him out. As long as he's with you and you bring him back, there's no harm in him spending time away from the Center. It might be good if he did, actually."

"I make no promises that an outing like that will make a difference for him, but I thought it might be good to try. He mentioned that he played for a team in high school. Maybe seeing that it's something he can still do—even in his wheelchair—will be eye-opening for him."

"At this point, I think we're willing to try anything that might give him a sense of hope and purpose. If it's basketball that gets him focused forward, then I'm all for it."

Tyler nodded then pushed himself up from the chair. "I'd better get going. I thought I was done for the day, but Marcus called so I have to head back to the office for a bit."

Melanie stood as well. "Thanks again for coming by."

"My pleasure." Tyler walked toward the door but instead of leaving her office, he placed a hand on the doorframe and turned back toward her. "Would you be interested in going for lunch tomorrow after your meeting?"

"Lunch?" Melanie's heart pounded. In the past, it would have been a quick acceptance, but now...

"Yeah. We haven't talked in a while." The smile that was usually on his face was missing, his expression serious. "Thought maybe we could catch up."

No.

That's what she should be saying. The word should have flowed easily because she'd practiced it with plenty of men over the years.

Instead, Melanie said, "Sure. I'd like that."

Tyler's smile lit up his whole face. "Great! I'll see you tomorrow then. You can text me when you're ready."

No. No. No. No. No.

It pounded against her skull like a drum, reminding her of what she *should* be saying to Tyler. Her mind might have been raging at that moment, but her heart was strangely happy.

Tyler made a rapid exit from Melanie's office. He had a feeling if he lingered too long, she'd change her mind about meeting for lunch the next day. Not that she couldn't phone or text to cancel, but for the next few hours, he was just going to enjoy the thought of spending time with her. If she ended up canceling, he'd just try again in a week or so.

All the recent talks he'd had with himself about this not being the greatest idea he'd ever had had fallen on deaf ears. Between Ryan and his mom, he was starting to feel that his life really was lacking something when that was anything but true. He had a job he loved. He kept active with the young men in his church, thoroughly enjoyed his basketball nights and was part of a group of people at the church that met regularly for fellowship and Bible study. It was full. It was satisfying. Until recently.

A couple of years ago when his heart had felt like it was healed enough to take another chance on love, he'd found that his mind just couldn't accept the risk of loving another woman who might leave when being with him became too difficult. But there was something about Melanie that made his heart clamor for him to take that chance. His heart...but his mind resisted.

As much as he liked Melanie, he sensed that there was something that she held back. Not just from him, but from everyone. After all, she was his age and hadn't—to his knowledge—had a serious relationship in all the time he'd known her.

What was keeping her from a relationship? He honestly wasn't sure he wanted to know. He couldn't ask her about it without having to reveal his own vulnerabilities and fears, and right now, he rather enjoyed the way she thought of him.

Melanie jerked on the jacket of the pantsuit she'd finally settled on after changing three times. Now she wouldn't have time to make her smoothie without being late. They usually had food at the weekly meetings, but often it was stuff she wouldn't eat. Doughnuts. Muffins. Bagels. Not the type of fuel she liked to put into her body.

Deciding she didn't care if she was late, Melanie went to the kitchen. Alex and Adrianne were just walking out the door and looked over at her.

"Running a bit late?" Alex asked with a lifted brow. "That's not like you."

"I'll be right behind you," she said as she pulled her fruit and veggies from the fridge. "I'm sure I won't miss anything too important if I'm a few minutes late to the meeting."

Adrianne laughed. "I'll be sure to let Marcus know you're on your way."

"You do that," Melanie muttered as she dropped her stuff into the mixer.

Once she'd started the machine, she looked down at herself. Her final choice of outfit was a pantsuit in deep plum with a jacket that was fitted through the bodice but had a peplum flared over her hips. The cream blouse she wore underneath it showed through the deep vee in the front of the jacket. It was one of her favorites and was comfortable to boot.

Adrianne also wore suits, but hers were usually paired with a skirt. Melanie, on the other hand, never wore a suit with a skirt. Inevitably, those skirts were usually pencil-thin and restrictive to movement. If she ever needed to *move*, she didn't want her progress impaired by a tight skirt. She did make a concession on the shoes, however, figuring that she could kick them off quickly and still be able to run if she had to.

When the mixer had done its job, Melanie dumped her smoothie into her travel mug then snapped the lid in place. She grabbed her briefcase and headed to the garage.

"Nice of you to join us," Marcus said as Melanie sat down in an empty chair next to Adrianne.

Though she nodded, Melanie fought the urge to scowl at the man. Unfortunately, he kinda scared her, so she kept her face expressionless. He might be her brother's best friend, but there was something about the man that put her on edge. Marcus and Alex were like night and day in her book. Literally. With his blond hair, blue eyes and his smile, Alex was sunshine. While Marcus with his intense nature set against dark hair and eyes made him like the night.

Light and dark.

Good and evil.

Okay, maybe the evil was going a bit far, but if he and Alex were cops, Marcus would definitely have been the bad one. Was it any wonder the man couldn't hold onto a secretary or assistant for more than a couple of weeks? No doubt all the women felt the same way she did about him.

"Anything we need to know about the Center, Melanie?"

Marcus's deep voice jerked her attention from her musings. She scrambled to remember the things she'd planned to make note of in the meeting.

"We are in the process of bringing in a couple of trained dogs to help with therapy."

"Dogs?" Marcus asked, his brows drawn together. "To what end?"

"In the past several years, there has been a rise in the use of dogs to help deal with PTSD. After talking with some of my counselors, we feel that there are a couple of vets who could benefit from having a trained dog."

Marcus leaned back in his chair, his steepled fingers touching his lips. His gaze was intent on her when he asked, "How is this accomplished?"

"The dogs are trained to recognize the anxious behaviors of their owners and will work to physically redirect them to something like petting or interacting with the dog. They also can be a physical barrier between their owner and the public if the situations become tense for them. People suffering from nightmares as a result of PTSD can also be calmed by the presence of the dog. Plus, for some, having a dog that needs their care and attention can help draw them out."

Marcus nodded. "And you haven't tried this type of thing before?"

"We've brought dogs into the Center to interact with the vets, but we've never actually provided them with a dog of their own. Right now we've chosen two vets to receive trained dogs. They will remain at the Center while they adjust to having them around so we can see firsthand how it's working. If these two cases are successful, we will look into expanding the program."

"And the funding for this?"

"I can answer that, Marcus," Adrianne said as she laid a hand on Melanie's arm. "We sent out information to our regular donors as well as a few new ones we thought might be interested in this program, and we had a remarkable response. We received enough money to initially fund five dogs so there is no additional cost to the Center or to the vet. If the program seems successful, we will do more to raise money for additional dogs."

"How much is the cost per dog?"

Adrianne glanced at Melanie before replying. "The value of a dog over the course of its life is around twenty to thirty thousand. The people we are working with receive no government funding so their costs are covered strictly through donations."

"So you raised over a hundred thousand dollars for this project?" Marcus asked.

Adrianne nodded. "We have. We feel that it is a worthwhile project for BlackThorpe to be involved in."

Marcus seemed to mull over her words, and Melanie felt her stomach churn. She did *not* want Marcus to shut this program down. He'd given them free rein over the Center when it came to programs and fundraising. She didn't want him to take that back now.

Finally, he nodded and sat forward. "It sounds like it was a good decision to move forward with it." His gaze landed on Melanie again. "I would like to speak to you a little further about it. Would you come to my office following the meeting, please?"

His request did nothing to settle her stomach, but Melanie nodded. Now, for the first time ever, she wasn't looking forward to the end of the meeting.

The rest of the meeting seemed to speed by and soon Marcus was dismissing them. Melanie took a minute to send a text to Tyler letting him know that she was going to be a bit late. Then, with a final look at Adrianne, she headed off to Marcus's office.

He had left the meeting almost immediately—which was normal for him—so he was already at his desk when she got there.

"Go ahead and close the door," Marcus said as she walked into his office. "And then have a seat."

Feeling a bit as if she was being called on the carpet, Melanie sat down in the chair indicated, her back ramrod straight. She waited for Marcus to begin the conversation because she didn't figure her attempts at small talk would go anywhere.

Thankfully, she didn't have to wait too long.

"So, you really feel that this program with the dogs has potential for people with PTSD?"

Melanie nodded. "Yes, I do. I did research on it extensively and met with people who had lived with trained dogs for over a year. It doesn't cure PTSD, of course, but it is another way for people to cope with it. So it does help improve the lives of people who have struggled with PTSD."

"I realize that you are probably looking at this strictly from the viewpoint of the people we help at the Center—namely vets—but would it work with someone who suffers from PTSD caused by something other than war?"

Again Melanie nodded. "The symptoms of PTSD, regardless of the origin, are often the same. I believe that a dog would also be beneficial for someone suffering PTSD from a trauma that is not related to war."

Marcus took a deep breath, and his gaze dropped momentarily. When he looked back up, the intensity was still there, along with a bit of vulnerability. Melanie hoped that her surprise didn't show.

"I have a sister—I'm not sure if you're aware of that."

Melanie actually knew very little about the man sitting across the desk from her, so hearing that he had a sibling was definitely news to her. "No, I didn't know that."

"Well, I do. She's several years younger than me and when she was thirteen, she experienced a trauma that has left her shattered."

Melanie stared at the man. With her own experience with teenage trauma, she wondered what it might have been that his sister had gone through. "I'm sorry to hear that."

Marcus nodded his acceptance of her remark and then seemed to be mulling over his next words. "I wonder if a dog might be something that would help her."

The knot that had been in Melanie's stomach eased. "We can definitely look into that for you if you'd like."

"I would. If you could send me some information to review, I would appreciate that."

Melanie assured him that he would have his information before the end of the day. "Was that all you wanted to talk to me about?"

Marcus nodded. "Please keep this confidential."

Melanie had already figured out that she would need to do that. There was a reason Marcus kept his sister's existence from them so she would honor that request without question.

As she stepped from his office, she took a deep breath and let it out. However, the nerves regarding the meeting with Marcus were quickly replaced by the flutters of anticipation about seeing Tyler. As she walked to the elevator to go down to the floor where Tyler's office was, she texted him a quick message to let him know she was on her way.

When the elevator reached the floor and the doors slid open, Tyler stood there, his hands in the pockets of his light gray dress pants. He wore a long sleeved dark blue button down shirt. Smiling, he stepped into the car with her.

"So you were meeting with the big guy?" Tyler asked as he pushed the button for the main floor.

"Yeah. He wanted some more information on the program we're setting up to match trained dogs with people suffering from PTSD. It went well, but meeting with him always makes me a little nervous."

Tyler laughed. "I know what you mean. Look up the word *intense* in the dictionary and you'd probably see his picture."

That made Melanie smile, glad for the easygoing conversation between them. *He's a great friend.* She repeated that to herself a couple of times as the elevator began its descent. Then she got a whiff of his cologne and her stomach clenched. *He's a great friend.*

Never had she been so grateful for the ability she'd cultivated to keep her face passive even when internally she was dealing with overwhelming emotions.

He's a great friend.

5

AS THEY WALKED through the doors of the small restaurant a short time later, Tyler was determined that this was going to be an easygoing, friendly lunch. That might be easier said than done, Tyler realized as he took in Melanie's stiff posture and how her eyes seemed detached from the smiles she gave. Her unease didn't make sense because they'd had lunches together in the past.

Something had changed. Unfortunately, he had no idea what that was.

Once they'd placed their orders, Tyler relaxed back on his side of the booth. "So Marcus was okay with the PTSD dog program?"

"Yes. He just wanted a bit more information on it." Melanie shifted in her seat and the familiarity of the movement let Tyler know she was crossing her legs under the table. "I'm actually quite excited about the program, particularly because we'll be able to monitor the interactions of the first two vets we've chosen to receive dogs. They are both staying at the Center so they'll be right there, giving us a firsthand view."

Tyler loved how Melanie's eyes sparkled and her face lit up when she talked about her work. There was never detachment there. She had been devoted to the Center's purpose even when she'd been just a student in college working toward her degree.

She continued to talk about the program but stopped when the waitress appeared with their food. They ate in silence for a few minutes before she said, "So are you flying to be with your mom for your birthday?"

Tyler would have been pleased that she remembered his birthday if it weren't for the fact that it was the same day as hers. "Nope. This year Momma and my stepdad are coming to me."

"Nice! Are you having a party while they're here?"

"Nah. Probably just have dinner with them and maybe Ryan." Tyler scooped up a forkful of mashed potatoes but didn't stick it in his mouth right away. "What about you? Any plans for the big three-o?"

"Really?" Melanie wrinkled her nose at him. "You had to remind me?"

"Hey, I survived turning thirty last year. It really wasn't that bad."

"Is your mother constantly on you about getting married and having kids? Cause my mom is. Although, to be honest, Adrianne is getting the brunt of it since she's older, but my mother is starting to spread it to all of us."

"I've already done the marriage thing," Tyler reminded her, not really wanting to admit that his mom was on the "get my kid married" kick as well. "Given how it ended up, I think my mom was just as glad no kids were involved. And my mom is pretty young still, so she's in no rush to become a grandmother."

"How old is she?" Melanie asked as she cut the piece of grilled chicken that had come with her salad.

"She's forty-five." Tyler waited for Melanie to do the math. They hadn't talked much about his mom in the past. He wasn't sure why, but it had just never come up, and Melanie had never had the opportunity to meet her since his mom preferred him to fly to where she was.

"She was...fourteen when she had you?" Melanie asked, her dark eyes widening.

"Yep. We kind of grew up together." She hadn't married until after Tyler had joined the military, so for a whole lot of years, it had just been the two of them. "Momma's more than happy to just let me do my thing—for the most part. All she wants is for me to be happy."

Melanie sighed. "My mom wants that too, but somehow in her books, being happy is equated with marriage and children."

Tyler tried to ignore the unsettled feeling in his gut and at the same time told himself this was a heavier more personal subject than they usually discussed. He really should turn it in a different direction. "So you're not interested in getting married? At all?"

Melanie twirled her fork in the salad on her plate. "It's not that. Well, it is partly that. I'm in no rush. I like my job and my life right now."

Tyler felt the same way about his life, but lately, the idea of a relationship was growing on him. This was a subject they needed to end, he decided and began to search for a new topic.

But it seemed Melanie wasn't done with it just yet. "To be honest, I am fairly particular about who I would marry—if I marry at all. My mom says I'm fussy."

Tyler swallowed the last bite he'd taken and murmured, "Standards are always good to have."

Melanie laughed. "Yeah, that's what I think, but my mom seems to feel that I'm getting to the age where having the standards I do will leave me a spinster."

"How is everything?"

When Tyler heard the waitress's question, he almost got up and hugged her. "Everything is just fine."

"Yes, it's great," Melanie added with a smile at the young woman.

After a glance at his watch, Tyler said, "If you could just bring me the bill, that would be great."

The woman nodded before she walked away.

"Hey, on the subject of parents, would it be okay to bring mine by the Center while they're here?" Tyler asked, grateful for the opportunity to move on from the topic of marriage.

"Sure. That would be fine." Melanie tilted her head, her brows drawn together. "If you are so close to your mom, why wasn't she here when you were staying at the Center?"

"Well, actually, it's because we're so close that she wasn't here. Her husband and I decided it would be better for her to not be around me while I was trying to get back on my feet. She would have hovered and made it hard for me to concentrate on what I needed to do. I would have been too worried about how she was dealing with things to be able to do that." Tyler smiled. "But I did talk to her on Skype pretty much every single day."

"In that case, I think it's mandatory for her to come see where you spent your time. And I can tell her what a great patient you were."

They stuck with small talk as Tyler took care of the bill and drove them back to BlackThorpe.

"Thanks for lunch, Ty," Melanie said as she stood beside his car. "I really enjoyed it."

"Me too. We should do it again soon."

Emotion quickly crossed Melanie's face, but Tyler couldn't put his finger on what it was.

"Yes, we should." Melanie paused. "Guess I'd better get back to the Center. Make sure the place is still standing."

"Speaking of," Tyler began, "I'll probably be back out on Thursday, and if Simon is interested, I'll see about taking him out on Saturday."

"That sounds great. Thank you again for being willing to meet with him."

A few minutes later, Tyler watched as Melanie's dark gray SUV headed for the exit. He shoved his hands into his pockets and let out a sigh. For the first time, he wondered if her standards included a man with two fully functioning legs. If that was the case, it was a good thing he wasn't interested in a relationship with her.

"Yeah, you just keep telling yourself that," the little voice in his head said.

Melanie tightened the belt of her robe as she made her way to the desk in her bedroom. One last check of her email before heading to bed. Her body felt pleasantly fatigued after another hard workout, and the hot bath afterward had been divine. It was too bad, though that her exercise regimen didn't occupy her thoughts as well as it did her body. Both last night and tonight, her thoughts as she'd worked out had been focused squarely on Tyler.

First, she kept thinking about the lunch they'd shared and then tonight all she could think about was that she'd get to see him the next day. Her behavior when it came to the man reminded her a lot of people who knew what the right thing to do was but chose the opposite because it felt so good. Like knowing that chocolate cake wasn't good for them, but choosing to eat it anyway because it tasted so wonderful.

Unfortunately, she found it a whole lot easier to resist the cake than she did Tyler.

She sank down on the chair at her desk and clicked to open her email program.

As unread emails filled her inbox, Melanie leaned close when a familiar but rarely seen name appeared. She ignored all the other new messages and clicked on that one first.

My Darling Lanie ~ It's been forever since we last were in contact, and I know that I'm the reason for that. Stupid me, I just assumed that if I cut off all contact with people from that time, I could forget. But I can't.

Can you? Have you figured out a way to forget?

I really don't know what to do. But I do know that I just can't go on like this. Most days I just don't want to go on at all.

Melanie's chest grew tight, and she fought to draw in a deep breath.

I can't trust anyone because the first person I ever really loved and trusted betrayed me. How do I learn to trust again? How do I not look at every man and wonder if he's just biding his time until he can lure me into another trap?

I'm too scared to leave my apartment because I know that some of the girls weren't lured the way we were but were outright kidnapped by strangers. How do I not know that that will be the way they come for me the second time?

I can't sleep because as soon as I do, the nightmares come. Too many times I fall asleep only to be woken by a huge figure looming over me. Afraid to fall asleep. Afraid to wake up. How am I supposed to survive?

I can hardly eat because of the drugs they put in our food. How do I know if what I'm eating is safe?

I've shaved off all my hair. I never wear makeup. I need to know that no one will look at me and see beauty again. Beauty was what led me into that trap. I don't ever want to hear anyone tell me I'm beautiful again.

It's been fourteen years, and I still can't get past the horror of it. Why am I so weak? How did the others manage to go on with their lives? Why is it just me who can't put the past in the past and move forward?

Please tell me what to do.

Loving you always ~ Jenni

Taking deep, gasping breaths, Melanie brushed at the tears on her cheeks. In her mind's eye, she could see Jenni as she'd been fourteen years ago. Her beautiful auburn curls had fallen to her waist, and her green eyes had been bright and full of life...at first. Yes, there had been fear there too.

They'd all had the fear, but Jenni had been full of life...until she wasn't.

After allowing that memory of Jenni to tumble through her mind, it was like the box she'd kept the memories in had split wide open. Memory after memory ripped through her. Curling in on herself, Melanie reached up and grabbed handfuls of her hair, pulling on it. She couldn't go down that path again. She just couldn't.

Melanie began to take deep, measured breaths.

In. Out. In. Out.

As the panic began to ease out of her body, she began to methodically pack away the painful memories. Then she went to that peaceful place in her mind. The place where nothing could hurt her.

Finally, Melanie straightened and took in one last deep breath and slowly exhaled, expelling the last lingering wisp of memory from her body. Now that she was calm and detached from the memories once again, she could look at Jenni's situation more clearly.

But really, how could she help her friend when she herself was still as messed up as Jenni? She just knew how to hide it better. The ways she'd chosen to cope were as unhealthy as the ways Jenni had, but her methods were more easily dismissed as lifestyle choices. The darkened hair. The colored contacts. The obsession with eating healthy and making sure her body was strong. The need to know how to use all kinds of weapons. The decision to not love a man again.

Although that last one was getting harder to stick to.

Jenni had chosen to hide away. Melanie had chosen to arm herself. The bottom line was that both of them were living their lives in chains to their shared trauma.

Melanie wished she had answers for her friend because then that would mean she'd have answers for herself. But nothing in her own personal counseling nor the years of training she'd taken had convinced her that she could accept her world and the people in it at face value ever again.

Knowing she didn't have the energy for a long response, Melanie just typed out a quick message assuring Jenni that she was not alone in her fears and that she loved her. She promised to write more at a later date and then tapped the button to send the email.

After a cursory scan of the remaining emails, Melanie closed her laptop and pushed away from the desk. Instead of going directly to her bed, she returned to the bathroom and stood in front of the medicine cabinet. It had been awhile and though she hated that they made her feel somewhat groggy the next day, Melanie opened the cabinet and pulled out the sleeping pills her doctor had prescribed.

At this point, it was more important that she sleep. She had to work the next day and trying to do so after a sleepless night was just not an option. After dumping two pills into her hand, she filled a cup with water and swallowed them. Once in bed, she opened the ebook app on her tablet and lost herself in a story until her eyes just wouldn't stay open a moment longer.

"So do you think you might like to come?" Tyler asked as he shook his pant leg down over the prosthesis on his right leg. He'd spent a little of their time together showing Simon the mechanics of having a prosthetic leg.

The man looked up at him, his brow furrowed. "I don't know. Am I even allowed out of this place?"

Tyler sat back down and nodded. "I already asked Melanie Thorpe if it would be okay. It might do you some good to get away for a little while. You don't have to play if you don't want. You can sit on the sidelines and cheer."

Simon scoffed. "You want me to be a cheerleader?"

Happy to see a bit of a smile on the man's face, Tyler shrugged. "Sure. I'll get you a pair of pompoms. Any color preference?"

"Not cool, man. Not cool," Simon said with a shake of his head, his mouth turned up slightly. "How about I give you a call on Saturday to let you know?"

"Sounds good," Tyler said as he got to his feet. "Just give me enough time to get out here to pick you up and still make it to the game."

"I will."

Tyler laid a hand on Simon's shoulder and squeezed. "Nice hanging with you again today."

Simon covered his hand briefly then nodded. "Thanks for coming by."

Tyler felt good about his visit as he left the therapy room. Simon still wasn't interested in dealing with the therapists or counselors at the Center, but he was opening up to Tyler and that was a good first step.

Hoping Melanie would feel the same way, Tyler made his way to her office. Heather smiled when he appeared in the doorway and waved him through.

"Hey, Melanie," Tyler said as he knocked on the doorframe.

She looked up and stared at him for a moment before smiling. "Hi. Come on in."

Tyler settled into the chair across from her, his gaze searching her face. There was something...off about her today. There was a puffiness under her eyes that he wasn't used to seeing, and she seemed tense. "Everything okay?"

Her eyebrows rose slightly at his question. "Yes. Why do you ask?"

He tilted his head, uncertain how to respond. "Well, you just seem like something is bothering you."

Her eyes narrowed at his observation. "You figured that out rather quickly."

Tyler shrugged. He wasn't sure why he'd been able to pick up on it at all, really. Lord knew he wasn't the most observant person around when it came to things like that. Maybe if he'd been better at reading his ex-wife, she might not have left him. As he thought about that for an instant, he realized that it probably wouldn't have mattered. He couldn't change what she didn't love about him.

"Anything you want to talk about?" Tyler offered, wanting more than anything to be supportive. To show her that he was there for her. As a friend.

Melanie gave an immediate shake of her head as she lifted a hand to her forehead. "Just a bit of a headache." She gave him another quick smile then asked, "How was your visit with Simon today?"

"He was more communicative today but still not too keen to deal with the people here."

"Did he want to go with you to the basketball game?"

Tyler shrugged again. "Not sure. I think part of him does, but there's that other part that so far has overruled everything else. The side ruled by guilt. Like if it's something that might make his life better or that he would enjoy, he doesn't feel right doing it since the guys that were with him that day can't do it."

"That's not an uncommon feeling among vets in his situation, but I think he has the worst case I've encountered since I started working at the Center."

"Yep. I've told him that the best way to honor the guys who lost their lives would be to live his life to the fullest. He doesn't agree. Everything is filtered through that perception of it not being right for him to enjoy life."

"At least it seems you're making some progress. I hope that he agrees to go with you."

"Me, too." Tyler pushed himself to his feet. "I hate to run, but I've got to pick up Momma and Hank at the airport at five-thirty."

A genuine smile spread across Melanie's face. "That's right. Tomorrow's the big day. I've been trying to forget about it."

"Celebrate life," Tyler said. "That's my philosophy."

"And it's a good one," Melanie said as she got up from her chair. "I hope you have a good birthday."

"You too." He paused for a moment then asked, "Would it be okay if I brought my folks by here tomorrow afternoon? I've taken the day off to spend with them so it would be a good time to come by."

"That would be fine. I look forward to meeting them." The smile she gave him supported her words though there was still tension on her face.

"Sounds good. I guess I'll see you tomorrow then." Tyler turned to go but then swung back around. He held Melanie's gaze for a long moment. "And if you need to talk, give me a call. I'm there for you if you need someone."

She didn't look away from his gaze, and he could see the softening of her expression as tension eased from her features. "Thanks, Tyler. I appreciate that."

"I mean it." Giving her one last smile, Tyler left her office. He wanted to make sure that she knew that he cared about her. As a friend, of course.

6

WHEN HER PHONE chirped an alert for a text message, Melanie reached for it but waited until she'd finished signing the form she'd been reading to see what it said.

I'm down at the front with my folks. Would you like to meet them?

Melanie smiled as she began to tap out a response. Before she could hit send, another message arrived.

BTW...HAPPY BIRTHDAY!

Her smile got bigger, and she felt a flutter in her stomach at the greeting.

I'd love to meet your parents. I'll be right down. TY for the HBD wishes. HAPPY BIRTHDAY to you too!!

After replacing the paper in its folder, Melanie stood up and slid her phone into her pocket. As she passed Heather's desk, she told her she'd be back in a bit and to phone if something important came up.

When she reached the top of the staircase, Melanie looked over and spotted Tyler standing with two other people talking to the receptionist. She walked down the stairs, her hand gliding along the smooth metal railing. As she stepped off the bottom step, she looked over to find Tyler watching her even though his parents were still engaged in conversation with Molly.

She felt heat rise in her cheeks as a smile spread across his face when their gazes met. Her heartbeat kicked up a notch, and it was hard to take a deep breath. Hopefully, nothing showed on her face.

"Hi, Tyler," she said when she reached his side.

"How're you doing today?" he asked.

"Not too bad." She wrinkled her nose. "All things considered."

"Already starting to feel the effects of old age, eh?"

Melanie jostled his elbow with hers but before she could say anything, a soft voice with the slightest southern lilt to it said, "Darlin', are you going to introduce us?"

Tyler took a step back and turned toward the petite woman standing behind him. "Sorry, Momma. This is Melanie Thorpe." He slipped his arm around his mom's shoulders. "Melanie, this is my mom, Shauna and her husband, Henry Wakeford."

The names sounded familiar, and she tried to place them as she shook hands with Tyler's parents. Suddenly, it hit her. *Adrianne's donors*. Tyler's parents were the two million dollar donors?

Her gaze met the older man's. His warm blue eyes twinkled as he smiled. He obviously realized she'd just put two and two together.

"It's a pleasure to meet you," Melanie said without divulging her revelation. She had no idea if Tyler was aware of their donation and didn't want to put anyone in an awkward position.

"The pleasure is all ours," Shauna said as she smiled. "We are thrilled to meet the people who helped Tyler so much."

As she looked at Tyler's mom, she didn't see too many similarities except for the color of their hair and their eyes. Clearly, Tyler had gotten his height and build from his father—whoever he was. Tyler had never spoken of him. His mother's petite stature put her quite a few inches shorter than her son. Henry Wakeford also dwarfed Shauna in the same way Tyler did.

That wasn't the only similarity between the men with regards to the dainty woman who stood between them. It was hard to miss the absolute devotion on the faces of both son and husband.

"It's so nice that you're able to spend Tyler's birthday with him each year," Melanie said. "He mentioned that you've only missed two birthdays."

Shauna looked up at her son, love clear on her face. "His birth made me a mother and there's no one I'd rather be a momma to than this boy." She lifted her hand and laid it on the side of Tyler's face. "I can't imagine not wanting to celebrate the day my whole world changed. For the better."

"You know, Momma, today is Melanie's birthday too."

Delight filled Shauna's face, her blue eyes sparkling as her gaze moved back to Melanie. "Really? Well, that confirms my theory that truly great people are born on this day. Are you having a party with your family?"

"Not today. I think my mom has something planned for tomorrow night." Melanie sighed. "I'm not really supposed to know about it, but my sister took pity on me and clued me in."

"Do you have plans for tonight then?" Tyler asked, his brows drawn together.

"Uh...not really."

"Then you must come with us," Shauna announced with a clap of her hands. She looked up at her husband. "Right, darling?"

"Absolutely, my love." As he spoke for the first time, Melanie heard the English accent and realized that they didn't just live in London, Henry was *from* the UK.

"I really couldn't intrude on your dinner," Melanie said as she looked to Tyler, hoping he'd see the plea for his help to decline the invitation.

Instead, he smiled at her and said, "It wouldn't be an intrusion at all. I'd love to have you along for my birthday dinner."

"It's just not right that you're not doing something special on the actual day," Shauna insisted. "Even if you are having a dinner tomorrow night."

Melanie knew she should just politely decline—that was the smart thing to do—but lately she'd been making some very un-smart decisions. This was just going to be one more. "Okay. You've convinced me. Where should I meet you?"

"We can pick you up," Tyler said.

"I appreciate the offer, but it would be easier if I just met you there." This was something Melanie wasn't going to budge on.

Tyler seemed to sense that because he nodded then said, "We're going to a place that Than recommended."

"The restaurant where he and Lindsay got engaged?" Melanie asked.

"Yep. That's the place," Tyler confirmed.

"I know where that is. What time are you planning to be there?"

"I made reservations for six-thirty."

"Sounds perfect." Melanie turned to smile at Shauna and Henry. "Now, would you like a tour of our facility?"

Tyler followed as Melanie led his mom and Hank through the Center. He felt pretty pleased with how things had turned out. Not only was he going to have his mom there to celebrate his birthday, but now Melanie would be celebrating with him too. He couldn't have planned it better if he'd tried. In years past, he hadn't been around for his birthday since he'd flown to be with his mom and Hank, so this was the first opportunity for them to actually celebrate together on the day.

He didn't add much as they moved from one area of the Center to another. Melanie was definitely the ultimate tour guide as she knew the place inside and out. In some ways, this center *was* Melanie. She had taken it from the small place that had only been able to accommodate a handful of vets to what it was now. Back then there had been a focus on therapy—physical and emotional—but what they had now was so much more. He hadn't even been aware of all the different aspects of the program that BlackThorpe now had in place at the Center until he'd gone on this tour.

Hank asked a lot of questions and it wasn't long before Tyler realized that his stepdad knew quite a bit more about the Center than he'd assumed he did. That surprised him since, to his knowledge, neither of them had ever been there aside from the first day when they'd brought him to the Center.

"Been doing your research?" Tyler asked when they stood at the front desk once again.

Hank looked at him and smiled. "I felt it prudent to keep up to date on what the BlackThorpe center was doing. After they did such a wonderful job with you, I wanted to make sure that they would always be able to accommodate others who had needs similar to yours."

"You've donated?" Tyler asked. He knew his stepdad was a very wealthy man, but for the most part, he had never availed himself of the money he had even when it had been offered. At most, he'd allowed Hank to buy the duplex that he and Ryan lived in.

"I most definitely have." Hank reached out and laid a hand on his shoulder. "You were the son I never had and then I—we almost lost you. The people here brought you back to us. They gave you the opportunity to put your life back together. How could I do anything but help them to be able to continue the good work they do here?"

Emotion clogged Tyler's throat, and he blinked rapidly. He'd always had respect for Hank and was so grateful for how he treated his mother, but Tyler had never thought that the man ever looked at him as anything more than his wife's son. The stoic British businessman had never expressed any sort of emotional connection to him. Because he was so visibly in love with Shauna, Tyler had just assumed Hank hadn't needed a grown son as part of the package.

"Thank you." The words were hard to force past tight vocal cords. Tyler felt a soft touch on his arm and looked to see Melanie smiling up at him. He could see emotion in her eyes too.

"You're welcome, my boy." Hank squeezed his shoulder then lowered his arm. "And Melanie, thank you so much for the wonderful tour. I'm convinced more than ever that our donations are going to the right place. Be sure to let us know of any special projects like the therapy dogs that are in need of funding."

"I will do that for sure, Mr. Wakeford. We are so very grateful for your support of the work we do here. It would have been impossible to expand the way we have without generous donations from people like you."

"First, please call me Hank. And second, it is all our pleasure."

Tyler swallowed hard to clear the remaining tightness from his throat and then said, "We'd better let you get back to work, but we'll see you at six-thirty. No backing out."

The smile she flashed told him she had been considering it, but she said, "I'll be there."

"Good. See you later."

Once his mom and Hank had said their goodbyes, he led them out into the bright afternoon sunlight. A quick glance at his watch showed he still had three hours before their dinner. Thankfully, he already had a gift for Melanie so didn't have to hit the stores to try and find something. They'd exchanged small gifts in years past, but this year he'd spent a little more time and effort to get her the perfect present. He just hoped she agreed.

When Tyler and his folks arrived at the restaurant, Ryan was already there waiting for them. Tyler had phoned earlier to add one more to their reservation so the table in the back of the restaurant was set for five.

"Nice to see you again, Ryan," his mom said as she sat down in the chair Hank held for her.

Ryan had stood at their approach and didn't sit back down until Shauna had settled into her chair. "You, too, Mrs. Wakeford."

"Oh please, call me Shauna. Mrs. Wakeford is Hank's mum." Tyler's mom leaned closer to the table. "And she never lets me forget it."

Tyler glanced at Hank and saw the man nod and smile. "That is very true. I love my mum, but she's a wee bit pretentious. A bit of a snob. According to her, Mrs. Wakeford should be a proper Brit, not some American."

"But the heart wants what the heart wants." His mom touched Hank's cheek. "Right, darling?"

Hank captured his wife's hand and pressed a kiss to her palm. "That's for sure, my love."

As Tyler watched them, he hoped that if he ever found himself in a relationship again, it would be like theirs. He thought he'd found that once, but looking back, he could see that things weren't that way for them even before his accident. His ex-wife had never been content to just sit and share quiet times. She had been an even bigger thrill seeker than him. He had enjoyed the adventures, but he would have been happy to sit in their own backyard around a fire pit just talking too.

Their lifestyle, even while dating, hadn't really allowed for much conversation. When the one thing they had in common was threatened, she'd hit the road. Tyler understood much more now how important it was to have a well-rounded relationship. One that could include the thrill of adventure but would also flourish in the slower less-exciting times.

"It looks like the birthday girl has arrived," his mom said.

Tyler turned to see Melanie making her way toward them with the hostess. She had changed from when he'd seen her earlier. She now wore dark fitted jeans that were tucked into knee-high boots, the heels of which gave her a couple more inches in height. The loose turquoise sweater she wore looked striking with her dark hair and eyes. But it was her smile as she approached the table that grabbed him.

Her eyebrows rose slightly when all three men got to their feet at her approach. Tyler stepped behind the chair next to his. "Good evening, Melanie."

She hesitated a moment before sitting down. "Hi, everyone."

Once they were seated, Tyler turned to her and said, "Glad you could make it."

She smiled, her gaze warm. "It was by far the best invitation I had for how to spend my birthday."

"It's your birthday too?" Ryan asked as he leaned forward.

"Yep. But Tyler's still older than me."

Before the birthday discussion could continue, a waitress appeared to take their drink orders. Tyler also ordered a couple of appetizers before the waitress left, promising to return when they'd had a chance to look over the menus.

As they waited for their drinks and then their meals, his mom regaled them with tales of her experiences living in London as part of the upper class. With a clear memory of how things had been for them when he was growing up, Tyler was glad that his mom no longer had to scrimp and save in order to provide for them. Even though she came off as somewhat flighty and lighthearted, he knew that underneath it all, she took her life and loves very seriously.

"Can you say grace, darling?" his mom asked as she laid a hand on Hank's.

Tyler had to smile at the indulgent nod Hank gave his mom. Saying grace out loud in a restaurant was something it had taken the man a while to get used to. However, Tyler was pretty sure Hank still wasn't used to his mom's insistence that they hold hands as well. But could anyone say no to Shauna Wakeford?

He took the hand his mom offered him and then turned to Melanie. Ryan had easily taken Hank's hand leading Tyler to believe that he too came from a family where grace—regardless of where it was said—included handholding. As both he and Ryan held a hand out to Melanie, she hesitated only briefly before slipping her hands into theirs.

As he listened to Hank give thanks for their meal and the birthdays they were celebrating, Tyler added his own silent prayer of thanks for the people God had brought into his life. People might look at his *disability* and feel sorry for him, but he knew that he was actually extremely blessed to have lost his legs because he was fairly certain that he'd never have met the people he had in his life now. Melanie. Ryan. Simon. They were all there as a result of what had happened to him. He couldn't find it in himself to wish away the one bad thing that had brought him so many good things.

Once they'd said grace for the food, his mom turned the conversation in another direction. "So, do you have family nearby, Ryan?"

Ryan took a drink of his water. "Depends on what you class as nearby. Most of my family lives in Winnipeg, which is about a seven or eight-hour drive north of here."

"Canada?" his mom asked.

"Yep."

"Do you have siblings?"

"I do. I kind of have a Brady Bunch thing going on with my family. I have one brother, two sisters, four stepbrothers, and two half-siblings, the Irish twins."

"The Irish twins?" Tyler was a little surprised at the sibling revelation. He'd known Ryan had a large family, but he hadn't known the exact makeup of it. "Is that because you all are Irish?"

"No." Ryan grinned. "Dalton was born just nine months after Danica. Siblings born within twelve months of each other are often called Irish twins. Dalton was two months premature."

"So there are...ten of you kids?" his mom asked.

Ryan nodded. "It was a good thing my step-dad was into construction. He had to build us a pretty big house when he and my mom got married."

"I bet there's a story there," his mom said, a dreamy look on her face.

Ryan laughed. "There is, and it was kind of fun being around to see it happen even though I was fairly young at the time."

"What brought you to BlackThorpe?" This time, Melanie joined into the conversation.

Tyler wondered if Ryan would answer the question since he was fairly quiet about his background. Ryan's gaze settled on Melanie, and Tyler felt a pinch of jealousy. If Melanie *was* interested in a relationship, Ryan would obviously be the better choice. And although he knew his friend wouldn't cross that line since he seemed to think Tyler had feelings for her, that didn't mean *she* wasn't interested in Ryan.

"My dad was in the US military." He twirled the straw in his glass. "He was an American, which is why I can work here. He was killed in action. After his death, my mom moved us back to Winnipeg, where she's from, but from very young I always hoped to be able to follow in his footsteps. Much to my mother's dismay, I enlisted and was sent to the Middle East. While I was there, I met Alex and when I decided that one tour was enough—particularly because of my mother—he offered me a position with BlackThorpe. So, here I am."

It was pretty much the same as what Ryan had told him when they'd first met. He still wasn't sure how his father had died, and Tyler was fairly certain there was more to the story of why he'd only done one tour. However, he wasn't going to pry too deeply if the guy wasn't interested in sharing.

"And he's the best neighbor I could ever ask for," Tyler said as he grinned at Ryan. "He brings me pizza and plays video games with me."

"Since you make me work out and eat halfway decent the rest of the time, I'm still trying to decide if you're the best neighbor *I* could ever ask for." Laughter floated around the table at Ryan's remark and accompanying pained expression.

Melanie shifted on her chair beside him and Tyler looked over at her. "Well, you should try *living* with your older siblings. Thrill a minute."

"You live with Adrianne and Alex?" Ryan asked as he tore a piece off the breadstick he'd taken.

"Sort of. We each have our own set of rooms, but then there's a large common area with a big kitchen, dining room, and a great room. Sometimes having our own rooms isn't enough when you need space. We had to lay down some ground rules not long after we moved in together."

"Ground rules?" Tyler asked. He'd known she lived with her siblings, but he'd never been to their home.

"Yep. We're not allowed to ask where anyone is going, for one thing. That was a biggie. I felt like I was living with my parents every time I went out, and Alex or Adrianne would be asking me where I was going and when I would be home."

Tyler tried to ignore the twist to his gut when Ryan and Melanie began to share stories about the joys of having siblings. It was one thing he had no experience with, and it had never bothered him until that moment when he wished he could have that in common with his friends too.

Thankfully, they didn't linger on that subject too long. Tyler really disliked being jealous of his best friend for any reason. He could sense his mother watching him and knew he'd have some questions to answer later.

They were discussing the merits of dessert when Tyler's phone vibrated. He slid it free of its holder on his belt so he could see the display. *Marcus.*

"Surely you don't have to take a call in the middle of your birthday dinner," his mom said with a frown.

"Sorry, Momma. He wouldn't call if it weren't important. I'll be right back." Tyler pushed back from the table as he tapped the screen to accept the call.

He walked towards the entrance of the restaurant, weaving among the tables as he went. "Hello, Marcus."

"Tyler. I hope I'm not interrupting anything."

"It's fine. What can I do for you?"

"I stopped by your office earlier, but they said you were off today."

Though it wasn't a question, Tyler felt obliged to give a reason for his absence. "Yes. My mom and her husband are here for a few days, so I took today off to spend with them."

There was silence then Marcus said, "I'll make this quick so you can get back to them. I've sent you two more names to add to the list you've been cross referencing telephone numbers for. And in addition to the names, I've included a number that I want you to watch for as you go through the phone records. If any of the numbers have called or received a call from that number, I want to know right away."

"Certainly. I'll get that started tonight."

"Thank you, Tyler, and I apologize for interrupting your time with your parents."

"It's not a problem. Have a good weekend."

After ending the call, Tyler checked his email for the names Marcus wanted added to his project. He didn't recognize them, but soon he'd know quite a bit about them...or at least their calling patterns. It didn't thrill him that he'd have to work on the weekend his mom and Hank were in town, but he knew this project was important to Marcus.

As he walked back to the table, his gaze lingered on Melanie as she sat perched on the edge of her chair, leaning forward slightly. He frowned as he recognized a telltale bulge right around her waist. Normally, he wouldn't have noticed it, but her position pulled her sweater more tightly across her back. She probably didn't even realize that her concealed weapon wasn't quite concealed.

What on earth was she doing wearing a weapon while out for a birthday dinner? Was she always armed? As he thought back over the outfits he'd seen her in, he realized that any of them could have concealed a weapon or two. He knew that BlackThorpe encouraged its employees to take weapons and self-defense training. He was fairly proficient with most weapons given his time in the military, and he spent time every couple of weeks at the BlackThorpe training compound, but he'd never seen Melanie there.

Melanie looked up at him as he approached the table. "Anything serious?"

Tyler shook his head as he sank into his seat next to her. "No. Marcus just wanted to let me know he'd added something to a project I'm working on. He hadn't realized I was off today."

"He expects you to work on the weekend?" his mom asked.

"Not normally, but this is a special project. I won't spend too much time on it, just need to work up some data for him by Monday."

Melanie leaned back in her chair. "I should ask Alex if Marcus ever stops working."

"You don't know Marcus very well?" Ryan asked.

"Not really, no. He's Alex's friend and well, he's not terribly social." Melanie lifted her glass and took a sip. "Although I've seen him at more social functions the past year or so with the all the weddings and engagement parties going on."

Tyler and Ryan laughed then Tyler said, "Yeah, there's been a slew of them recently."

"Seeing two confirmed bachelors bite the dust in quick order means that just about anyone is fair game," Ryan said. "They're taking bets on our floor on who'll be next."

"What?" Melanie's eyes were wide as she stared at Ryan. "Bets on who'll get married next?"

Ryan shook his head. "Nope. Bets on who'll fall in love next."

"Who are people betting on?"

"Well, since there are only four of you left…" Ryan grinned at her.

"Seriously?" Melanie's brows drew together. "You guys are betting on whether Marcus, Alex, Adrianne or I will be the next one to fall in love?"

Tyler held up his hands. "I'm not part of that."

Melanie stared at him for a moment then looked back at Ryan. "Do I even want to know who the odds-on favorite is?"

Ryan chuckled. "Probably not."

With a groan, Melanie sank into her seat. "Well, here's an insider tip for you. Of the three of us—I haven't a clue about Marcus—Adrianne is the only one who is actively dating."

"Nice try, Melanie," Ryan said, "but Justin is proof that even someone who has no interest in a relationship can succumb. People think you're next in line."

Melanie frowned. "The joke will be on them when Adrianne's the one who falls first."

Tyler listened to the conversation with interest. Likely more interest than he should have. He shouldn't care about Melanie's outlook on relationships and falling in love. Six months ago, he wouldn't have cared. Three months ago, he wouldn't have cared. What was happening to him?

He let out a sigh, hoping this conversation would end quickly. The last thing he needed was for his mother to hear anything more about Melanie. She was already getting ideas that he really wasn't sure he wanted her to have. It was one thing for her to ask if he'd met a "nice young lady," quite another for her to ask specifically about Melanie in their weekly conversations.

Melanie found herself relaxing as the evening wore on. She'd been surprised to see Ryan at the table when she'd arrived, but realistically she shouldn't have been. It was no secret that Ryan and Tyler were great friends.

She hadn't spent much time with Ryan but found him easy to talk to. She could see why he and Tyler got along so well together. It had been a bit unsettling to hear about the bets going on, and that she was the odds-on favorite for the next person to fall in love.

Not long ago she would have laughed about it, confident in her ability to protect her heart. Lately, though, she wasn't as sure. She just needed to stay strong, reminding herself that even though her heart might want to love, it couldn't be trusted.

If she was honest with herself, she really was too messed up for any sort of relationship. She watched Shauna and Hank, seeing the love and affection between the two of them. Melanie had no doubt that Hank would do everything within his power to protect Shauna, to give her anything her heart would desire. And when she saw the way Tyler looked at his mom, she knew that Shauna was blessed with the love of two men.

She wondered what that would be like. Even her own mom and dad didn't seem to have that type of relationship. Oh, she was sure they loved each other, but it seemed that they kind of lived their own lives. Her mom had her interests and her dad had his. It seemed that what brought them together most of the time was the three of them.

Though her heart longed for what Shauna had with Hank, she knew that it wasn't meant for her. She had too many secrets. Too many things she couldn't share with anyone. Too many pieces of herself that she needed to guard.

"So your big party is tomorrow night?" Tyler asked.

It took a moment for Melanie to realize that Tyler was asking *her* that question. "It won't be a big party. Just my family. At least that better be all that's planned."

She waited for someone to ask why, if it was just family, they hadn't been able to gather on the day of her actual birthday. Thankfully, no one posed the question. In reality, she had no idea why they hadn't planned something for tonight. Her mom had just said that it would be more convenient if they did it on a Saturday night, and given that she had no interest in celebrating at all, Melanie had gone along with it.

And honestly, spending the evening with Ryan, Tyler, and his parents was a lot more fun. Given Adrianne's latest upset with their mother, the dinner party would no doubt have its tense moments.

"Well, I'm glad you were free to join us this evening," Shauna said with a smile.

"Me too," Melanie said, her words full of sincerity. It had been awhile since she'd last enjoyed an evening like this.

Shauna's brows drew together. "I wish I'd had the time to get you a gift."

"Oh, I'm glad you didn't go to any trouble," Melanie told her. "There's really nothing I need."

"Birthdays aren't about getting things you need, sweetheart. They should be about being indulged with the things you want." Shauna looked at Tyler. "I think Tyler has a gift for you, though."

"Momma," Tyler said, a slight reproof in his voice, but his mom just smiled.

Melanie turned to look at him. "You bought me a gift?"

"Uh...yes." He reached down beside his chair and lifted a gift-wrapped box. "Here you go."

Melanie stared at the box for a moment, uncertain what to make of it. She scooted her chair back a bit so she could set the box on her lap. "Thank you."

"Don't tell me you're one of those people who carefully removes each strip of tape," Ryan said with a groan as she slid a finger under the paper. "That's no fun."

"Well, it seems a shame to just rip right into it."

"I give you permission," Tyler said with a grin.

When her stomach lurched at the twinkle in his eyes, Melanie swallowed and said, "Well, if you insist."

It *was* a lot more fun to rip the paper, just as Ryan had said. She smiled as the contents of the box was revealed. She looked up at Tyler. "You remembered?"

Tyler shrugged. "You did mention it more than once."

She lifted one of the delicately formed candles out of the box and sniffed it. "And it smells like my perfume. Did you have these specially made?"

"Well, maybe?" He ducked his head. "It's not like I'd ever forget your birthday, and I knew you were a year younger than me so this was a big one for you."

"Thank you, Tyler." Melanie was touched and a little worried, but she shoved those thoughts aside for the moment. She was going to enjoy the evening without trying to dissect it. "I actually have a gift for you too."

Tyler straightened and his eyebrows rose. "Really?"

She reached into her purse and pulled out the card she'd gotten for him earlier. "Sorry, you don't get to madly rip into a wrapped present."

As he took it from her, he grinned. "Well, we can't all have that fun."

He opened the flap and pulled out the card. Melanie had agonized over it, trying to find one that was masculine and friendly without being flirty or romantic. Hopefully, the gift inside would distract from the card itself.

Tyler looked up at her when he realized what she'd gotten him. "Tickets to a Timberwolves game? And what are these? Almost courtside?"

"Almost," Melanie said. "I figured that since you were a basketball fan..."

"I can't accept these. That's too much, Melanie," Tyler said as he stared down at the tickets.

"You *will* accept them," she insisted. "Just like I'm accepting this gift that you probably paid far too much for."

Tyler was quiet for a moment, and Melanie wondered if he was going to continue to protest. Finally, he looked up and their gazes met. The determination in his caused butterflies to come to life in her stomach.

"Okay. I'll accept these under one condition."

Melanie didn't like the sound of that. "What's the condition?"

A corner of his mouth lifted. "You come with me."

"You want me to go to the game with you?" Melanie stared at him. "I'm not really a basketball fan myself."

"Then it's about time you went to a game to see what it's all about."

"I thought maybe you could take Ryan or Simon."

"Are those for the first pre-season game?" Ryan asked. When Tyler nodded, he said, "I've got tickets to that already. My brother is coming to town for that game, so don't worry about me."

"See?" Tyler said as he turned back to her. "Ryan's already going. So...?"

Spend an evening with Tyler? At least it wouldn't be a romantic thing. She couldn't think of anything less romantic than watching a basketball game. It wouldn't be fair to give Tyler the wrong idea. Although, considering the gift he'd given her, it was possible he had different ideas about their friendship than she did.

"Are you sure that Simon wouldn't want to go with you?"

"It would be difficult at this point for him to go. We'd need to be able to get a wheelchair to the seats. So unless you bought a ticket for some sort of handicap seating, I don't think it would work for him."

"Well, if you're absolutely positive there's no one else to go with you..."

"I'm positive."

Melanie knew the date for the game was a couple of weeks away, so there was always the possibility that she could weasel her way out of it. Even if her heart was telling her to grab hold of the chance.

When the evening finally drew to a close, Melanie found she was disappointed. It had been a long time since she'd been able to just relax and enjoy time with friends.

"I'll be right with you," Tyler said to his mom and Hank as they left the restaurant. He pointed his keys at his car and the lights flashed. "It's unlocked."

"No rush, sweetheart," Shauna said as she leaned her head against Hank's shoulder.

"See you at home, Ty," Ryan called out.

Tyler lifted a hand in acknowledgment then turned to Melanie. "Can I walk you to your car?"

Melanie thought about pointing out that her car wasn't that far away—and she was armed—but instead, she just nodded. Tyler didn't say anything as they walked the short distance to her car. She pressed the button on her fob to unlock her door then automatically rearranged the keys in her hand so that she gripped the small canister of pepper spray attached to her keychain.

When they reached her car, Tyler rested his hand on the handle of the door. "Listen, Melanie, if you really don't want to go to the basketball game, just say the word. I really didn't mean to pressure you into it."

Melanie looked up at Tyler. The streetlight was behind him, casting him in shadows so she couldn't read the expression on his face. She should be grateful for the 'out' he was giving her and definitely should take it, but instead Melanie said, "You didn't pressure me. I just wanted to make sure that there wasn't someone else that you might want to take. I hope you didn't feel obliged to ask me because I'd given you the tickets."

"Nope. I asked because I wanted you to go. I think you'd enjoy it." Tyler paused and his head dipped toward her. "But..."

"But?" Melanie prompted when he didn't continue.

"If something like this is going to make you uncomfortable, I'd rather not do that. So if the flipside to you going to the game is going to be you stepping back from our friendship then tell me now, and I'll find someone else to go with me."

Melanie's heart clenched at his words. Did their friendship really mean that much to him? "That's not what will happen. I'll be happy to go to the game as long as you're willing to explain it all to me. I haven't paid much attention to the game or the teams."

Tyler straightened as he chuckled. "No worries. I'll make sure you get the drift of what's happening." He opened her door then and held it as she got behind the wheel. "Thanks so much for joining us tonight. It was fun to have someone else to celebrate with."

"Yes, it was. I'm the one who should be thanking you for sharing your evening with me. It was great to get to know your mom and Hank."

"Well, I think the feeling was mutual." He eased the door forward a few inches. "Drive safe. See you next week."

At her nod, he shut the door completely then turned to walk to where his car sat. Though Melanie was tempted to sit for a few minutes to process the events of the evening, she started up her car and headed for home. She still had to do her workouts for the day and that would give her plenty of time to think over it all.

7

SHE'S A LOVELY GIRL," his mom said as Tyler drove back to his place. She sat on the seat beside him while Hank was in the back. His step-father's down-to-earth attitude was something else Tyler really appreciated about the man.

He'd thought that they would want to stay in a hotel since Hank could, realistically, afford to *buy* most of the ones in the city. Instead, when his mom had asked to stay with him, he'd been more than happy to accommodate them.

"Yes, she's been a good friend." He was glad that in at least that regard, he didn't have to lie to his mother.

"Any chance she might be *more* than a friend? She did say she wasn't dating anyone."

Tyler wasn't too surprised at his mom's question given her not-so-subtle queries over the past few months regarding his dating life. He supposed he should be grateful that it took her as long as it had to start to focus on that part of his life following his divorce.

He didn't disagree with her on the surface, but it would take a special woman to take him on considering he was a double amputee. While he didn't view himself as disabled, his need for prosthetics for both legs made certain adjustments necessary. He still used a wheelchair at home sometimes since once he took off his prosthetics at night, he wouldn't put them on just to go to the bathroom or get a drink during the night.

A woman would have to accept all of that. And being honest with himself, Tyler had to admit that part of what drew him to Melanie was her devotion to helping people like him. She understood the challenges that came with living with prosthetics, and she also knew just how far he'd come since that day six years ago when he'd first arrived at the Center. He wouldn't need to explain anything to her and, whether it should be or not, that was a definite positive.

"Well, I think her point about dating was that she's chosen not to date, not that she is currently between boyfriends," Tyler explained. "As far as I know, she's never dated in the years we've been friends. I don't think she wants to."

"You could always change her mind." His mom was nothing if not persistent.

"If something like that is meant to be between the two of us, she'll have to change her own mind. I'm not going to try to talk her into something she's not interested in. Her friendship is too important." He didn't really want his mom to pick up on his own reluctance to pursue a relationship. Better to let her think it was all on Melanie's side.

"Well, if you're not opposed to the idea, I think I shall make Melanie a focus of prayer," his mom said.

His mom's words did cause Tyler to think, wondering what Melanie might make of a comment like that. He really wasn't sure where Melanie stood in her faith. From comments she'd made, he was fairly certain that she attended church. But he knew from experience that attending church didn't make someone a Christian.

"Momma, I would never tell you to not pray for something if you feel you should." Tyler pressed the remote to open the garage as he turned into his driveway. "But just remember that God might have an entirely different plan in mind."

"But, of course, darling. I am the poster child for how a person's plan for their life can be very different from what God has planned."

Tyler drove into the garage and stopped the car. "Well, I think both Hank and I would agree that we are very happy for that, regardless of the circumstances that brought us into your life."

Hank got out of the back seat and opened the door for his mom as Tyler turned off the car and pressed the button to close the garage door. He followed them from the garage into the house, punching in the alarm code to deactivate it.

"Do you want anything to eat or drink?" Tyler asked as they walked into the kitchen.

"Nothing for me," his mom said. "I'm actually pretty tired. Still a bit on London time, I guess."

"I'm fine too," Hank said, slipping an arm around his wife's waist. "I'm going to do a quick look over my email and then call it a night as well."

"Momma, you're still okay with me being gone for a few hours tomorrow night?" Tyler asked. Since Simon had agreed to go to the basketball game, he wanted to make sure he could follow through on his invitation.

"That's perfectly fine, sweetheart. I think Hank and I can entertain ourselves for the evening." She came and gave Tyler a kiss on the cheek. "Sleep well. See you in the morning."

Tyler watched them walked through the living room to the hallway that led to the three bedrooms. He had the master bedroom, but the guest room they occupied was also fairly large and comfortable. The third bedroom he used as an office though he usually worked on his laptop in his bedroom.

He grabbed a bottle of water from the fridge, set the alarm and shut off the lights in the rest of the house. Though he thought about going to the basement he shared with Ryan to see if his friend was hanging out there, he really wasn't in the mood to work out or chat, so he retreated to his room instead.

After putting the water bottle and phone on his nightstand, he went to the bathroom to prepare for bed. His routine was fairly simple but necessary so that he didn't have to get back up out of bed for anything. After he was finished in the bathroom, he sat on the bed and carefully slid his pants down over the prosthetics, then went through the process of removing each of them, setting them beside the wheelchair next to the bed.

Though being without them restricted his ability to get around, it was a relief to be free of them now that his day was nearly over. Using his arms, he pushed himself to the headboard and reached for the portable laptop desk that sat on the unused side of the bed.

He logged into his work email to read over the email from Marcus. Once he had done that, he realized he needed to access his work programs. After a couple of extra steps, he was able to remotely log into his computer at BlackThorpe.

As Tyler inputted the information Marcus had sent him, he knew that he was going to have to take some time to compile all this data for Marcus. The man wasn't putting undue amounts of pressure on him, but Tyler knew him well enough to read the underlying current of impatience. By Monday morning, he needed to have something to give the man.

As he quickly skimmed over the results that the computer had come up with from the previous information, Tyler was confident he'd be able to give Marcus a full report. He still wasn't sure what he was looking at—even with the additional information Marcus had given him earlier that night—but there were a few connections between the phone numbers that might interest Marcus.

Once he'd restarted the program running with the new information, Tyler logged out of his remote connection. He clicked to his Facebook page and spent a few minutes thanking people for the birthday wishes and commenting on a few posts from his friends. He wasn't a big one for social media, but he did enjoy being able to keep in easy contact with friends who lived far away.

On a whim, he typed Melanie's name into the search bar but wasn't surprised when none of the possible profiles that popped up were hers. Alex and Adrianne both had Facebook profiles and were fairly active on them, but for some reason, Melanie was absent from social media. He'd asked her about it once, but she'd just brushed aside his questions, muttering something about it being a waste of time.

It was just one more way she was different from her two older siblings. Not that that was a bad thing. In fact, it made her that much more interesting to Tyler.

Okay, so that might not necessarily be a good thing...

Tyler was feeling pretty good when he drove through the security gates into the BlackThorpe complex on Monday morning. Simon had come to the game and even though he hadn't physically participated in it, he had shouted encouragement from the sidelines. He'd been the most animated Tyler had seen him to date. From Simon's reaction, Tyler was fairly certain it wouldn't be too long before he got more involved.

His mom and Hank had gone to church with him and then they'd gone out to eat before spending the rest of the day back at the house visiting. He'd said goodbye to them when a car had arrived earlier that morning to take them to the airport for their flight back to London. Though it was never fun to say goodbye, Tyler had enjoyed having them come to his home for a change so he had plenty of good memories of their short visit.

After parking his car, he went into the main building and pressed the button to call the elevator.

"Morning, Tyler."

He glanced over to see Than Miller standing next to him. Though the man looked impeccably dressed as usual, his countenance lacked the lopsided grin that Tyler had come to expect from him.

"Hey, Than. You don't look your usual sunshiny self," Tyler said. He motioned for the man to precede him into the elevator when the doors slid open.

"Don't ever get married, Tyler, my friend," Than muttered as he punched the button for Tyler's floor and then his own.

"Actually, I've been there, done that." Tyler watched as Than digested that information, his dark brows drawing together.

"You're married?"

"Not anymore. She couldn't deal with the changes in my lifestyle after I lost my legs."

"I'm sorry to hear that, man. That's just wrong."

Tyler just shrugged. If it had been his choice, he would have stayed married, but now that they'd gone their separate ways, he didn't dwell too much on how their life would be now if they hadn't gotten divorced. "So what's soured your views on the institution?"

Than ran a hand through his hair. "It isn't actually the marriage, it's the wedding. If we didn't think our mothers would kill us, Linds and I would just elope. Things are getting way out of hand with the wedding plans. Weddings are a huge thing in Filipino culture, so my mom is making sure ours is a big one. It doesn't help any that money doesn't appear to be an object. And since Linds is an only daughter, her mom is right in there too. My mom and her mom...look out wedding world."

Tyler couldn't keep from laughing. "So not a bridezilla thing?"

Than shook his head. "No way. Lindsay is perfect." The smile that accompanied the statement lit the man's eyes.

"She's trying to take it all in stride, but there just comes a point where it's too much—even for me! Twelve bridesmaids? That's crazy."

"You have my sympathies, man," Tyler said with a grin as he stepped off the elevator when it stopped on his floor.

The grin stayed on his face until he settled behind his desk and put the final touches on the report he'd compiled for Marcus. He'd already told Marcus he had something for him, so now it was just a matter of waiting for the summons.

Melanie got on the elevator after the Tuesday meeting. She meant to press the button to go to the garage, but instead, she pushed the one for Tyler's floor. She wasn't entirely sure why, and when the doors slid open, she hesitated briefly before stepping out.

When she reached Tyler's door, a quick glance inside revealed it was empty. Telling herself that feeling disappointed was ridiculous, Melanie turned to retrace her steps.

"Hey, Melanie!"

She stopped and looked over to see Ryan heading toward her. "Hi, Ryan. How are you?"

He jogged the last few steps to her side and gave her a smile. "I'm good. How about you?"

"I'm good."

Ryan put his hands on his hips. "Were you looking for Ty?"

Though she wanted to deny it, his question was no doubt a rhetorical one and lying might fall under the "protest too much" category. "Yeah. Is he around?"

"Just left him in the lunchroom." Ryan gave a jerk of his head in the direction he'd just come from. "He'll be back in a minute or two. In the meantime, I can keep you company."

Melanie laughed. "Well, then how was your weekend?"

"It started off with a fun birthday party dinner. Which, by the way, if I had known it was your birthday along with Ty's, I totally would have gotten you a gift."

"I really don't do birthdays, Ryan, so you're safe."

"Did you have a good dinner with your family?"

Melanie wrinkled her nose. It had been everything she'd been expecting, so no, she wouldn't exactly call it good. The dinner on Friday night had been a lot more enjoyable. "Let's just say I'm so glad I only have a birthday once a year."

"My mom likes to make a big deal out of birthdays, so with ten kids, that's a lot of parties."

"I can't even imagine having nine siblings. The two I've got are more than enough most days."

Ryan laughed. "Well, let's just say that growing up there was always someone around to do something with. A lot of built-in playmates. Two of my stepbrothers are twins and were just a year older than me so my mom said it was like having triplets. We got into a lot of trouble together."

"Hey, you two."

Tyler's voice kept Melanie from responding as she turned to see him headed their way, coffee mug in hand.

He smiled as he came to a stop next to her. "What brings you to our floor?"

"I just wanted to stop in and thank you again for Friday night."

Before Tyler could reply, Ryan gave a small bow and said, "On that note, I'll return to my office. See you later."

"C'mon in," Tyler said as he motioned to his office.

Melanie walked through his doorway and sank into a chair while he rounded his desk. She waited until he had settled before she said, "I really did appreciate the dinner Friday night. I had a lot of fun. And it was so great to meet your mom and her husband."

"They enjoyed getting to know you too. Hank couldn't stop talking about the Center and the good work you're doing there. He was very impressed with the tour you gave them."

"You know, your stepfather has been a donor for several years. One of our bigger ones, in fact. I just never made the connection between him and you."

Tyler tilted his head. "It doesn't make a difference, does it?"

"No. Not at all. I just think it's great how our helping you has in turn allowed us to help so many others because of donations like those from your parents."

"I learned a few new things about Hank on this visit," Tyler said, a thoughtful expression on his face. "Because I was already out on my own when he married my mom, I've never really thought much about the relationship between him and me. I mean, he was good to my mom and made her happy and that's all I really cared about, to be honest. She had a rough life, and I was thrilled to finally see her find love and happiness."

"She was young when she got pregnant with you," Melanie remarked, recalling their earlier conversation about his mom. "I'm sure it wasn't easy being a teenage mom."

Tyler nodded. "It wasn't. In fact, I'm pretty sure it was horrible for her."

"Did her parents help her out?" As soon as she said the words, Melanie realized that maybe this wasn't a subject Tyler was interested in discussing. "Uh, you know what...no need to answer. That's really none of my business."

Leaning back in his chair, Tyler stared at her for a moment. "No, it's fine. Her parents tried, but when she realized that they would never view me as a person in my own right, she moved out and did her best to raise me on her own."

Melanie frowned. "View you as a person in your own right? What does that mean?"

Again Tyler paused. "My mom got pregnant with me as a result of rape. Unfortunately, her parents were convinced I'd turn out just like him."

Of all the things she'd expected him to say, that hadn't been anywhere on the list. Her stomach churned at the new revelation. "Did they catch the guy?"

Tyler shook his head. "Not until a few years later when they were able to use DNA to nab him. It didn't result in a conviction though because he was killed in a standoff with police because of another assault."

"I'm so sorry, Tyler, I didn't mean to pry into something so personal."

Tyler shrugged. "It's not something we've ever hidden. In fact, I'm so proud of my mom and the difficult decisions she made at such a young age. Obviously, there was lots of pressure to abort given the circumstances, but she always told me that in her mind, there was no choice. That while I may have the DNA of the rapist, I also had part of her."

Even though she'd already thought Shauna was a wonderful person, Melanie's respect for the woman sky-rocketed. She wasn't sure she would have had the strength to make the choice Shauna had at that age. And as she sat there staring at Tyler, she realized just how glad she was that Shauna had chosen life for the baby she'd carried.

"Your mom is amazing," Melanie said with a smile.

"Yes, she definitely is." Tyler's answering smile sent warmth spiraling through her. "I thank God every day that He gave me to her."

"I really didn't mean to delve into your life that way." Melanie clasped her hands in her lap. "But thank you for sharing."

"Well, if we're sharing," Tyler said with a mischievous grin on his face. "Are you gonna tell me any secrets about yourself?"

Melanie hoped her smile didn't change or that the color wasn't leeched from her face at his comment. Any secrets she had were going to stay in the past where they belonged. "Sorry. A woman's gotta keep her secrets. Preserving the mystery and all that."

Tyler tilted his head back as he laughed. "Ah. So men have to be open books while women get to preserve the mystery?"

"Something like that," Melanie said, glad he hadn't seemed to notice her reaction to his question. She felt her phone vibrate in her pocket and slipped it out to see a text from Adrianne. "Oops, I'd better scoot. Adrianne is looking for me. I promised I'd go for lunch with her today."

Tyler got to his feet as she did. "It was nice having you stop by for a chat. I thought maybe you were coming to back out on the basketball game."

"No. I said I'd go and I will."

"Good." Tyler shoved his hands into his pockets. "Ryan's brother is coming into town, and Ryan suggested that we go for dinner beforehand since we won't be sitting together during the game. You up for that?"

"Sure. Sounds like fun." Melanie thought about declining, but if it was all about being friends, going to dinner with the three guys shouldn't be an issue.

After saying goodbye, she headed for the elevator, tapping out a message to Adrianne as she went.

This is not a date.

Tyler had been repeating that to himself for the past hour as he got ready for the dinner and basketball game. He was still surprised that Melanie hadn't backed out, and he was going to make sure that she didn't regret this decision. He just wanted the evening to go smoothly and be fun for her.

Remembering that he'd planned to call her, Tyler grabbed his cell phone from the top of his dresser and tapped the screen to bring up her contact information. Once the phone was ringing, he put it on speakerphone and laid it back down on the dresser. As he waited for her to answer, he threaded his belt through the loops on the black jeans he wore.

"Don't tell me you're calling to cancel," Melanie said when she answered.

"Nope. You wouldn't get that lucky. I have a different reason for calling."

"What's up?"

"I, uh, just wanted to make sure you knew you can't get into the Target Center if you're carrying."

"Carrying?" Melanie asked.

"You know. A concealed weapon."

She didn't answer right away but then said, "How do you know I carry?"

"I happened to see it the night of our birthday dinner. I know that BlackThorpe likes its management team to be armed, but the security at the Target Center will likely not let you in if you've got any type of weapon on you." He paused. "Is that going to be a problem?"

"No, Tyler. It's fine. I actually checked their website to see what their security measures were and left my weapons at home. I think I'll be okay without them tonight. I'm with three big strong guys, right?"

Weapons? She had more than one that she wore concealed? "Sure. Well, I haven't met Ryan's brother yet so it might just be two big strong guys."

She laughed at that. "Actually, I'm pretty adept at taking care of myself. With or without weapons."

Tyler could only imagine. He was making a few discoveries about Melanie that made him wonder exactly how well he actually knew the woman. "Well, let's hope no fights break out at the basketball game. We'll leave that to the hockey fans."

"Sounds good. I'm already on my way, so I'll be at your place in a little bit."

After she hung up, Tyler went into the bathroom to check his appearance one last time. It might not be a date, but he didn't want her to be embarrassed to be seen with him. He probably should have gotten his hair trimmed since it was almost long enough for him to pull back with an elastic band.

"Yo, Harris!" Ryan's shout drifted down the hallway to his room.

Tyler grabbed his wallet, phone and the tickets from his dresser and walked out to the living room. Ryan stood talking with a man who was a couple of inches taller than him and just as broad.

"Hey, Ryan," Tyler said as he joined them.

Ryan swung around. "Hey, Tyler. This is my brother, Gabe Callaghan. Gabe, this is Tyler Harris."

Tyler took the hand Gabe held out and gave it a firm shake. "A pleasure to meet you."

Since he knew they weren't biological brothers, he wasn't surprised at the differences in their appearances. While Ryan had brown hair and dark blue eyes, Gabe had blond hair not much lighter than his own and his eyes were a light shade of green. The man was tanned like Ryan though and looked like he enjoyed working out as much as his brother.

He also had an easy grin that crinkled the corners of his eyes as he said, "Nice to meet you too. I'm glad to see Ryan has someone close by to keep him in line."

"I'm not the one that needs to be kept in line," Ryan scoffed as he dug an elbow into Gabe's side. "This guy is an adrenalin junkie. Out of the ten of us, he is single handedly responsible for every gray hair our parents have on their heads."

"Hey, what's life without a little adventure?"

"Melanie's not here yet?" Ryan asked.

"She said she was on her way when I talked to her a few minutes ago."

As if on cue, the doorbell rang. Though he would have preferred to pick Melanie up for the evening, keeping in mind that she didn't view this as a date, he didn't protest when she turned down his offer.

This isn't a date.

He had to remind himself of that when he set eyes on the woman standing on his porch. She wore a pair of fitted blue jeans tucked into knee high boots he'd seen her wear before.

The cropped jean jacket she wore covered the top part of a light green T-shirt that lay loosely across her hips.

"C'mon in," Tyler said, hoping she hadn't noticed him staring. They might not be on a date tonight, but anyone looking at them together was going to think he was one lucky dude.

8

MELANIE'S SMILE as she stepped passed him into the house warmed Tyler. *This is not a date.* Trying to keep the reminder front and center in his head, Tyler shut the door then followed her as she walked to where Ryan and Gabe stood.

"Well, Ryan, you didn't tell me we were going to have the pleasure of the company of such a beautiful woman," Gabe said, a wide grin on his face. He stuck his hand out as Melanie neared them. "Gabe Callaghan. Ryan's brother."

"Melanie Thorpe. Nice to meet you." Melanie took his hand but didn't hold it longer than a quick shake.

"We ready to go?" Tyler asked, suddenly eager to be on their way. The quicker they got through the part of the evening when they were all together, the quicker they got to the part where it was just the two of them at the game.

"Are we taking one vehicle?" Ryan asked. "We could save on parking if we did. Just meet up back there after the game."

It wasn't Tyler's first choice, but it did make sense. "Sure. We can take yours if you want."

Tyler set the alarm then waited for the other three to exit the house to lock the door. He had just shoved his keys into his pocket when he heard Gabe say, "I don't know whose wheels those are, but that's the one I want to go in."

"That's mine."

Tyler turned to see Gabe staring at the sleek ivory colored truck parked in his driveway, his own eyes widening as he realized what Melanie had just said. The truck was *hers*? He was pretty sure she'd been driving a smaller SUV of some sort the night of the birthday dinner.

Gabe sidled up to Melanie. "I don't suppose you'd let me drive, would ya?"

Melanie laughed. "Sorry. Not a chance." Then she turned toward Tyler and held out her hand, a keychain dangling from her fingers. "You, however, I will let drive it."

Gabe groaned. "Really? Why him and not me?"

Ryan grabbed Gabe by the arm and pulled him toward the truck. "Put a cork in it, buddy."

Tyler waited until they were a short distance away then asked in a low voice, "Are you sure?"

Melanie's brows drew together as she pointed the fob in her hand toward the truck and unlocked the doors. "Well, sure. You know how to drive, right?"

"Of course, but that truck looks like it cost a fortune." Tyler looked at the vehicle again, watching as Ryan and Gabe climbed in the back seat. "I'd hate to ding it up."

"Are you in the habit of dinging up cars?"

"No—" Tyler turned back to Melanie as her hand gripped his to turn it over. She pressed the keys into his palm then curved his fingers around them.

"I have no idea where we're going," she said, her expression serious. "If anyone were to ding it up, it would be me."

Tyler hesitated, but this time it was because he didn't want to lose the warmth of her hand on his. "Okay. I'll drive."

She smiled up at him then headed for the truck. As they neared it, Tyler reached out to open the door for her. Melanie grasped the handle above the door then stepped up on the running board to smoothly lift herself onto the seat. It was a lot of truck for someone like Melanie.

When he opened the door to get behind the wheel, Melanie said, "You might want to adjust the seat back before you get in."

Chuckling, Tyler did as she suggested. "Only way I could drive with the seat this close up would be to take off my prostheses."

There was a fair bit of traffic as they headed downtown, but having attended a lot of games over the years, Tyler knew how best to get to where they were going and found parking easily. He and Ryan had settled on a restaurant not far from the Target Center. It was one they'd gone to in the past and enjoyed.

"An Irish pub?" Gabe said as they approached the restaurant. "You're gonna be making me feel right at home, boyo."

Ryan groaned. "Seriously? I'm beginning to regret inviting you along."

"Ah, you don't mean that, Ry." Gabe turned to walk backward in front of them, a big grin on his face. "Everything is better when I'm around."

"Not sure that's entirely true," Ryan said. "But it *is* usually more interesting."

When they reached the entrance, Gabe held the door for them. Because Tyler had made reservations, it wasn't long until they were shown to a booth. Melanie slid in one side and Tyler joined her while Ryan and Gabe settled across from them.

"I've never been here before," Melanie said as she looked around then glanced down at the menu. "What do you recommend?"

Tyler bent toward her and pointed to a spot on the menu. "I'm partial to the chicken pot pie or the shepherd's pie. Both are delicious."

"Not the healthiest things around," Melanie observed.

"Well, you gotta splurge every once in a while," Tyler said. "I won't tell anyone."

"Honestly, I doubt anyone would care." Melanie seemed to consider his suggestions. "I guess I'll go with the chicken pot pie."

"Good choice. I think you'll really like it."

By the time the waitress had brought them drinks and taken their order, the restaurant was pretty much full. Tyler was glad they'd decided to come a little early.

"So, Gabe, what do you do for a living?" Melanie asked.

Ryan dropped his head forward with another groan. "What doesn't he do...."

Once again, Gabe grinned. "Yep. I do a little bit of everything. My passion is living life to its fullest which means I don't generally tie myself to a desk unless absolutely necessary."

"What do you mean?" Melanie asked.

Tyler was curious himself. Ryan had talked about Gabe at different times, enough for him to know that the two were close, but he hadn't really given specifics about the man.

"Some say I'm an adrenalin addict."

Tyler felt his stomach clench. He had a feeling he knew where this was going.

Melanie tilted her head. "You like to do risky things?"

"Yep. The riskier, the better. And that's not just in terms of activities, but I also like to help businesses take risks to grow."

"He also helps failing businesses," Ryan said. "Usually using unconventional methods to turn them around."

"What's life without taking a few risks?"

"A few?" Ryan's tone was incredulous as he turned to Gabe. "That's just a bit of an understatement."

"Well, I'm afraid I'm not much of a risk taker," Melanie said. "Probably the most risk I take is going to the shooting range or taking a self-defense class."

"You haven't lived until you've felt the surge of adrenalin as you face death and win."

Melanie seemed to consider that for a moment before she said, "Sometimes facing death and winning is overrated. It can leave a person with scars that never completely heal."

Tyler's brows drew together at her words. Was she talking about him? He was certainly glad he'd faced death and won, even with the scars his body still carried.

"Maybe it's different for me because I'm the one choosing when and where I'm facing death." Gabe paused. "Sometimes, if a person has had to face death in a way not of their choosing, they can take back that control by taking a risk that they *do* choose."

"I'm sure your family must worry about you."

"We do, Melanie," Ryan said. "But that doesn't stop him from jumping off cliffs, out of airplanes or climbing mountains."

Before the conversation could continue, the waitress appeared at their table with the appetizers they'd ordered. Gabe offered to say grace and then, thankfully, the topic of discussion changed. However, Tyler couldn't keep from wondering exactly what Melanie had been referring to with her comments.

Melanie wasn't sure how she felt about the way the evening had gone so far. Part of her wished it had just been her and Tyler for dinner. Not that she necessarily wanted to be alone with him—this wasn't a date, after all—but at least with just the two of them, the meal would have been more enjoyable.

Gabe wasn't anything like she'd expected, not that she'd put a lot of thought into it, but after meeting Ryan, she'd just thought he'd be like him. Of course, they weren't biological brothers, but Gabe's outlook on life had taken her by surprise. Maybe it was his cavalier approach to death. As someone who had at one time prayed for death only to stare it right in the face and ultimately escape with her life, she just couldn't fathom Gabe's attitude.

"Looks like it's time to head over to the arena," Tyler said as he lifted his hand to get their waitress's attention.

"Too bad we don't have seats closer together," Gabe said as they walked out of the restaurant.

"Oh, I think Melanie and Ty are probably grateful we don't." Melanie shot Ryan a look as he hooked his brother around the neck with one arm. Hadn't Tyler told him that this wasn't a date? "I'm sure they're thinking that if you're this hyper over dinner, you're going to be out of control during the game."

"What's the fun of going to a game if you can't yell at the refs or the players?" Gabe hip-checked Ryan, sending him stumbling toward Melanie.

Tyler quickly stepped between them so Ryan bumped into him instead. "Did you say there's ten of you? I can only feel deep sympathy for your parents."

They stood at a light, waiting for the signal to change for them to cross.

"Most of us are fairly calm. It's only when we're all together that things kind of get out of hand. And even then, it's usually Gabe and Kenton who are the instigators."

"Kenton?"

The light changed, and Melanie stepped off the curb with the other people who had been waiting. She glanced back to see Tyler still standing there. He suddenly moved forward and jogged a couple steps to catch up with them.

"Kenton Callaghan?"

"Yep," Gabe said with yet another grin. "The one and only."

"Seriously?" Tyler asked, grabbing Ryan by the arm. "Why didn't you tell me?"

"Tell you what?" Melanie stepped up on the curb, sticking close to Tyler so they didn't get separated by the crowd of people all heading in the same direction as them. "Who is Kenton Callaghan?"

"Only one of the best defensive hockey players in the NHL."

She didn't know much more about hockey than she knew about basketball, but even Melanie was impressed. "Your older brother plays for the NHL?"

Gabe fell into step beside her. "He plays for the Kings at the moment, though I'm pretty sure Mom and Dad are praying he gets traded to Winnipeg soon. And if Kenton is doing any praying these days, he's likely praying that he'll be traded anywhere but there. I might live my life on the edge, but Kenton is the party dude. He works hard and plays harder."

Before Melanie could ask anything more, they reached the doors of the arena. They followed Ryan and Gabe into the building then went their separate ways after agreeing to meet back at her truck.

As Ryan and Gabe moved away, leaving her alone with Tyler, Melanie let out a long breath. When Tyler chuckled, she looked up at him.

"Gabe's a bit over the top, isn't he?" Tyler asked as he laid a hand on her back to guide her to the doors that would take them to their seats.

Trying to ignore his closeness, Melanie nodded. "Just a bit. I'm not sure I've ever met someone so...alive? I'm not sure if that's the right word, but he certainly does bring life to the party."

Tyler seemed to know exactly where they were going and led the way down the aisle to their seats. He stood at the end of the row and let her precede him. She'd gotten an aisle seat for him, not knowing how comfortable he'd be in the middle of the row. Once she'd settled into her seat, he sank down beside her.

He turned to look at her, his eyes sparkling. "These are terrific seats. Thank you."

She couldn't help but return his smile. "I did a little research and was able to see the view on some 3D viewer they had so that helped."

"Not sure you could have gotten any better seats than these." Tyler looked out at the floor, his elbows resting on his thighs.

"Where are Ryan and Gabe?"

Tyler glanced over his shoulder at her then pointed across the arena. "They're in seats that are about ten rows up from ours. The seats they have are good." He looked at her again and smiled. "But ours are better."

Movement to her right drew Melanie's attention. A large group was filing into the row from the other end, and the guy leading the way smiled broadly when he spotted her. As he settled into the seat next to her, Melanie could see the interest in his eyes as his gaze raked over her from the top of her head to the soles of her boots.

Uneasy with the man's attention, Melanie moved closer to Tyler, her shoulder bumping into his. He turned to look at her and then his gaze moved past her to the man on her other side. His eyes narrowed as he straightened and leaned back in his seat. Melanie turned toward him, crossing her legs and giving the man her shoulder.

Tyler looked down at her. "You okay? Want to change seats?"

"I'm fine." Hopefully, the man would back off and stick to his own group. "How about you give me some idea of what the game's all about."

"That I can do." Tyler bent his head toward her as he pointed things out on the floor.

Melanie tried to focus on his words, even as she thought about how she didn't think they'd ever been this close before. Close enough that she could see the little lines that creased the skin by his eyes when he smiled. And the scent of his cologne was tantalizing.

This is not a date. I'm not interested in dating.

The noise around them grew as Tyler explained the scoring and talked about who they were playing. Clearly the man took his sports seriously. Suddenly, the lights dimmed and an announcer began to talk over the PA system.

"Player introductions," Tyler said, his breath warm across her ear.

Shivers raced up and down her spine at his nearness. Melanie tried to keep her attention solidly on what was happening on the big Jumbotron and the floor below them. Flashing lights and pulse-pounding music helped keep her attention off Tyler for a bit. There was lots of excitement building as the announcer worked his way through the opposing team's players.

The Jumbotron above the court began to flash with the team's trademark wolf. The announcer's voice kicked up a notch as he introduced the first of the Timberwolves' players. There were cheerleaders on the court now, shaking their pompoms along with their bodies as player after player ran out onto the court.

By the end of introductions, people all around were on their feet, Tyler included. Melanie got to her feet as well, clapping along with the crowd that was clearly ready for the game to start.

It wasn't too long before they got their wish. Though Melanie was pretty sure she'd never become a rapid fan of the sport, she enjoyed watching Tyler get into it. He certainly didn't hold back his thoughts on certain plays and calls. She could only imagine how it would have been if they'd actually had seats next to Ryan and Gabe. She felt a bit bad that he likely would have enjoyed the game a bit more if he'd been with someone who was as enthusiastic about the game as he was.

She quickly realized that even though the scoreboard said twelve minutes for the quarter, it took a lot longer than that to actually count down those minutes. At some point, the guy next to her left for a bit. Melanie relaxed a little without him right beside her.

As the seconds ticked down to halftime, Tyler explained they had fifteen minutes before the second half started.

"Do you want to go get something to eat or drink?" he said as the whistle blew to end the half.

"I wouldn't mind something to drink."

With a nod, Tyler got to his feet and stepped into the aisle. He angled his arm toward her. "Hang onto me so we don't get separated."

Grateful, Melanie slid her hand between his arm and his side and gripped his arm just above his elbow. She could feel the muscle there work as he held his arm against his side so her hand wouldn't slip away.

"Just something to eat? Or can I interest you in popcorn? Nachos? A hotdog?"

Melanie wrinkled her nose at the last option. "Popcorn would be fine."

With a nod, Tyler began to move them through the crowd of people. He seemed to know where he was going and soon they were in line at a concession stand. Though they'd agreed that he would pay for dinner since she'd paid for the tickets, Melanie wasn't sure what to do about the snacks.

Given the number of people milling around, Melanie was surprised at how quickly they made it to the front of the line. Tyler rattled off a few items then asked what she wanted to drink. After she had told him, she let go of his arm to reach into her boot to pull out the cash she'd slid in there earlier with her driver's license since she hadn't wanted to bother with a purse.

"I've got it," Tyler said as he pulled his wallet from his back pocket.

Figuring it wasn't the place to argue, Melanie just nodded and waited as he paid. She glanced around at the people standing at the concession with them. Her brows drew together when she noticed a young woman standing not too far from Tyler watching him, her gaze clearly appreciating what she was seeing.

Melanie had to admit that Tyler looked good in his blue jeans, white button down shirt and black leather jacket, but it didn't sit well with her that she was bothered that other women thought he did too. The urge to slide her hand back around his arm screamed of wanting to claim him as hers...which he wasn't. And never would be.

"Here you go." Tyler handed her a drink and then stuck out his elbow again. He held the food he'd ordered in both his hands. Without hesitation, she took his arm and allowed him to lead them back to their seats. She resisted the urge to look over her shoulder at the woman who'd been eying him...but just barely.

They were back to their seats with a couple of minutes to spare, according to the countdown clock on the scoreboard. Tyler let her go into the row first and reclaim her seat before he handed her the popcorn. As he sat down next to her, she looked at the food in his hands. Nachos. A hotdog. Pop.

"I only eat this way when I'm at a game," Tyler said, a sheepish expression on his face.

She looked up to find him watching her. As she unscrewed the lid of the bottle of water he'd gotten her, Melanie lifted a brow at him but then grinned. "Hey, none of my business if you choose to ingest artificially flavored and colored food and drink. Besides," she lifted the popcorn, "who am I to judge?"

As they settled back in their seats, Tyler asked, "Are you enjoying your first NBA game?"

"I am, surprisingly enough."

"You didn't think you were going to enjoy it?" Tyler's brow furrowed. "Why did you agree to come then?"

"You're a hard one to say no to, Tyler," Melanie said with a smile. "And you presented a compelling argument for why I should attend with you."

"If you say so." He didn't seem convinced as he turned his attention back to his food.

Holding the bag of popcorn between her knees, she laid her hand on his arm and waited for him to look at her. "I'm glad I came. I don't get out to stuff like this much. And coming with you has been fun. You're the only friend I have that would go with me to something like this."

He stared at her for a moment, his blue gaze intent. "Well, we'll have to make sure you get to do it again sometime."

The buzzer sounded and soon the game was underway once more. A couple of minutes later, the seats beside her that had been blessedly empty were filled once again. It quickly became apparent what they had used their time out of the arena for.

"Hey, sweetheart. What's your name?" Clearly the guy had imbibed some liquid courage while he'd been gone. He swayed in his seat toward her.

Melanie pulled away, once again bumping into Tyler. He turned toward her and groaned when he saw the man making a nuisance of himself once again.

"Back off, buddy. She's with me," Tyler said as he glared at the guy.

"Really now." The guy arched a brow. "Doesn't seem to me you're paying much attention to her. I was just trying to make sure she knew she was more interesting than some basketball game."

Tyler frowned as he looked from the man to Melanie and then back to him. "She's not interested in your attention. Leave her alone."

"And if I don't?" the man taunted him. "What're you gonna do about it?"

"Oh, I won't have to do anything. She's perfectly able to take care of herself. I'm just trying to save you the embarrassment of being beat up by a girl."

Melanie almost laughed at Tyler's words. Clearly he'd been paying attention when she'd mentioned taking self-defense and weapons training. When the man shot her a questioning look, all Melanie did was smile.

"Whatever," he mumbled under his breath as he turned to his friend in the seat on the other side of him.

"Switch seats with me," Tyler said in a low voice. "He's not drunk enough to try hitting on me."

That did make Melanie laugh. She got to her feet and stepped into the aisle so Tyler could get to her seat. The drunken man glared at the two of them as she sat down in the aisle seat.

She leaned her head toward Tyler. "Thank you."

"You're welcome. I want to make sure you enjoy this game so you might consider coming to another one sometime."

A roar from the crowd drew Melanie's attention, and she looked up at the scoreboard to see that the game was now tied. For the remainder of the game, Tyler seemed to make sure he divided his attention between her and the game. Did he think the guy's comments about him not paying attention to her had bothered her? She hoped not, because that certainly hadn't been the case.

By the last few minutes of the game, Melanie was on her feet beside him as they cheered the home team on to victory. She was still grinning as they joined the crowd heading for the exits. Once again Tyler offered her his arm as they walked up the aisle and out of the arena. She didn't let go until they were almost at the truck. Gabe and Ryan were already there, watching them as they approached.

"Well, that was a game worth stopping in for," Gabe said from the back seat as Tyler guided them out of the parking lot along with a ton of other cars.

"When do you go home, Gabe?" Melanie asked.

"Ryan and I are heading out tomorrow."

Melanie turned in her seat to face Ryan. "You're going to Winnipeg?"

He nodded. "It's Canadian Thanksgiving, so I took Monday and Tuesday off."

"I decided to fly here from Hawaii and then drive up with Ryan," Gabe said.

"Will everyone in your family be there?"

"Everyone except Kenton. NHL is in full swing now so he won't be able to make it," Gabe said. "Mom and Dad are disappointed. Kenton...not so much."

"He doesn't like to spend time with your family?"

Ryan and Gabe exchanged glances in the dimly lit cab of the truck then Ryan said, "He lives his life in a way that he knows Mom and Dad don't approve of. The dumb thing is that they would just be happy to have him home for a bit. They know that he is aware of how they feel about his life. They're not going to lecture him every time they see him. Kenton, however, seems to feel that they will."

"It's the guilt talking," Gabe said. "He knows better than to be doing what he is."

"What exactly has he done?" Melanie couldn't help but ask.

"He's a big partier. Never has a girlfriend for longer than a month."

"Let's not forget his brushes with the law," Gabe added. "Nothing he's been arrested for, but I'm sure that's only because of who he is. One day he's going to regret living his life like this. He's not going to be playing hockey forever. Especially since he's already had one serious concussion."

Melanie decided that she was going to do a search on Kenton Callaghan when she got on to her laptop later. Listening to his brothers talk about him had definitely made her curious about the man. She also found it curious that Ryan hadn't even let Tyler know that Kenton was his brother. As far as she knew, Ryan and Tyler were close, so that was a bit surprising. Of course, the whole evening had been full of surprises.

Back at Tyler's, Ryan said goodnight to her and dragged Gabe to his side of the duplex. Once they were gone, Tyler turned to her.

"I had a great time. Thank you for the birthday present."

"I really enjoyed myself too. We'll have to do it again sometime."

"Consider it a date." Tyler paused then said, "Uh...no, not a date. Um...you know, an appointment. Wait..."

Melanie laid her hand on his arm, trying not to laugh at his flustered attempts to backpedal. "I know what you mean. No worries. I'm not considering it a date. Just two friends hanging out, having some fun."

"Exactly." Tyler nodded his head vigorously. "That's what I meant."

"On that note, I'm going to head for home. Have a good night."

"You too." Tyler held the keys out to her. "Thanks for letting me drive her."

Not wanting it to turn awkward, Melanie snatched the keys from him. "Her, eh? Well, I guess she is a bit too pretty to be a boy." She rounded the front of the truck, giving the hood a pat then opened the door.

With a quick movement, she slid behind the wheel and started it up. The headlights showed Tyler still standing in his driveway, his hands in his pockets watching as she backed out. She gave a final wave, not sure he could see her, and then accelerated away.

9

"STACI'S PREGNANT," Eric McKinley announced to the group gathered for their regular Tuesday morning meetings.

As everyone offered their congratulations, Melanie looked at the broad smile on Eric McKinley's face. His joy over the news was unquestionable. What would it be like, she wondered, to know that a little person was growing inside of her? A person who carried part of her and part of the man she loved? A little boy or girl who was the physical manifestation of the love between the parents? Although, as her thoughts went to the circumstances of Tyler's birth, she realized that not all pregnancies were the result of a happy union.

As Marcus called the meeting to order, Melanie gave Adrianne a sideways glance. Her sister sat with her head bent, her lower lip caught between her teeth. Her heart ached for Adrianne. She wasn't sure why Adrianne wasn't able to find a guy who she could get serious with. Her sister was cute and fun to be around—as long as she wasn't in a mood after their mom got to her—and she did a lot of good with her work.

Her mind wasn't on the meeting until she heard Tyler's name mentioned. Perking up, she turned her attention to Marcus.

"I've been working with Tyler Harris to see if he can find any connection between people that Alex and I feel might have something against BlackThorpe and might be instigating the attacks we've had over the past year." Marcus stared down at the file in front of him, his brow furrowed. "He couldn't find anything to link Ben Stevenson or Patrick O'Neal, at least through their phone records. And he went back over the past two years. I realize they could have used burner phones to communicate, but with those records and the background checks into the men, it just doesn't seem likely that they are working together against us. Ben, who has a wife and three kids, has an established career as a police officer in California. I feel confident saying he isn't involved."

"What about O'Neal?" Justin asked.

Marcus shook his head. "He's a bit more suspect. He hasn't held down a job for more than a couple of years and in amongst all the calls on his phone are a few that Tyler says were made to burner cells. That makes him a little more suspicious. What we can't figure out is who he's working with. Not to disparage the man, but he wasn't one to do much of the dirty work. I really don't think that if he's behind these attacks that he's acting alone."

"Do you sense another impending attack?" Eric tapped the notepad in front of him with his pen.

Melanie didn't really like the look that Marcus and Alex exchanged. She'd be having a conversation with her brother at home later.

"While the last attack was a major one since it injured both Alex and me," Marcus began, "we don't believe that was his endgame. He needs for us to know that it's him. We have a few big things in the works that he might try to sabotage."

"Is the fundraiser at risk?" Adrianne asked, her expression all business now.

"We don't know," Alex answered instead of Marcus this time. "But it's definitely a possibility. It's our highest profile event of the year."

Marcus nodded. "We're going to tighten security significantly. Anyone we hire to work the event will have to be vetted from the coat check person to the chef who's in charge of the food." He paused. "I realize it will make more work for you, Adrianne, and I'm sorry for that, but safety is paramount. If you need extra people to help you, just let me know, and I'll make it happen."

"What else is at risk?" Given Justin's role in security, Melanie wasn't surprised he was asking for more details. The last attack had occurred under his watch, and she knew it still chafed him even though he'd been injured along with Alex and Marcus.

Again Alex and Marcus exchanged a look. For the first time, Melanie wondered if they were concerned about the people in the meeting with them. Were they questioning the loyalty of those they'd handpicked to be part of the management team? That thought didn't sit well with Melanie at all. Her gaze circled the room, and she knew there was no way anyone present would betray them in that way. Surely Alex and Marcus knew that.

"We have two huge defense contracts that we've bid on," Alex said. "Obviously any sign that we're having issues with our own security or that data stored with us is not secure would jeopardize our chances at winning those bids."

"I want each of you to double and triple check the security you have in place. We're going to high alert until the bids have been decided." Marcus turned to Trent Hause, who was in charge of the company's network security. "I want someone monitoring the network twenty-four seven. If there is another hacking attempt, I want to know about it immediately and not wait for the alarm to trigger."

Trent nodded. "I'll put three guys on an eight-hour rotation."

"Melanie."

She looked from Trent to Marcus when he said her name.

"We're going to need to tighten security at the Center. I know you prefer to keep things low-key out there, but we can't have any part of the company vulnerable to an attack."

Marcus was right, she didn't like the people staying at the Center, or the friends and family who came to visit, to have to jump through extra security hoops. "What are you thinking of putting in place?"

"You'll need to call a meeting with all the staff and residents. If you'd prefer, Alex or I can come speak with them. Basically, we'd outline the new protocols which will include producing photo ID before entering the grounds. We will also ask each resident to provide a list of approved visitors that we will then vet."

Thankfully, Melanie knew that most the residents would understand the increased security given that they were all ex-military. It would be a bit of a hassle, but she didn't want to take a chance with the safety of any of her staff or the people residing at the Center for the purpose of receiving help.

"I'll set up a meeting and let you know."

Melanie made some notes as the meeting began to wind down. When Marcus finally dismissed them, she followed Adrianne out of the conference room.

"You doing okay?" she asked as they walked side by side down the hallway to the elevators.

"Yeah." Adrianne glanced at her. "Why?"

"Just seemed like maybe Eric's announcement caught you off-guard."

Adrianne let out a sigh as she pressed the button to call the elevator. "I'm happy for him and Staci. You know how it is. Or maybe you don't because you don't seem to care about getting married or having kids."

"You're right. That's not really something I'm anxious to do, but I know it's different for you."

As they stepped into the empty elevator car, Adrianne said, "And why is that? Is it because of what happened with you know...the kidnapping?"

Melanie jabbed at the button for the floor where Adrianne's office was. "I guess that might be part of it."

"It's just so hard to be the only one of my group of friends who's not married or having kids. It's like I don't have anything in common with them anymore." Adrianne sighed again. "Any decent single man I come in contact with probably senses the air of desperation I no doubt wear, and runs for the hills."

"You do not act desperate," Melanie told her. "Believe me, if I thought you were, I would be giving you a swift kick in the butt."

Melanie was glad when Adrianne laughed at her comment.

"What about you and Tyler?" Adrianne asked.

"What about us?" Melanie really didn't want to get into this discussion.

"Didn't you go out with Tyler on Friday?"

"Yeah, but it was actually Tyler, Ryan and his brother, Gabe. We just went for dinner and then to the Timberwolves' game."

"Seriously? I can hardly get a date with one man and you went out with three?"

"Well, it certainly wasn't a date which is probably why the three of them agreed to it."

"Was he cute?" Adrianne asked.

"Who?"

"Ryan's brother."

"Oh, don't make me kick your butt. Besides, I'm pretty sure he's not what you're looking for, plus he's too young for you." As the doors slid open on Adrianne's floor, Melanie gave her a quick hug. "Have patience. I'm sure there's someone out there who's perfect for you."

Adrianne flashed her a smile. "From your lips to God's ears."

With that, her sister turned and disappeared down the hall. As the elevator doors slid closed again, Melanie's finger hovered over the buttons. Part of her wanted to see Tyler, but maybe it was too soon for her to just drop in to chat. Ignoring the disappointment in the pit of her stomach, she pressed the button for the parking garage, leaned back against the wall and closed her eyes. She'd just wait and see him when he came out to the Center to see Simon.

Except he came the next day while she was in a meeting and all she got was a text. *Sorry to have missed seeing you. They said you were in a meeting and I need to get back to the office. Chat later!*

They exchanged a few texts over the course of the week, but between meetings to set up the new security protocols and Tyler's own work, there was no time for anything more. The one good thing that came as a result of the distance was that Melanie felt more in control of her emotions again. Eric's baby news had stirred something in her the way the engagements of Than and Justin had. She couldn't—she *wouldn't*—allow herself to pine for a relationship the way Adrianne did.

But in spite of not having seen Tyler, he managed to occupy her thoughts most nights as she made her way through her workout. Sunday night was no different and she had the same old arguments with herself.

She needed to trust someone completely in order to consider being with them, and the only man in her life that met that requirement was Tyler. Yet still, she knew a relationship wouldn't work. The issues in her life that she kept carefully hidden from everyone would also keep her from being with Tyler. And who knew if he even wanted to be with her? Nothing he'd said or done had led her to believe that he wanted her as anything more than a friend.

A text flashed across the screen where she'd propped her phone while she ran on the treadmill. *Someone here to see you.*

It was from Adrianne, and Melanie figured it was a just a joke of some kind. She wasn't expecting company. But as punishment for interrupting her workout, she had half a mind to drag Adrianne back up to her room to join her. She hit the button to slow the machine so she could step off. Grabbing her phone and a towel to wipe the sweat, Melanie left her room.

The house was quiet as she made her way downstairs to the main living area. There was a murmur of voices coming from the kitchen so she headed that way, figuring she'd find Alex and Adrianne there. As she rounded the corner, she froze in shock.

"Ryan?" Melanie was instantly aware of her attire and how she must look with her hair plastered to her head and sweat dripping down her neck to soak into the tank top she wore.

"Hey, Melanie. Sorry for stopping by unexpectedly." Ryan gave her a quick smile. "Looks like I interrupted something."

"Just my workout." Melanie dragged the towel across her face then looped it around her neck. "What's up?"

Ryan shifted his weight, uncertainty crossing his face. "I need to ask you a favor."

Melanie looked at Adrianne, who shrugged, then back at Ryan. "What kind of favor?"

"It's about Tyler."

"Is he okay?"

"Uh, not so much." Ryan paused. "He's caught some kind of bug, and it's really kicking his butt."

"A bug?"

"There were a couple of kids at the youth meeting on Friday night who got sick while they were there. We figured it was food poisoning or something. Tyler took care of them and then drove them home. Unfortunately, it seems that whatever they had, he now has."

"So it's a stomach bug?"

"Yeah. He called his doctor today, and he said that it's likely some gastrointestinal thing." He shifted his weight again, looking down as he lifted a hand to rub the back of his neck. "Tyler will probably kill me for this, but I don't know what else to do. I'm leaving tomorrow with Eric for meetings in London, so I can't keep an eye on him. The biggest problem with this is dehydration. I'm just worried he won't be able to help himself since...you know...he uses a wheelchair when he's not wearing his prosthetics, and I'm not sure he'll be able to maneuver well enough. He's been running a high fever and vomiting." He lifted his head, his gaze meeting hers. "If I give you a key to my place, would you be willing to stop in and check on him tomorrow?"

Melanie's stomach clenched at the thought of Tyler suffering on his own with no one to take care of him. "Yes. Sure. I can do that."

Relief spread across Ryan's face. "I hope he doesn't give you any hassles. You know how independent he can be, but I'm just worried about leaving him on his own when he's this sick."

"Yeah, I know he likes to take care of himself," Melanie said.

Ryan held out his hand, keys dangling from a finger. "Here are the keys to my place. I'll text you the alarm code and then you can go through the basement and up to Tyler's side."

Melanie took the keys, wrapping her fingers around them so tightly that the edges bit into her palm. "Do I need Tyler's alarm code as well?"

"Only if you want to go in and out of his door. I'll text you that as well."

Melanie gave him her number since he didn't have it, hoping she could be the help Tyler needed. Or rather, she hoped he'd accept the help she offered. During her early years at the Center, she had helped with the physical care of residents which had included everything from changing dressings to cleaning up bodily fluids when necessary.

"Eric is picking me up at six, so I'll make sure he has water with him before I go, but if you could check on him in the afternoon, that would be great."

"Don't worry. I'll make sure he's taken care of."

"Thanks so much, Melanie. I know he considers you a close friend which is why I'm hoping he won't object to your help. My other option was to call Shauna, and I figured he would get mad at me for sure about that one."

"Yeah, no doubt," Melanie said with a laugh as she walked with him to the door. "Thanks for letting me know, Ryan. I'll text you to let you know how he's doing."

"Thanks." He seemed to be about to say something more but then just nodded.

10

IT WAS CLOSE to noon before Melanie was able to make it over to Tyler's, but at least she didn't have to return to the office if she needed to stay with him for any length of time.

She used the key to get into Ryan's front door and then used the code he'd sent to turn off the buzzing alarm. It didn't take her long to find the stairs to the basement. She wasn't too surprised to see it set up as a gym with a massive television on one wall.

As she climbed the stairs to Tyler's side, Melanie pressed a hand to her stomach. She really hoped Tyler wasn't going to be upset that Ryan had asked her to check on him.

When she stepped into the kitchen on Tyler's side, Melanie wrinkled her nose as the smell of sickness assailed her senses. She set her purse on the counter along with a bag of supplies she'd picked up on her way over.

"Tyler?" she called out softly as she moved further into the house.

She had to poke her head into a couple of rooms to find the one that was his. It was dark with only a single shaft of light spilling from another door, and the smell was even stronger here. "Tyler?"

Bracing herself, Melanie walked into the room and saw right away that the bed was empty. She turned to where the light shone through an open doorway and saw his wheelchair there.

"Ty?"

She heard a moan then and approached slowly, looking around for something to cover him if necessary. She hadn't really thought this part through since she'd helped care for men before, but suddenly it was different now that it was Tyler.

Thankfully, when she reached his side, she saw that he wore a pair of shorts and a muscle shirt. She laid a hand on his shoulder and could feel right away that his fever was raging. He was just sitting slumped there so she squeezed past the chair and dropped to her knees. An empty water bottle lay on the floor.

Melanie reached out to touch his cheek and when she did, his head lifted. His blue eyes were glassy as he stared at her.

"Melanie?"

"Yeah. Hi. Ryan asked me to stop by and check on you."

"He shouldn't have done that," Tyler said as he lowered his head again. "I'm fine."

Melanie gave a huff of laughter as she pushed to her feet. "Yeah. I can see that."

"I'm not helpless, you know," Tyler said, his tone defensive.

Melanie looked around the bathroom and found a stack of washcloths. She picked one up and ran it under the water. "I know that. But you are alone. No one should have to be sick by themselves."

When she turned back to him, she saw that he'd grabbed a towel and draped it over his legs. The thought that he felt he had to hide his stumps from her hurt a little bit. She handed the cloth to him. "Here. Wipe your face."

He hesitated a moment before taking the cool cloth from her hand. His hand shook a bit as he wiped it over his face. Melanie would have happily done it for him, but something told her that right then, he wouldn't have appreciated the gesture.

"Can you open that drawer there and grab an elastic for me?" Tyler asked.

Melanie pulled out the drawer and saw a package of hair elastics. She took one out and handed it to him.

"Thanks. My hair keeps getting in the way when I'm sick." He lifted his hands to gather his hair back, but Melanie could see his arms shaking with the effort.

"Can I do that for you?" she asked.

It hurt her to see him struggling when she knew what a strong man he really was. When Ryan had said this bug had brought him down, he'd meant it.

"Let me help you, Ty. I know you can do this for yourself, but I'm here. Let me help. That's what friends do."

Without looking at her, he held out his hand and let her take the elastic from his fingers. Melanie squeezed back around to the other side of the wheelchair and with quick movements, pulled his curls back into a short ponytail.

Then, leaving him in the bathroom, she went back to the kitchen and pulled another bottle of water from the fridge. She could tell that he'd been sweating at one point and given that he was sitting in the bathroom, she'd assume that he'd been sick to his stomach as well.

When she got back to the bathroom, she loosened the cap on the bottle and handed it to him. "Drink up. Ryan said the doctor told you that dehydration was something you needed to avoid."

"Yeah." He took the bottle but didn't drink any of it. "The problem is, every time I drink something, it comes right back up."

Melanie could hear the weariness in his words. She sat on the edge of the tub next to the wheelchair. The bathroom was a little on the small side for her and the wheelchair to both fit comfortably. "You still need to drink. Do you want some crackers so you have something more solid in your stomach? Might make it a little less sloshy."

"I'm not sure if I have any."

"No worries. I made a stop on the way here and picked up a few things."

"You shouldn't be here." His voice stopped her as she got to her feet.

"We've been over that already, Tyler. You need help. I'm here to help. It's what friends do. It was what Ryan was doing before he had to leave."

When he didn't say anything right away, Melanie turned to leave the bathroom, thinking she'd gotten her point across.

"I don't want you to get sick." His voice was so low she almost didn't hear the words he spoke.

"I won't. I've read up on the precautions I need to take. And if I do, well, my mother's close enough to take care of me."

Again he was silent but then said, "If you could just get me my pills and put some more water in here and by the bed, I should be fine. You don't need to stay."

Melanie glared at his bent head. She'd expected that he wouldn't be entirely happy with her being there, but dealing with it directly was difficult. She just wanted to help.

Before she said anything to upset him more, she left the bathroom and went back to the kitchen to get the crackers she'd bought. She took them into the bedroom, frowning when she saw that the door to the bathroom was now shut. With a sigh, she set the crackers on the bedside table and then snapped on the lamp.

Realizing that the sheets on Tyler's bed needed to be changed, she went in search of a linen closet. Thankfully, Tyler seemed to be a fairly tidy housekeeper. She found a set of fresh sheets in the closet and then went back into the kitchen to grab the gloves and mask she'd picked up. She washed her hands first with the antibacterial soap she'd purchased then pulled on the gloves and mask.

Back in the bedroom, she made quick work of stripping the bed then took the dirty linens to the washing machine she'd seen in a closet in the hallway. After adding some bleach to the load, she set it for the hottest water, discarded the gloves and washed up again.

When she returned to the bedroom, she could hear the sounds of retching from the bathroom. She wanted to burst through the door and demand he let her help him, but instead, she remade his bed then got the disinfectant spray she'd bought and began to use it liberally on all the appropriate surfaces. She also opened the window to let in a little fresh—albeit slightly cool—air.

Though the bathroom door remained closed, she could hear movement so at least he was still alive. Frustrated that he wouldn't let her help more, she went and grabbed her laptop bag and her phone. She owed Ryan an update and if Tyler was still holed up in the bathroom, she'd spend a little time checking her email to see if anything needed her attention.

She did a little figuring in her head to determine how late it was in London. Realizing it was early evening, she tapped out a message to Ryan.

It's probably not a good sign when the nurse wants to strangle the patient, right?

It wasn't long before a message appeared. *Not being the most cooperative patient, eh?*

Melanie huffed out a sigh as if Ryan could hear it. *That's putting it mildly. He's locked himself in the bathroom and won't let me help him.*

Even as she hit send, Melanie realized she didn't know for sure that the bathroom door was locked. She'd just assumed it was. Hopefully, he'd just closed it for effect but not locked it. If she had to get to him in a hurry, a locked door wouldn't be a good thing.

Are you really upset with him? Should I be apologizing for asking you to check in on him?

No. Well, yes, I am upset, but only because he needs help and won't let me do anything for him.

There was a bit of a delay before his reply showed up. *I'm sure he doesn't like to be seen as weak in front of you. It's a man thing.*

*No. It's a dumb thing. He's the least weak person I know. Being sick doesn't make a person wea—*Melanie looked up from her phone as she heard water begin to run in the bathroom. She really hoped he wasn't taking a shower. If something happened while he was in there, she would be calling Alex to help him out. She was pretty sure that their friendship wouldn't survive her stepping in to help him in a situation like that.

She finished her message and hit send before setting the phone on the dresser. Moving as quietly as she could, she made her way to the bathroom door and bent her head close to it. She breathed a sigh of relief when the water shut off. Hopefully, he'd just been washing his hands.

Not wanting to be caught lingering outside the door if he came out, Melanie grabbed her phone and tapped out another message to Ryan.

What's your guys' wireless information here? I brought my laptop to do a little work.

Tyler still hadn't opened the door, so Melanie settled down on the floor with her laptop and using the information Ryan had given her, she logged into their network.

Mr. Tyler Harris was about to find out just how stubborn she could be.

Tyler looked longingly at the shower, but he knew better than to press his luck. He couldn't remember the last time he'd felt so weak. The effort to simply lift his arms just about did him in.

He took another small sip of water from the bottle Melanie had brought him. He supposed it was too much to hope that he was hallucinating her presence in his house. No doubt he had Ryan to thank for her arrival, which had shocked him once he'd realized it was really her.

The lack of movement on the other side of the door had him thinking she'd taken him up on his request that she leave. He took another sip of water and waited to see if his stomach was going to reject it once again.

After repeating the sip and wait routine over the next several minutes with no negative results, Tyler decided that he'd make an attempt to get back to his bed. He really was exhausted and his body ached, but he didn't dare fall asleep in his chair. The last thing he needed was to fall out of it and add a broken bone to the mess he was in.

He managed to get his wheelchair swung around and reached out to open the door. His gaze swept his room as he wheeled out of the bathroom. He noticed that the lamp beside his bed was on and then he saw her.

She sat cross-legged on his floor against the wall at the foot of his bed. Looking over the top of her laptop, she seemed to be daring him to say something to her. Instead, he just rolled closer to the bed, noticing as he did that the air smelled sweeter, fresher than it had earlier. And then he saw the bed had been remade.

He looked back over to where Melanie sat. "Thank you."

"You're welcome."

"I'm just going to go to bed and see if I can sleep some of this off."

Melanie set her laptop on the floor next to her and got to her feet in one smooth motion. "Have you been able to drink anything?"

He nodded. "I'm hoping that if I take a pill now, I'll be able to keep it down."

"Do you want to try some crackers?"

She moved toward him, her movements slow as if she was afraid of frightening him off. If only she understood that it wasn't that he didn't want her there. He wanted her there too much. That was dangerous ground for him to be on.

"I think I'll just stick to the water and a pill." He wheeled himself over to the bed, glad that his arms didn't shake too much with the effort.

"Let me just go get you a couple more bottles of water," Melanie said and slipped from the room before he could respond. He suspected she'd done that to give him privacy as he got into bed. He appreciated that she didn't make a big deal out of it.

Moving as quickly as his aching, weak body would allow, he lifted himself from the chair onto the edge of the bed. He swung his legs up onto the bed and then pulled the blanket over his lower body. Tyler wasn't sure why he didn't want Melanie to see his stumps. She knew about his prosthetics. Had worked with him as he'd learned how to put them on and take them off. Why he was trying to hide them from her now was beyond his fevered mind to grasp.

When she came back into the room, she had two bottles of water in her hands. She set them on his bedside table within his reach.

"Do you have a basin or something like that? So if you get sick, you don't have to try and make it to the bathroom?"

"Yeah. There's one in the tub. I had used it earlier and rinsed it out."

"Okay. Let me get that for you."

He lay back against the pillows and watched as she grabbed a bag from the floor and disappeared into the bathroom. The water began to run then he heard some spraying and more water. When she returned, she carried the basin and a large towel. She went around to the other side of the bed and spread out the towel before setting the basin on it.

"Can I get you anything else?"

"No, I think I'm good. Thank you."

She came back to the night table on his side and snapped off the light. Then she pulled the door of the bathroom almost shut, leaving just enough light for him to see if he needed to use the basin or drink some water.

Exhaustion pulled at him and the last thing he remembered was seeing Melanie pick up her laptop.

When Tyler woke later, he lay still for a moment, waiting to see if his stomach was going to rebel on him. When nothing tried to surge up into his throat, Tyler pushed himself up and reached for a bottle of water. His mouth was drier than the Sahara, but he still just took tiny sips. He'd learned his lesson earlier about gulping it down.

He looked at the wall at the end of his bed to see if Melanie was still there, but there was no sign of her. There was, however, an enticing aroma in the air. He hadn't eaten anything since early Sunday morning when he'd realized that the boys on Friday night hadn't been sick with food poisoning. The smell was tempting, but he wasn't sure what his stomach could tolerate just yet.

As he sat up and turned to the edge of the bed, Tyler toyed with the idea of putting his prosthetics back on. But when he bent down to grab one then sat back up, his head spun. Obviously the lesser of two evils—the wheelchair versus falling flat on his face—was to use the wheelchair. He maneuvered himself onto it and then grabbed a blanket from the foot of the bed to cover his legs.

Once settled, he sat for a minute to give his body a break before he pushed it some more. He could hear movement beyond his bedroom so knew Melanie was still hanging around. With a sigh, he pushed on the wheels and made his way out of the bedroom and down the hallway.

"Hey! You're awake," Melanie said when she spotted him, a smile on her face. "How are you feeling?"

"A bit like a truck hit me." He lifted a hand to run it through his hair and, realizing that most of it was still held back by an elastic, he tugged it free. "You didn't have to be at work today?"

"My work goes with me," she said with a motion toward the table.

He looked over to see that her laptop sat open on his dining room table with papers spread out around it. "I'm sorry you had to leave work just to check in on me."

She went to the stove and gave the contents of a pot there a stir. "Actually, it's worked out just fine. I was able to get some stuff done without interruptions like there have been at work lately. All the new security protocols have meant I've had a steady stream of people in and out of my office. The peace and quiet here has been welcome. I've been able to work through files that needed attention but have been pushed aside by distractions."

He hoped she was telling the truth and not making it up so he didn't feel badly about her being there. "What are you making?"

"Homemade chicken noodle soup. My mom swears it cures everything. If you're feeling up to trying something in your stomach, I can dish you up a bowl."

"You made it yourself?"

"No, the elves helped me out but they scurried away when they heard you coming."

Tyler chuckled at that. "Okay, fine. I apologize for doubting your cooking skills."

"That's okay." She tossed him a smile. "Most people don't know that I can cook. In fact, I prefer to cook from scratch rather than eat prepared foods. It's healthier for you."

"I've always thought you were a bit of a health nut," Tyler said as he wheeled himself closer to the table. He was still trying to figure out if his stomach would be receptive to food or not.

After she opened and closed a couple of cupboards, Tyler said, "Far corner."

Once she found the bowls, she set two on the counter and ladled some soup into each. "I believe in giving my body the fuel it needs to run properly."

"Are you the female version of Justin?" Tyler asked as she carried the bowls to the table. It was slowly dawning on him that perhaps the friendship he thought they had wasn't quite as deep as he'd imagined. Lately, he was discovering more about her. It was both interesting and disconcerting.

"It's possible. Without the muscles anyway. And I think I probably eat healthier than he does." She filled two glasses with water and set one next to his plate before taking the seat across from him.

She looked at him expectantly, and Tyler realized she was waiting for him to pray. Suddenly feeling the intimacy of the situation, he quickly bowed his head and thanked God for the food and for Melanie's help. He couldn't say for sure that the worst had passed, but he sure hoped it had.

"It seems you're into self-defense and weapons as much as Justin is." Tyler dipped his spoon into the bowl, allowing the liquid to fill it. He'd try the more solid pieces of the soup once he saw how the liquid did.

"Well, I do think a woman should be able to take care of herself."

"Do you think every woman should learn how to shoot and carry concealed weapons like you do?" Tyler wasn't sure if his questions were making her uncomfortable, but he was curious about this side of her that had really only come to light recently.

"No," she replied with confidence. "A woman should only carry a gun if she's really prepared to use it. If she's armed and yet hesitates to use the weapon, it can be used against her."

"So you're prepared to use the gun you carry?"

Her brown gaze met his straight on. "Yes. If need be, I can and will use any of the weapons I carry."

Something about the way she talked had Tyler wondering how much more he didn't know about Melanie. He hadn't known she carried concealed until their birthday dinner, and now he sensed that there was a reason she felt so strongly about being able to protect herself. Would she tell him about it if he asked?

11

THEY ATE IN SILENCE for a few minutes as Tyler cautiously tried a carrot and a small piece of chicken. So far so good, but Tyler figured he'd be better off not pushing it. He finished the bowl she'd given him but declined any more. "I think I'd better not push my luck."

"I'll put the leftovers in your fridge for later."

Without thinking, Tyler reached over and laid his hand over hers where it rested next to her bowl. "Thank you. I know I wasn't very grateful earlier, but I really do appreciate you taking the time to make sure I was okay."

She stared at their hands for a moment before lifting her gaze to his. "It's what friends do. The other option was to call your mom."

Tyler pulled his hand back and groaned. "Yeah. Thanks for not doing that. As it is, I missed our weekly Sunday call. I'm surprised my phone hasn't been ringing off the hook."

"It kind of has been vibrating a lot," Melanie said as she got to her feet to grab his phone off the counter and hand it to him.

It didn't take long to see that his mom had called and texted several times with the last text twenty minutes ago. That one carried the threat of getting on the next plane if she didn't hear from him by morning.

Hoping to prevent that from happening, Tyler quickly tapped his contact list to call her. He knew it was likely late in London, but he also knew she'd accept his call whatever the time.

"Tyler Devon Harris! Where have you been? Why haven't you answered my calls?"

"Sorry, Momma. I kinda came down with some sort of bug and have been under the weather. I spent most of yesterday and today trying to sleep it off."

"I'll be on the next plane out." He heard rustling and then, "Sweetheart, can you get me on a flight to Tyler in the morning?"

"Momma!" He spoke loudly into the phone. "Hey!"

"What? I'm just getting Hank to make arrangements to come see you."

"You don't need to do that. Ryan and Melanie have been taking turns caring for me. I'm much better today."

"Ah, I knew she was a sweet girl. Thank her for me."

"I'll do that, Momma. But don't come. I really am doing much better than I was."

"Who is there with you now?"

"Melanie."

"Perfect. Let me speak to her please."

"Uh..."

"Now, Tyler."

"Yes, Momma." With a sheepish grin, Tyler held the phone out to Melanie. "She wants to talk to you."

A grin crossed Melanie's face as she placed the phone to her ear. "Hello, Shauna."

Tyler wished he'd hit the speakerphone button so he could hear what his mother was saying to her.

"Yes, he wasn't doing too well earlier, but he slept several hours and just now finished a bowl of homemade chicken noodle soup. So far it's stayed down." She paused, listening as his mother no doubt offered medical advice or asked questions he'd rather she didn't. "Yep. He had a few moments of being a difficult patient, but he came around."

Tyler rolled his eyes at her. As he listened to her chat with his mom, he realized that Kelly would never have spoken to his mom like that. She'd hated when his mom would ask to speak to her.

He looked away from Melanie, trying not to frown. Why was he comparing Melanie with Kelly? That was a road that led to nowhere good.

"Okay, I'll tell him." Pause. "Give my regards to Hank." Pause. "You take care too. Bye."

As Melanie handed the phone back to him, Tyler asked. "Tell me what?"

"That you're supposed to do what I tell you and stop giving me grief about helping you out."

He lifted an eyebrow at that, trying to figure out if she was making that up or not. Unfortunately, he could almost hear his mom saying those very words to him.

"I'm trying to be better." He reached for his glass and took a sip of the water. "I really am feeling a lot better."

Melanie tilted her head. "Don't overdo it, though. I think you should stay home tomorrow just to make sure that you're really on the road to recovery."

"Yeah, that's probably a good idea."

She stood and carried their bowls to the kitchen then began to put away the leftover soup. "I probably should get going soon. What can I do to help you out before I go?"

"I think I'm fine. I feel almost human again."

"Keep your phone handy so if you need help, you can call. I'll even add your number to my list of people whose calls will override the do-not-disturb set up on my phone."

"You mean I wasn't already on that list?" Tyler asked with a grin as he watched her put the last of the dishes into the dishwasher.

She closed it and swung around to look at him, a smile on her face. "Well, considering I figured I wouldn't be high on your list of people to call in an emergency, I never saw the need."

"By the way, how did you even get in here?"

Melanie sat back down at her laptop and began to gather the papers that were spread out next to it. "Ryan came by Sunday night to ask if I'd check on you and gave me the keys to his place."

"Really?"

"Yep." She glanced at him before focusing back on the laptop. "He was quite worried about leaving you alone."

Warmth filled Tyler. He hadn't expected Ryan to go out of his way to make sure he was alright while Ryan was on his trip. "He's kinda like the brother I never had."

She smiled at him again as she pressed the lid of the laptop shut. "Siblings can come in handy on occasion." It wasn't long before all her things were back in her bag. "Make sure you take water with you. Oh. I'll just switch over the laundry before I go. I forgot all about that earlier."

Tyler grabbed her wrist as she walked past him. "You don't need to do that."

"It will only take a minute, and it's one less thing for you to think about."

She didn't jerk her arm away but stood staring down at him. Tyler let his hand slide away, brushing his fingertips across her fingers.

"Thank you."

Something had changed in her gaze, but Tyler had no idea what it meant. She gave him a quick smile before walking to the hallway where the washer and dryer were. He wheeled himself to the fridge and pulled out a couple more bottles of water. There was a stack of three containers with the leftover soup. Hopefully, he'd be up to enjoying more of it tomorrow.

"Okay, the dryer's on so you've got clean sheets there if you need them." Melanie picked up her bag and looped the strap over her shoulder. "I guess I'll go back out Ryan's side so I can set the alarm."

As she walked past him, she rested a hand briefly on his shoulder. When she didn't remove it right away, Tyler looked up at her. "You call me if you need anything. Seriously. I'll give you a call in the morning so make sure you answer."

Her brown eyes held his gaze, an expectation in them. "Yep. I'll be sure to do that."

With a squeeze of his shoulder, she said goodnight and headed for the stairs that led to the basement. Tyler wheeled around to watch her go, suddenly finding the quiet of the house oppressive. It wouldn't have been right for her to stay the night, but he couldn't deny that it had been nice to have her there once he'd gotten over his early objections.

With a sigh, he went to check that the alarm was set on his door, pausing to watch the sweep of headlights as Melanie backed out of the driveway. He turned off the lights as he made his way back to the bedroom. Thanks to whatever Melanie had done earlier, his room didn't carry the heavy odor of sickness it had early. He definitely owed her big time.

The question was...would she let him pay her back?

Melanie made it home in time to still be able to get her workout in. As usual lately, her thoughts kept wandering to Tyler. She hoped that he would be okay overnight. He had seemed much better than when she'd first arrived. Hopefully, that meant he was on the mend, but she also knew relapses weren't uncommon with something like what he had.

With sweat dripping down her face and back, she made her way into the bathroom. She washed her hands thoroughly then removed her contacts, rubbing her eyes with relief. She looked in the mirror and met her own—now blue— gaze. These brief glimpses of her true eye color were always a bit disconcerting. She'd worn her brown contacts for so many years now it always felt like her blue eyes were the imposters.

She ran her hands through her hair, lifting the damp strands from her scalp. Once she washed it, her blonde roots would be evident. She was due for a touch-up but hadn't had the time to go yet so she'd relied on temporary color to keep the roots hidden. When she'd been younger, she'd just used the cheap hair coloring from the store and had begged her parents for the colored contacts. They hadn't understood, but at that point they were so glad to have her safely home that they gave her anything she asked for.

Unfortunately, the one thing she'd wanted above all else was a guarantee that nothing like that would ever happen to her again. No one had been able to make that guarantee for her, so she'd done what she could to make sure that if it did, she would at least have a fighting chance.

Once the sweat was washed away and she'd had a nice soak, Melanie wrapped herself in a thick robe and sat down at her desk. She owed Jenni an email. After she'd sent her the short email earlier, another one had come back the next night as long and rambling as the first. And now again tonight, there was another one. Concern ramped up in Melanie as she read through it. Her friend was holding on by a thread. After nearly fourteen years, something had triggered this downward spiral.

The counselor in her recognized the warning signs. Pushing back from her desk, Melanie grabbed her phone and left her room in search of Alex.

"What's up?" he said when she found him in the kitchen making a cup of coffee.

"I need to take a couple of days off. Actually, maybe more like three or four."

Alex's brows drew together as he lifted his mug to take a sip. "Why?"

Her first instinct was to tell him it was none of his business. They never—ever—discussed what had happened to her all those years ago. That was mainly due to her parents not wanting her to be upset by talking about it, and she'd been happy to not have to constantly rehash what had happened.

"Jenni needs me," she said.

"Jenni?" Alex set his mug down, his gaze serious.

"She was one of the girls who was kidnapped like I was."

Alex's eyes widened. "What's happened?"

"I'm not sure, but the last few emails from her have me concerned."

"You're still in contact with the other girls?" It seemed that the idea that she maintained contact, surprised him.

"Yes. Not all of them, but there are a few of us who email back and forth. No one else understands what we went through and how it has impacted our lives."

He leaned a hip against the counter and crossed his arms over his chest. "You've never talked about it with us."

"You didn't need to know everything that happened." Melanie could hardly believe she was having this discussion with Alex after all these years.

His eyes narrowed. "There was more that happened to you that you didn't tell Mom and Dad?"

Her heart pounded as Melanie carefully considered her answer. "Yes. You knew why the kidnappers wanted us, Alex. Think about it."

His jaw clenched, and Melanie could see the muscle jump in his cheek. "You said you weren't raped."

"I wasn't, because they wanted virgins, but they wanted us to be knowledgeable. Think sex ed on steroids."

The color leeched from Alex's face. "You never told me."

"And I'm not sure why I'm telling you now, but Jenni is in the middle of a meltdown, and I need to go to her."

Alex gave a jerky nod. "Are you okay to go by yourself?"

"Yes. I'm able to protect myself now, and I've made sure that I'm not what they want anymore."

As his gaze flicked to her hair, comprehension dawned on his face. "Why didn't you ever tell us, Lanie?"

"There was no reason for you to know. There was nothing you could do to help me."

"But..." Alex's arms dropped to his side as a helpless look crossed his face.

Melanie moved to his side and laid a hand on his arm. "I'm fine. I figured out how to deal with it, but Jenni hasn't."

Alex reached out and pulled her into his arms and held her tight. With her arms trapped between them, she couldn't return the embrace, but in reality she was so surprised by the move, she probably would have just stood there not knowing how to respond anyway.

"Take all the time you need."

"Thank you."

She felt him press a kiss to the top of her head before he let her go. His blue eyes stared down at her. "And you need to trust us more. We love you, Lanie. Probably more than you'll ever realize. Yes, it's hard to hear these things, but none of that changes how we feel about you." Alex sighed. "You can tell me anything. Anything. I'm here for you."

"I just didn't want to burden you guys with the knowledge of stuff that had happened to me that you could do nothing about."

"Maybe we couldn't do anything about it, but we could help carry that burden with you so you would know that you're not alone. Just like you're going to help Jenni, we want to be there if you need our help."

"I'll try to remember that." Melanie laid a hand on Alex's cheek. "But old habits are hard to break."

"Do you need me to get Lisa to book you flights?" Alex asked.

"No. I'll book the tickets myself tonight." She paused. "But there is one thing you can do for me."

"What's that?"

"Can you check on Tyler tomorrow if I need you to? He was pretty sick today. Although he seemed better by the time I left, I'm worried he'll relapse. I'll check in with him in the morning, but if he seems bad again, you might need to go over there."

"Is there something I need to know about you and Tyler?"

The question was getting a little old, so Melanie just grinned and said, "Yeah. We're good friends."

The tension eased from Alex's face. "Well, I'll be sure to check in on your good friend tomorrow if you need me to."

As she sat at her computer a short time later making ticket reservations, Melanie felt a heavy sadness in her heart. Given what she'd been reading from Jenni, there was really only one way this situation would have a positive ending. Jenni would probably hate her, but at least she'd be alive.

Tyler popped his head into Melanie's office after his visit with Simon Thursday afternoon. He was feeling one hundred percent better, pretty much back to normal after three days off on sick leave.

"She in?" he asked Heather.

Melanie's assistant shook her head as her brow furrowed. "She's been out of the office since Tuesday morning."

"Is she sick?" That had been his biggest concern with her having come over to his place.

"No. She had to take care of some personal business out of town. In an email I got from her this morning, she said she's hoping to be back in the office tomorrow."

"Okay, thanks," Tyler said before he left the office.

As he made his way out of the Wellness Center, Tyler tried to figure out why Melanie hadn't said anything. He'd talked to her Tuesday morning, and she hadn't told him about going away. She'd also called for a quick chat on

Wednesday, and again, there had been no mention of being anywhere but Minneapolis.

With a frustrated sigh, he jerked open the door to his vehicle and climbed behind the wheel. Her standard response to him, when she'd come to help him out, had been *it's what friends do*. Well, friends also told each other if they were going out of town or if something was going on.

"Thank you for your help with this, Tyler," Marcus said as he brought their meeting to an end the next morning.

"I wish I could have given you more definitive answers or more clear connections."

Marcus shrugged. "Sometimes the connections that aren't made can be as helpful as the ones that are. Just keep an eye on things. You know the drill."

He did. Picking up the file that sat on the edge of Marcus's desk, he got to his feet. After shaking the man's hand, he left his office. As he walked down the hallway to the elevator, he recognized the woman headed toward him, head bent over her phone. He stopped and waited for her to get closer.

"Hey, Melanie."

Her head jerked up as she came to a stop. "Tyler! Hi."

Right away he saw the tension in her face and the dark circles under her eyes that even makeup couldn't hide. "Everything okay?"

She smiled. "Yep. Just have a meeting with Marcus about the service dog program."

"I stopped by your office yesterday after visiting with Simon."

"Yeah, Heather mentioned you'd come by. Sorry I missed you."

"Can you come by my office when you're done with Marcus?"

Her brows drew together briefly before she nodded. "Sure. It shouldn't be a long meeting."

He watched as she walked the rest of the way to Marcus's office and disappeared inside. He wondered what exactly her trip had involved considering that she'd come back looking drained and tense. Would she tell him if he asked?

12

WHEN MARCUS ASKED her if everything was okay, Melanie realized that perhaps her makeup wasn't doing such a great job of hiding the stress and sleepless nights of the past few days. Thankfully, he wasn't one to prod when she said that she was fine.

The meeting didn't last too long. He had wanted to let her know how things were going with his sister and the dog they'd gotten for her. Melanie had been relieved to hear that it was going very well. Having this be a success with Marcus's sister would mean his unqualified support of the service dog program and its financial needs.

As she left his office, she remembered Tyler's request that she stop by and see him. Melanie took a deep breath and let it out slowly. She had a ton of work waiting for her at the office, so she really should head there. But when she stepped into the elevator, she didn't hesitate to press the button for

Tyler's floor. She'd just have to work over the weekend to get caught up.

As she neared his open door, Melanie saw Tyler focused on his monitor. Rather than knock, she walked in and settled into the chair across from him. His gaze flicked to her briefly then, as if registering it was her, he turned his chair toward her with a smile.

"Hey! Done already?" he asked as he reclined back in his chair. He looked a whole lot better than when she'd last seen him on Monday night.

"Yep. Was just a quick update meeting." She relaxed into her chair, crossing her legs as she rested her hands in her lap. "So, you're looking remarkably better."

"I'm feeling better too. Took me a good three days to feel like I had my energy back, but yesterday I felt well enough to come back to work."

"How is Simon doing? I assume you were there to see him yesterday when you stopped by my office."

"He's coming around. Slowly, but surely. I think he agreed to have a session with a counselor."

Melanie smiled. "That is good news. Definitely a step in the right direction."

"Yep." Tyler's brows drew together. "When Heather said you were out of the office, I was worried you'd come down with the bug I'd had."

"No. I managed to avoid getting that." She hesitated, knowing he was no doubt wondering where she had been the past three days. "I had to go out of town to help a friend."

"Heather mentioned you'd gone out of town. I was just surprised you didn't mention it when we talked on Tuesday or Wednesday."

This was treading perilously close to things she really didn't want to share with him...or anyone, for that matter. "It was kind of a depressing and stressful trip."

"All the more reason to share about it with your friends. At the very least we could pray for you."

Friends? "I had to go to Seattle to help a friend who was on the verge of suicide."

Tyler's brows drew together. "Suicide? Were you able to help them?"

"I'm not sure she thinks I helped her, but yes, with her family's support, we got her some psychiatric care."

"It looks like it took its toll on you. Have you known her long?"

"I...met her when we were teenagers. She was a gentle, fragile soul back then but unfortunately, it's made her unable to cope well with certain things." Melanie's thoughts went back to the moment Jenni realized what was happening. Her last memory of Jenni was her screams of how much she hated Melanie and how she'd betrayed her.

Tyler pushed back from the desk and came around to sit in the other chair, pulling it so it was right next to hers. Before she could adjust to his nearness, his arm slipped around her shoulders. "I'm sure that was difficult for you to deal with."

Melanie felt the mask she'd tried to keep in place the last few days melt under Tyler's caring words and supportive embrace. She took a deep shuddering breath. She couldn't fall apart now, couldn't show how much seeing Jenni had shaken her.

His hand rubbed up and down her upper arm as he continued to murmur encouragement to her.

"She said she hated me." The words slipped out on a whisper, but Melanie knew he'd heard her when his hand tightened on her arm.

The tears she'd been holding back since that moment flooded her eyes. Melanie bent her head and leaned against Tyler. Without hesitation, his other arm went around her and she felt his cheek rest on the top of her head.

"Heavenly Father, we come to you today to ask that you ease the pain Melanie is feeling."

When Melanie realized that Tyler was praying for her, a fresh flood of tears escaped her eyes.

"Please give her peace in knowing that she did the right thing for her friend. We can't know the turmoil of her friend's soul, but You do. You know the pain Melanie is feeling right now as well. We ask that you bring comfort to Melanie and give her the courage to continue to do the tough things. Assure her of Your love and presence, we pray. In Jesus' name, amen."

Though she hadn't prayed much in the years since the kidnapping, she'd prayed a lot the past few days with Jenni. And now to hear Tyler pray for her, she felt as if she wasn't alone, that even without knowing all the details, Tyler was willing to step up and ask God to help her.

"Hey, bro!" Ryan's voice interrupted the silence that had fallen at the end of Tyler's prayer. "Oh. Sorry. I'll come back later."

"Ryan, it's okay." Melanie straightened, rubbing her hands over her cheeks.

She looked over to see that Ryan had dropped to his haunches next to her, concern on his face. "Everything okay?"

Though Tyler's arm was no longer around her shoulders, she could still feel the warmth of it where it lay on the back of her chair. "It will be. Just had a couple of rough days."

His gaze shot to Tyler then back to her. "You didn't get sick, did you?"

"No, nothing like that."

"That's good." He laid a hand on Tyler's desk and pushed to his feet. "You take care of yourself."

"Thanks, Ryan."

"I'll be back to talk to you later, bro."

"Sounds good."

As Ryan left the office, Melanie gripped her purse and tried to keep from looking at Tyler. "I really should go."

"Hey, how about dinner and a movie tomorrow night?" Tyler asked as she got to her feet.

Melanie glanced down at him, not sure how to respond.

As if sensing the reason for her hesitation, he said, "I think you could use a night out, and I owe you a thanks for taking care of me."

"You don't owe me anything," Melanie said. "That's what friends do."

Tyler stood up, making her have to tilt her head to look at him. "Well, friends also try to help friends when they're going through a rough patch. I think dinner and a movie would be just what you need after this week."

"Don't you have basketball tomorrow night?" Melanie asked.

"You're lucky. As it happens, we had already canceled because too many of the guys had other things going on. I was just going to sit at home with Ryan watching television and eating bad pizza. You'd be doing me a favor."

Melanie laughed for what felt like the first time in years even though she knew it had only been a few days. "Well, if it will make you feel better."

"It would."

"Do I get to pick the movie?" Melanie asked.

"If you must." A pained look crossed Tyler's face, but it quickly slid into an indulgent smile. "I'll pick you up at five tomorrow."

Melanie nodded. "Sounds good." She took a couple of steps toward the door then turned around. Tyler stood with his hands on his hips, his gaze on her, a serious expression on his face. "Thank you."

A small smile curved his lips. "You're welcome."

As Melanie walked to the elevators, she realized she felt lighter than she had since...well, in a long time. Was it Tyler? Or his prayer? Or both? She didn't know for certain, but she was going to enjoy the feeling for as long as it lasted.

Melanie took a break from the work she'd brought home with her and headed down to the kitchen. She found Adrianne sitting at the table with a bag of Oreos and a glass of milk. Frowning, Melanie sat down across from her sister.

She reached for the bag of cookies, but Adrianne pulled them away.

Staring at Adrianne in surprise, Melanie said, "What's going on? I thought you were going out tonight?"

"I was. Julie and Liz were supposed to meet me for dinner."

"What happened?"

Adrianne sighed. "Julie's little guy is sick, and Conrad ended up getting the night off unexpectedly so Liz decided she'd rather spend the evening with him."

Melanie felt for her sister. She knew something like this just rubbed salt into an already open wound when she had neither a child nor a husband. "So why can't I have one of the Oreos?"

"Because." Adrianne glared at her. "You'll eat just one and stop. Meanwhile, I plan to eat about ten. Or the whole pack. I don't need to be reminded of yet another way in which I'm failing." She plucked one from the package and twisted it apart to lick the frosting. "I should take your approach to friends."

"My approach? I don't have an approach."

Adrianne stared at her then said, "Who's your best friend?"

Melanie answered without hesitation. "You."

"I'm your sister. Aside from me, who's your best friend?"

She shifted in her chair. What was Adrianne trying to prove? "I guess I don't really have one."

"Exactly. You don't have friends because you don't want to have to open yourself up to them. Or, you choose to have guy friends because they don't tend to ask you to share about your emotions and stuff."

Well, that wasn't completely true, as Tyler had proved earlier that day. But she figured Adrianne's words had merit. She had lots of acquaintances at work, but she'd long accepted that she'd never have that best friend who would know everything about her.

"I'm beginning to think that not relying on friends might be a good thing."

"Adrianne, stop." Melanie reached out again and this time managed to snag the Oreo package. "You need to snap out of this funk you've been in lately. And don't tell me that it's easy for me to say. You didn't use to let stuff like this bother you. You use to be confident and outgoing. This has turned into a never-ending pity party. It's so unlike you."

Adrianne dunked one side of an Oreo in her milk. She did it a few times until part of the cookie softened so much it disappeared into the white beverage. "Do you remember how I was back in high school?"

Melanie managed not to wince as an image popped into her mind. They'd all had awkward years growing up, but Adrianne's had seemed to last a whole lot longer. She'd struggled with her weight, had bad acne, glasses, and braces. Pretty much any one of those might have led to some teasing, but all four? Yeah, she was sure those years hadn't been the easiest for her sister.

"You're nothing like what you were in high school," Melanie tried to assure her.

"On the outside maybe. But inside? I can still hear what the boy I asked to the Sadie Hawkins dance in graded ten said to me. He couldn't just have turned me down. No, he had to take the knife he'd shoved into my chest and twist it."

Melanie frowned. "What did he say to you?"

With a sigh, Adrianne dropped the remainder of the Oreo into the milk and looked at Melanie. "He said that no guy would ever want to be seen with me. That I was going to just get fatter and fatter, and that I'd never get married or have children because no man would ever want to touch me. And that was after he'd told me he wouldn't have gone with me to the dance if I'd been the last female on earth."

Melanie's jaw went slack, and it felt like she'd been slugged in the stomach. "Who was it?"

Adrianne shook her head. "Not going to tell you that. Let's just say that as each year clicks by, I'm hearing his words louder than ever."

"But he's wrong. Teenage boys can be such..." Melanie bit down on her tongue.

"At least the ones I had the pleasure of being around."

"Hey. Did Alex know him?" When Adrianne didn't answer right away, Melanie said, "He was a friend of Alex's? Oh, my word. Did you tell Alex what he said to you?"

"One of the reasons I approached him was because I thought he'd be safe since he and Alex were friends." Adrianne brushed a tear away from her cheek. "I'm sorry. I know I've been difficult to be around lately, and I've taken some of my hurt out on you. Sometimes I wonder if you work at changing your appearance so you don't look like me."

Melanie was speechless. She stared at her sister, aching for the inadvertent role she'd played in her distress. "No, it had nothing to do with that." Melanie paused as she realized that she was going to be letting down another one of the walls she'd kept in place for so long. But she had to. If she could ease this part of the hurt Adrianne was feeling, she would do it for her. "You want to know why I color my hair, keep it short and wear colored contacts?"

Adrianne's eyes were wide as if she recognized the significance of the moment. "Only if you want to tell me."

"They wanted girls with beautiful long blonde or red curls and blue or green eyes. It was those things that made me a target and then a victim. I do this," Melanie waved her hand around her face and hair, "so I won't ever be a target for them again."

Now it was Adrianne's turn to stare. "I never knew."

"I know everyone thought it was just a phase. That after what I'd been through it made sense that I would go through an emotional stage. It wasn't a stage, and it had nothing to do with being goth though I did play that up at the time with the black nail polish and dark makeup since it seemed easier to explain. And now," Melanie shrugged, "it's just who I am. Well, minus the nails and makeup."

"Is what happened the reason you don't go out on dates now? Do you not plan to ever get married or have kids?"

"Partly. I'm just not comfortable with guys in a romantic way. I mean, how many men would want a woman who keeps a gun under her pillow?"

"I don't know. That may turn some guys on."

"I'm not sure I'd want to be with a guy like that." Melanie wrinkled her nose. "Honestly, though, I have so many issues as a result of what happened, I'm not sure I could contribute to a healthy relationship."

"What about Tyler?"

Melanie hoped she didn't reveal in any way what the sound of his name did to her. "What about him?"

"You seem pretty close to him."

She shrugged. "We've been friends for a long time, but I think you're right about what you said about me being closer with guys than girls."

"So you only see Tyler as a friend?"

"Yeah. And that's how he views me."

"Well, the BlackThorpe gossip mill is saying differently."

Melanie frowned. "What?"

"Someone saw you in Tyler's office. They said it looked like more than a friend moment."

Irritation flowed through Melanie. She grabbed an Oreo out of the bag and gave it a twist to separate it. "They need to mind their own business. I was upset about something, and Tyler was...praying for me."

Adrianne's eyes widened as her mouth dropped open. "He was *praying* for you?"

Melanie understood why Adrianne was so surprised by that. "Yeah. That was a new one for me."

"That was really sweet, honestly."

"Yes, it was." Melanie hadn't ever had someone pray for her like that. She knew that Tyler was fairly involved with his church and that his faith was an important part of his life because of things he'd said during the conversations they'd had over the years.

Melanie glanced over toward the door leading to the garage when she heard it open. Alex walked in, his briefcase in hand. He still wore his suit from the day though he'd abandoned the tie at some point.

"Hot date?" Adrianne asked as he set his briefcase down on the floor.

Alex shot her an exasperated look as he yanked open the fridge. He pulled out the jug of orange juice and took a glass out of the cupboard. "I was at Marcus's going over some contracts."

After pouring himself some juice, he put the jug back and came to sit at the table with them. He eyed the package of Oreos. "Having a girl chat?"

"Yep. Spilling secrets all over the place," Adrianne said as she pulled an Oreo out and offered it to him. "Your turn. Why don't you ever go out on dates?"

"Oreos and Orange juice? I think not," Alex said with a wave of his hand. "And I don't go on dates because I don't want to."

Melanie figured it was only fair to let Alex keep his secrets. They all had them even though she and Adrianne had shared a couple. She wondered what Alex would do if he ever found out what one of his friends had said to his twin sister. He was still in contact with some of them from high school, but not all of them. It was possible that the guy who'd so badly hurt Adrianne was long gone from Alex's life. She hoped that was the case because she couldn't bear the thought that Adrianne might encounter him again if he happened by to visit Alex.

"So I hear you had an interesting meeting this afternoon," Alex said.

"Me?" Melanie asked. "You mean with Marcus? Did you see Scout?"

"Yes, I did. He's working well with Meredith. Marcus spent a good ten minutes raving about the program and the work you've done with it." Alex took a sip of his orange juice. "But that wasn't the meeting I was referring to."

"Not you, too." Melanie's shoulders slumped as she scowled at him. "Never figured you guys would be gossiping grannies."

Alex and Adrianne shared a look and then started laughing. Melanie fought the age-old urge to give them both a kick in the shins. It had been her go-to move as a kid when she'd felt they had ganged up on her.

"Don't do it," Alex said with a grin, obviously recalling the twin kick move. "Or I'll tell Mom that Tyler's more than just the friend you keep saying he is."

That threat pretty much guaranteed Melanie wouldn't do anything. And their knowledge of the office gossip meant she wasn't going to tell them that she and Tyler were going out for dinner and a movie the next night. Maybe she should text Tyler and tell him she'd meet him at his place or at the restaurant.

"Well, on that lovely note, I'm going back to my work." Melanie shoved the package of Oreos over to Adrianne.

"Thanks for the chat," Adrianne said.

Melanie glanced over at her to see if she was just joking, but her expression was serious. "You too. Have a good night."

After having a late-night conversation with Ryan about the latest office gossip, Tyler half expected to get a text from Melanie canceling. That she hadn't done that, either meant she hadn't heard the gossip or she didn't care. He really hoped it was the latter.

As he pulled his vehicle to a stop in front of a set of closed gates, Tyler stared in surprise—even though he shouldn't have been—to see the tight security around the Thorpe residence. Uncertain what to do, he glanced around to see if there was a way to contact the house. His gaze landed on a panel set into the stone pillars flanking the gates.

Tyler was just about to get out of his car when the gates began to open, and he spotted Melanie walking out. Once she was through the large gates, they began to close behind her.

Tyler got out of the car as she got closer and quickly rounded to the other side to open the door for her. He noticed that she wore familiar knee high boots over jeans and a light blue sweater with a collar that draped softly below her neck. Her black jacket just skimmed her waist, no doubt in deference to the cooler fall temperatures that had rolled in that day.

"I was wondering how to get through the gates," he said as she neared him.

"Yeah, Alex has really upped the security around here in recent months. You can just press the button on that panel to call someone at the house to open it. We have cameras on the property so we will know if someone entering is expected or not."

"Got all the bases covered," Tyler said as he waited for her to settle into the passenger seat. "Probably a good idea given what's been happening."

"Yeah," Melanie said as she reached for her seatbelt.

Tyler closed the door once she'd buckled up then went around to slide behind the wheel. He put the car into reverse and backed out of the driveway.

"I thought maybe you'd cancel tonight."

"I did consider it," Melanie confessed.

"Because of the rumor?"

"Yeah. Both Alex and Adrianne asked me about it."

Tyler looked over at her. "And you still didn't cancel?"

"Honestly, it's none of their business." Melanie shrugged. "I need this evening out, and we know the truth of things, so I'm just going to ignore them and do what friends do."

Tyler wondered if she used the *what friends do* phrase to remind him or herself what this evening was all about. "I like the way you think."

"It's a little more difficult with those two, especially when they gang up on me."

"They didn't ask where you were going?" Tyler guided his car into the traffic on the highway.

"That's rule #1 in our household. No asking for the details of each other's social life."

"And you all stick to the rule?"

Melanie laughed. "Well, not as much as we should. Fortunately, both of them are out tonight so I didn't have to sneak past them like a teenager trying to get out of her house."

Tyler was glad to see Melanie so relaxed. After the tension he'd seen in her the day before, he hadn't been sure how she'd be. He had prayed that she'd be at peace in spite of the stresses the week had held for her. It was good to see that his prayers had been answered.

"So where are we going for dinner?" Melanie asked as he took an exit off the highway.

Tyler had thought long and hard about a suitable spot for their dinner. He didn't want it to have an overtly romantic ambiance, but he still wanted it to be a good place for them to visit. In the end, he'd settled for a chain restaurant that was a few steps up from fast food. When he told her the name, she didn't seem to have a problem with it.

Thankfully, there wasn't much of a line when they arrived, and the hostess quickly seated them in a booth in a back corner. The booths had higher backs on them which gave them some privacy from the other restaurant patrons. A recap of the sports of the day was playing on the televisions over the bar in the Center of the room.

It didn't take them long to place their order with the waitress. After she'd picked up the menus and left the table, Tyler leaned back in the booth.

"So have you spent your Saturday playing catch-up like I have?" he asked.

Melanie groaned. "Yeah. Up late last night and then all day today. I was actually able to do some work while I was away, but not enough to be caught up when I got back."

"Me, too. By day two of my sick leave, I was going a bit stir-crazy so I logged in from home to do some work, but still had lots to follow up on when I got back to the office. Is it any wonder none of us ever take long vacations?"

"That's so true, though as a counselor I would have to say that those vacations are necessary to recharge batteries." A corner of her mouth lifted. "But I'm as guilty as the next person of not taking my vacation time."

They continued to talk about work-related things until the appetizers arrived. Out of habit, Tyler held out his hand. She obviously understood what he was doing because she laid her hand in his and bent her head. Tyler took a moment to say a prayer of thanks for the food before they dug in. Their conversation turned to Simon as Tyler filled her in with a little more detail about the time they'd spent together.

Once their meals arrived, Tyler changed up the conversation, asking a question he hoped she'd feel comfortable answering.

"How's your friend doing?"

13

MELANIE GLANCED UP from the piece of chicken she'd been cutting. "Jenni?"

"Yeah. Is she getting the help she needs?"

"No. I talked to her mom earlier today and she said that Jenni's still refusing medication and won't talk to anyone." Melanie's brow furrowed. "I'm not sure if she's going to be able to get back from this mind set of hopelessness. I mean, she has to *want* to, but I sense she just thinks life will never be any better than what it's been so why hang around to live it."

"Do you mind me asking what exactly happened to her?"

Melanie stuck a piece of chicken in her mouth and chewed, obviously taking time to figure out her response to that. After swallowing, she lifted her glass and took a sip of water. "She was abducted when she was fifteen years old."

"I'm guessing from the severity of her trauma that it wasn't a parental abduction."

"Not even close." Melanie paused again. "She was taken as part of a trafficking ring."

Suddenly, Tyler wasn't sure he wanted to hear more. He knew enough about what something like that would entail without needing to hear about the details from Melanie.

But what kind of attitude was that? Stuff like that flourished because people ignored it. If it didn't happen to someone they knew or loved, it was easier to turn a blind eye. Click away from the links to stories about it. Pretend it only happened in third world countries, not countries like the US.

If Melanie wanted to talk about it, he would listen. And after a pause, it was apparent she wanted to.

"It was a very specialized ring, apparently. They had been sent by some super wealthy men from the Middle East, who had very specific requests in the girls they wanted." Melanie twirled her fork through the pasta on her plate but didn't lift any of it to her mouth.

"Hey." Tyler reached across and covered her hand with his. "You don't have to talk about this if you don't want. I'm willing to listen, but I don't want you to feel compelled to talk about it."

She stared at him for several moments before she shook her head. "I want to share...her story with you. So you understand. But it's not a pretty story, and you've heard the ending already."

Tyler nodded then pulled his hand back and waited.

"There were two types of girls they wanted. Blonde or redheads with long hair and light eyes. Jenni had...has beautiful red hair and exquisite green eyes. They also wanted young girls, in the fourteen to sixteen-year range and...inexperienced. Virgins."

"How would they know if they were virgins before they took them?"

"Jenni and her family were churchgoers. A young man joined their youth group and took an immediate liking to

Jenni. He was the quintessential gentleman, she said. Even her family liked him. And he told her that he would never pressure her for sex because he believed in saving himself for marriage. When she told him she felt the same way, that she was a virgin, he knew he had what he needed. What better place to find potential victims than a church that had an active 'waiting for marriage' program for their youth. These guys did their research."

"So he just abducted her?"

Melanie shook her head. "It was all so elaborate even though it unfolded over a relatively short period of time. After a few weeks, the guy had her set up a weekend at a friend's. After a romantic dinner between just the two of them, he drugged her, gave her something to make her feel sick, like the flu. Jenni said he told her he'd take her home, but suggested she phone her friend to cancel their planned weekend. Once she'd done that, he took her to a waiting car. It was two days before anyone realized she was gone. Her parents thought she was at her friend's. Her friend thought she had gone home sick. It wasn't until her parents looked for her after church on Sunday that they realized what had happened. By then, she was a long way from Seattle."

"That's a pretty slick operation," Tyler said. Looking at it with his experience in intelligence, there was no doubt that a lot of money and effort had gone into Jenni's abduction. "How did they find her?"

"Well, the kidnappers had an order for twelve girls. They managed to snag them from all over the US. No two girls were taken from the same city or state, so no one tied the kidnappings together. Apparently, the kidnappers had access to a very secure compound not far from New York City. They would bring the girls there as they found them and begin to train them."

Tyler swallowed and tried to stop from asking the obvious question. "Train them?"

Melanie got a faraway look in her eyes before she answered his question. And after she had, Tyler could understand better than he had before why Jenni was struggling to recover. Anger burned in his stomach that there were people out there willing to inflict such horror on young girls. But he knew from his own experience of being in the Middle East and dealing with some of the rebel groups there that money and the absolute devotion to a cause could get people to do almost anything.

"Were the kidnappers from the Middle East?" Tyler asked.

Melanie slowly shook her head. "I think that's one of the reasons Jenni struggles so much. The boy—although it seemed he was more of a man who looked young for his age—was paid to play the part up until he put her in the car after drugging her on their date. He looked just like any other young man on the street. I'm not sure he knew what he was doing. The police never found him."

"How did she get free?"

"They'd gathered the twelve girls over the course of two or three weeks. Jenni had been drugged at times so didn't know how much time passed before they had all they needed. But then one of the girls committed suicide. Suddenly, they didn't have twelve anymore and according to what the girls heard, they were supposed to leave within twenty-four hours. I guess the kidnappers decided to take their chances and snatch someone off the street in New York, hoping she would be what they needed."

"And that's where their plans fell apart?"

Melanie nodded. "They happened to snatch the daughter of a wealthy family who had equipped their daughter with some sort of GPS thing in her jewelry. All she had to do was press it to activate it, and she managed to do that before they knocked her out. The company monitoring was alerted to what was going on and immediately called the police who followed the signal right to the house."

"So they were able to free all twelve girls?"

Melanie nodded. "But not without some bloodshed. Though the girls were safe, all the men involved in the kidnapping were killed in the standoff. The cops weren't able to discover if there were other rings operating across the country. The person who owned the house said they were paid more than sixty thousand dollars in cash for a month's use of the home so they didn't request any sort of identification. It was all a dead end."

"That's got to be difficult for Jenni and the other girls."

"Jenni was one of the first girls taken so she suffered more and the damage to her psyche—which wasn't strong to begin with—was significant. She's been in and out of psychiatric care ever since."

As Tyler mulled over everything Melanie had shared, something niggled at him. He watched as she continued to play with her food, her head bent. "Did any of this make the news?"

Her head jerked up. "No. Well, not with the specifics of the girls who'd been abducted. The families wanted to keep their names out of the press so that the girls would have a chance to recover without the media hounding them. There were police statements issued warning people of the scam that had been used. But since there were no kidnapper survivors of the raid and the rental information was a dead end, there was no trial."

"Jenni's fortunate to have a friend like you," Tyler said.

"She doesn't think so, but her last few letters were alarming. She'd shaved her head and was refusing to leave her apartment. It's a cycle for her, but this go-around was taking her much lower than other ones had."

They ate in silence for a few minutes. Tyler was glad to see that Melanie was actually putting food into her mouth instead of just playing with her food. He felt a bit bad to have brought up such an emotional subject.

"How's your food?"

A smile flashed across Melanie's face as she looked up at him. "It's pretty good. How is yours?"

Conversation from that point drifted to less intensive topics. At one point, Tyler managed to convince her to share a dessert with him when she balked at eating a whole one by herself. There were several empty tables so Tyler didn't feel pressured to bring an end to their dinner though it was getting late.

"Still want to go to a movie?" Tyler asked as he ate the last piece of the dessert. "We could make the late show."

Melanie seemed to think about it. "If you'd like to go, I'm up for it."

"I'm enjoying just sitting here talking actually," Tyler said.

"After this week, so am I." Melanie relaxed back against the booth. "Thankfully, there were no major fires while I was gone."

"So," Tyler began, "I hope the rumor floating around BlackThorpe didn't upset you too much. I apologize for putting you in that position."

Melanie laughed. "Not your fault. I think people were looking with dollar signs in their eyes given that I'm at the top of that bet they've got going. There are far worse rumors that could be circulating. People are going to think what they think, and me trying to convince them it's not true just brings more attention to it."

Tyler was glad she wasn't bothered by it, but a part of him wished that the rumor was true. Would taking their friendship in the direction of a relationship ruin it? Their friendship had morphed over the years, so there was no reason why it couldn't continue to grow and pull them closer together. But he kinda figured he was alone in that thinking.

"Alex and Adrianne thought it was pretty funny," Melanie said. "But that's siblings for you."

Tyler shrugged. "I've never had the pleasure given I'm an only child. Ryan's kind of become the brother I never had."

"And am I the sister you never had?" Melanie asked, a grin on her face.

"Um..." Tyler regarded her seriously. "Not exactly."

Her brown eyes widened briefly at his response then her brows drew together. She tilted her head to the side as she stared at him. "Yeah, I suppose I don't exactly view you in the same light as Alex."

Tyler would have liked to take hope from that, but he had a feeling that she still kept him squarely in the friend-zone.

In the meantime, he'd keep praying and waiting for the right opportunity even though there was a little voice in his head that just kept saying to go ahead and ask about the possibility. If she said no, well, then he'd know, and hopefully, they could still be friends. But if she said yes... If she really was willing to consider something more than a friendship, then they would only have wasted time if he waited.

The waitress finally slid the bill onto the table around ten-thirty, and they agreed it was time to call it a night. This time when they approached the Thorpe property, Melanie pulled a device from her purse and soon the gates were swinging open. He steered the car around the bends in the driveway until he came to a stop in front of a large...huge, really...house. Though it was dark, he could see that it had an odd structure to it that he would have liked to explore.

"Thanks so much for dinner," Melanie said as she opened her door.

Tyler got out of the car as well and walked with her up the steps to the house. "You're welcome. I enjoyed the evening. Definitely what I needed."

"Me, too." She hesitated, then gripped his arm while she went up on her toes to brush a light kiss across his cheek. "See you next week."

"You bet." Tyler watched as she opened the door. "Will I need to do anything to close the gate?"

"Nope. I'll watch the monitors and close them once you're gone."

After a final goodbye, Tyler waited until she was inside with the door shut before he returned to his car. He resisted the urge to press his hand to his cheek. Did friends kiss each other? He followed the loop in the driveway and headed back to the gate. Okay, well, did *female* friends kiss their guy friends? He knew that Ryan wouldn't be kissing him. At most they did a quick guy hug.

He thought back and realized that Kelly had kissed him when they were still friends, but that was slightly different as they'd both seemed well aware of the direction their relationship was going. And of course, his mom kissed him. But Melanie never had.

Tyler let out a sigh as he turned onto the ramp leading to the highway to go home. Thirty-one years old and the female species of the race still managed to confound him more often than not.

"You're free to go in," the guard at the entrance to the BlackThorpe training compound said as he stepped back from her truck. The security had been upped to include guards at the gate in addition to the hand scan in order to gain access to the compound.

After parking in the lot, Melanie got out and grabbed her gun case from the back seat along with her purse. She hadn't been out here to shoot in quite a few weeks. Because her training was more intense than most realized, she usually went to a shooting range/self-defense center in St. Paul. Today, she just wanted to shoot.

She walked into the main building and greeted the two guards before heading for the door that would lead to the shooting range. As she neared the range, she could hear the muffled shots of others practicing. As long as there was one lane open for her, she'd be happy. When she pulled open the door, her gaze went to the left and the windows there that looked out on the shooting range.

"Well, imagine seeing you out here."

Turning, Melanie saw Justin standing behind the counter where they stored the ear protection among other things. She was a bit surprised to see him since it was a Sunday afternoon and he didn't live at the compound anymore.

"I could say the same thing to you. What are you doing out here on the weekend?"

Justin smiled, something he did more frequently since the gentle Alana had come into his life and captured his heart. "Alana was getting together with some of the ladies so I'm out here to meet with the guys. Than and Trent should be here in a bit."

Melanie was surprised at the pang of longing that briefly took up residence in her chest. She was happy that Alana had found some friends in the wives and girlfriends of the men at BlackThorpe. It shouldn't bother her to not be part of it, but for the first time, it did. However, she had no one to blame but herself for the lack of friends.

"I'm just out here to do a little shooting." Melanie looked back at the windows, uncertain what her expression might reveal.

"Everything okay?"

Trust Justin to pick up on it. They've been friends ever since he'd come to work at the company. It had kind of been like her friendship with Tyler. It had started as acquaintances and gradually worked its way up to friendship. She glanced back at him and smiled. "Yep."

Justin crossed his arms over his chest and stared at her with narrowed eyes. "That was only a half-smile. What's up? Does it have anything to do with the rumor floating around?"

"Really, Justin?" Melanie intentionally arched an eyebrow at him. "Listening to rumors?"

If she'd expected him to look abashed, she was in for a disappointment because the dude grinned at her and said, "Sorry, but hearing you linked romantically to someone kinda made me pay attention."

"There's nothing to it," Melanie retorted. "Never gonna happen."

"Never say never, Melanie," Justin said, the grin still firmly in place on his face. "Look at me. All it takes, if it's God's will, is meeting the right person."

Well, she could hardly argue that with him. Justin had been a confirmed bachelor if there ever had been one. Seeing him take the plunge headfirst into the pool of love had been somewhat amusing. And the spiritual side of him was yet another change since he'd met Alana. He'd never spoken much about his faith, at least not the way he did now.

"The best thing you can do is to pray and ask God to prepare your heart for the man He has for you—if it's His will."

"You keep saying that. *If it's His will.* Do you believe that sometimes it's not His will for a person to fall in love and marry?"

Justin shrugged. "God calls us all to different walks of life. Sometimes it will be alone. Sometimes it will be with a spouse. I wouldn't presume to know what might be the case in your situation, but don't deny yourself the possibility of a relationship for any reason other than you feel that it's not God's will for you."

Her thoughts drifted back to her evening with Tyler and then the time she'd spent at church earlier that day. She hadn't gone to her parents' church—the one she usually attended—but she'd gone with Alex to his. There were subtle differences between the churches and she'd felt more receptive to the message the pastor there had brought, but that could have less to do with the church itself and more with where her heart and mind had been lately.

The pastor had also spoken about finding God's will for one's life. He'd talked about how God could see the whole picture while people only see a little bit at a time. *How much wiser*, the pastor had said, *to let the person who sees the whole picture guide you through the decisions in your life.*

Of course, it made sense, but Melanie had no idea how to actually do that. Before she could ask Justin more about it, Than and Trent showed up, exuberant in their greetings and once again bringing up the rumor.

"I need to get a T-shirt printed that says *No, it's not true*," Melanie grumbled.

Than laughed. "Or, you could say *hey, that Tyler dude is a pretty nice guy. Maybe I should consider something with him.*"

"Oh, I know Tyler's a pretty nice guy. We've been friends for years. It has nothing to do with whether or not he's nice."

"Going from friends to something more can be a scary thing," Trent said with a gentle smile. "But sometimes you just need to take the plunge and pray for God's will to prevail."

There is was again. "Well, it's kind of a moot point since Tyler hasn't shown any interest in that either."

Trent shrugged. "Could be he's as reluctant as you to put a friendship on the line."

It struck Melanie once again that unlike Adrianne with her girlfriends, she was getting relationship advice from three guys. Not that she'd asked for it. Besides, where did God's will fit into the horrific abduction she'd endured? She hadn't asked for that. In fact, it was her efforts to date a boy who shared the values and morals she'd been taught that had gotten her into trouble.

"I'll keep all this in mind," Melanie said with a smile she hoped didn't reveal the turmoil within her. Right then she was as confused about her relationship with God as she was about one with Tyler. "And on that note, I'm going to do some serious damage to paper bad guys."

Though Justin looked like he might have wanted to continue the conversation, he didn't say anything more about it while he got her some ear protection.

"We're going to the gym to spar and work out," he said once she was set. "If I don't see you before you go, enjoy the rest of your weekend."

Once she was in a lane ready to shoot, she lifted her weapon, aimed and began to fire. The paper form had a face in her mind. Several different ones, in fact. Each face was indelibly etched in her mind. She even knew what they looked like dead. When she and the other girls had been led from the house after the raid, the cops had tried to shield them from the dead bodies sprawled on the floor, but Melanie had *needed* to see them. If she didn't see with her own eyes that they were dead and would never again be able to reach her, she knew they would haunt her dreams.

Of course, that didn't take away the fear that someone *else* would one day try to insert themselves into her life again. You'd think that the fear of a man coming after her again would have prevented her from being able to be friends with men—would have sent her in the direction of female friendships only. But the men she claimed as friends had come into her life by circumstances that couldn't be faked or because Alex or Marcus had trusted them.

Ryan was probably the one person in her life currently that she didn't know much about. But he wasn't pursuing her, and he seemed to be a good friend to Tyler, so until he proved otherwise, she would extend limited trust to him.

Melanie laid her gun down and lowered her ear protection as she waited for the paper target to come toward her. The range had fallen quiet, and she wondered if she was the only one still shooting.

"You aiming at anyone in particular? You're amazingly accurate."

She jerked in surprise and glanced over her shoulder to see a tall, muscled man with a brush cut standing behind her. He stood like Justin often did with his arms crossed over his chest. Suddenly uneasy and unwilling to give him her back, Melanie turned sideways while she reloaded her gun.

"I always find it helps to imagine a bad guy. And there is no shortage of those in the world today."

"Well, you'd be doing a bang up job if you were shooting them in real life," the man said, his lips curving up into a wide smile. "Name's Eli Bennett."

The man held out his hand. Melanie hesitated just a moment before she reached out to shake it. Surely if the guy was this deep into the BlackThorpe compound, he'd been cleared to be there. Still, there was something about him that put her on edge. "I'm Melanie. Melanie Thorpe."

The man's eyebrows rose at that. It was a good sign that he apparently hadn't realized who she was. "Thorpe as in Alex's sister?"

Melanie nodded. "One of them anyway."

Eli glanced around. "Is Alex here today?"

"Nope." Melanie lowered her gun to rest against her thigh, barrel pointed at the floor. "So you know Alex?"

The man propped his hands on his hips. "We've met a few times. I'm in with a group from D.C. We're doing some security training."

"Well, Eli, it was nice to meet you."

"You, too." His head tilted to the side, his gray eyes regarded her with interest. "Hey, would you be interested in going for coffee? Sorry if I seem a little forward, but I feel like I know you a little bit because of Alex."

Melanie tried to give him a friendly smile even though everything inside her was screaming for her to get away from him. "Thanks for the invite, but I'm not available."

Eli's eyebrow arched. "Is this a recent development? Alex mentioned that you weren't dating when we talked a few weeks back."

Melanie stared at the man. Was he for real? What was Alex doing discussing her personal life with this man? "You talked with Alex about me?"

"Not directly. I was just bemoaning the fact that I couldn't find a woman who shared my interest in things like this." He waved his hand to indicate the gun range. "Alex said he had a sister who was single and liked shooting. Guess he doesn't know you're not available."

Now she was really regretting that she hadn't gone to her usual shooting place. This was definitely a first. "I guess perhaps I should clarify. I'm not available for a short-term fling, and I'm not interested in anything long distance."

Before Eli could respond, Melanie's phone rang. She picked it up and turned it over to see the display. *Tyler.*

Keeping Eli in her peripheral, Melanie tapped the screen to answer the call. "Hey, Tyler. How's it going?"

"It's going fine. You?"

"Good. Just out at the range shooting." Melanie saw Eli shift his weight, but he didn't leave.

"Sounds like a...fun way to spend a Sunday afternoon."

"No doubt you and Ryan were hunkered down watching some sport and eating pizza."

Tyler chuckled. "You know us too well."

"Sports and food. What's to know?"

"True. So true. But listen, I called because I forgot to ask you last night if you thought it would be okay for me to pick Simon up for the evening. There is a men's group meeting at the church tonight and when I mentioned it, Simon seemed interested in attending."

"Sure that would be fine. I'm glad to hear he's wanting to interact with people. That's a definite improvement."

"Yes it is, so I'd like to take advantage of this."

Melanie looked over as she heard someone call Eli's name. A man stood not too far from Eli, but Eli's gaze was on her. "Just hang on, Les. I'm waiting for Melanie to finish up her phone call. Still trying to convince her to go for coffee." Eli winked at her and made no move to leave.

Melanie was sure Tyler heard the comment.

"Uh, sounds like you're busy. I'd better let you go."

"I'll talk to you later," Melanie said, not happy with the sudden distance in Tyler's voice.

When Tyler ended the call, Melanie stared down at the display for a moment before laying her phone back on the small shelf. In her mind, she was already rehearsing the moves she'd use on the man if he didn't back off. She was not in the mood for games like that.

14

MELANIE RAISED her head and met his gaze. "Not cool, Eli. Definitely not cool. I'm not going to change my mind about having coffee with you. If there was any man I'd go out with it would be the one I just got off the phone with." She narrowed her eyes. "Alex must have neglected to mention that I don't like it when people don't take no for an answer."

"Fair enough," Eli said as he lifted his hands. "Sometimes women need to play hard to get."

"But for most women, no means no. Plus, your approach is akin to a bulldozer. Try something with a little more finesse on the next woman."

"I'll take that under advisement." His expression told her that he didn't quite take her seriously. And that annoyed her even more.

"Here's one other thing to take under advisement." She clasped her gun between both hands and lifted it slightly. "You only get one warning. Stay away from me."

She still wasn't sure he took her threat as seriously as he should, but he gave a nod of his head, his eyes sparking with something that looked suspiciously like anger, before turning toward the man waiting for him. Melanie didn't take her gaze from Eli as he walked away. When Eli passed the other man, Les turned to her and gave her a big grin and a thumbs up. Clearly, he'd enjoyed seeing Eli Bennett taken down a notch.

As she stood there, the silence of the range settled around her. She took a step back out of her lane and looked in both directions, confirming she was on her own. A frisson of unease skittered down her spine. She snatched up her phone and quickly scrolled through her contacts to call Alex.

"What's up?" Alex said when he answered.

"What's up? *What's up* is that I just had a run in with one of the most arrogant men I've ever met. And he said he knew you."

"Who are you talking about?"

"Eli Bennet. That's who I'm talking about. The guy was not interested in taking no for an answer after finding out that I was your single sister who enjoyed shooting. What on earth, Alex? Why are you talking to guys about me? Especially guys like *that*."

Alex groaned. "You're out at the range?"

"Yeah. Imagine my surprise when he said he knew you and then told me what you'd said about me."

"Sorry about that. I didn't mean it in such a way that I thought he'd ask you for a date. I just mentioned I had a sister who enjoyed things like shooting."

"Yeah, well, he apparently thought that was the green light to try and pester me into going out for coffee with him."

"What did you tell him?"

"What do you think? No. And when he finally figured out I was serious, I also told him he'd better stay away from me. And I might have sort of indirectly threatened him with my gun."

"Seriously, Melanie? Why would you do that?"

"Nothing else was making him back down. He seemed to take my negative answer to his date invitation as a joke. As if I wanted him to try harder to convince me to go out with him. Keep him away from me, Alex. You'd better make sure he gets the message, because I won't be responsible for what I do if he doesn't."

"I'll talk to him." Alex sighed. "Just don't shoot him. He's part of an important contract."

"Well, might I suggest that you let him know that all BlackThorpe female employees are off limits to him? I would hate to have him go after a woman who didn't have my ability to say no. You might end up with a whole other issue on your hands."

"True. Sorry, Melanie. But I gotta say, I'm proud of you for standing up to him. He's a pretty formidable guy. I've seen men cower under his attention."

"Yeah, well, he ticked me off. And he did it while I was holding my favorite gun."

"That's my girl."

Melanie smiled at the affection in her brother's voice. "Well, I'm going to do a little more shooting. I'm feeling a little bit aggressive at the moment."

Tyler climbed behind the wheel of his SUV and backed out of the driveway. His jaw hurt from clenching his teeth ever since hanging up the phone with Melanie. He really had no right to be upset by the comment he'd overheard. He had no claim on Melanie. If she wanted to go out for coffee with a guy, that was her prerogative. But that didn't mean he had to like it, because he most certainly didn't.

"Everything okay, bro?"

Tyler shot Ryan a quick look before nodding. He didn't plan to tell Ryan about what he'd heard. Given their past conversations, he was pretty sure the guy wouldn't have any sympathy for him. Ryan had said on more than one occasion that he should just ask Melanie out on a date. Maybe if he'd done that, he wouldn't be in this predicament.

Ryan gave him a light punch on his upper arm. "You do know, right, that usually when I ask you that question it's because I know that everything is *not* okay."

"How would you know that?" Tyler said, his tone a little more defensive than he'd meant for it to be. "You can't read my mind."

"True, but I can read your body."

"Excuse me?" Tyler turned his head to stare at his friend before looking back at the road.

"It's my thing," Ryan said mildly.

"Reading bodies is your thing?"

"Well, reading body language. And between the tight grip you've got on the steering wheel and the tense set of your jaw and shoulders, something is definitely not okay."

"And that's supposed to be a special talent? Seems pretty basic to me."

"You make it easy since I know you, and you're usually pretty easy going. Seeing you tense makes it simple to deduct that you're upset about something."

Tyler looked at Ryan to see if he was pulling his leg. "And when you say it's your thing? Like it's your job?"

"Part of it. It became a big part of my job when I was in the military."

"No kidding?" And Melanie thought women were supposed to be all mysterious. Ryan was right up there with the stuff Tyler didn't know about the guy even though they'd been friends for over six months.

"No kidding."

"So how do you do it?" Tyler was more than happy to grab onto any subject except the one Ryan had been previously focused on. "I'm assuming it's more than just your average *hey, you look angry* sort of thing."

"Hard to explain. It's just like I can read their bodies and absorb their emotions. Ever since I was a little kid, I've been able to do it."

"Do you use this with BlackThorpe?" Tyler asked, somewhat surprised he hadn't known this about his friend.

"To some degree. I analyze videos. Sit in on interviews. And observe the employees."

Tyler's eyes widened as he stared at the traffic ahead of them on the highway. "Observe the employees?"

"Yes. Marcus and Alex aren't convinced that there isn't someone within BlackThorpe that has been feeding information to someone. They want me to interact with the employees to see if I can pick up on anything."

"So I guess since you're telling me this that I checked out," Tyler said with a laugh.

"You, my friend, are an open book. Very easy to read," Ryan said. "Which brings us back to my original question. What's wrong?"

Sighing, Tyler tried to loosen his grip on the steering wheel as he gave Ryan a brief rundown of the conversation he'd had with Melanie, what he'd overheard.

"You need to chill, dude. If you're right in what you're saying, it sounded like the guy was trying to convince her to go with him. Not that he'd succeeded. My guess is she turned him down flat."

"You can't even see her. How do you know that?"

"I just do. And honestly, if you think about it, I think you know that too."

Ryan was right, but he wasn't about to tell him that. No need to give the guy a swelled head. Tyler felt some of the tension ease from his shoulders. One thing he did know as a result of all of this was that he needed to ask Melanie if she'd consider going out with him. Sooner or later there was sure to be someone who would come along that she would say yes to. If he left it too long, it wouldn't be him.

Melanie stared at the number on her cell phone display, not recognizing it. After a short debate, she tapped the screen to accept it.

"Melanie?" The voice was soft and tentative but familiar.

"Jenni? Is that you?"

"Yes. I'm calling to apologize." Jenni paused. "I don't hate you."

Though not often given to tears, when dealing with Jenni and her situation, they were always near the surface, and this time was no different. They had been through so much together. Thinking that Jenni hated her had been gut-wrenching. But she understood why Jenni had felt that way. She'd wanted to be free from the pain this life was causing her, and Melanie had stopped that from happening. "Oh Jenni. I'm so glad to hear that."

"I know you were only doing what was necessary. And I know it wasn't easy for you. My mom told me that you were crying when you told them what needed to be done."

Melanie swallowed hard, emotion clogging her throat. "I wanted to take away your pain, but I couldn't let you do it that way."

"I know. I'm getting help now. I don't think I'll ever be able to live my life the way you live yours, but hopefully the overwhelming fear will go away. Maybe for good this time."

"You're stronger than you think, Jenni. You know I have my own ways of coping with what happened that aren't exactly healthy."

"Will you come see me again soon?"

Melanie smiled even though Jenni couldn't see it. "You bet. Maybe in a couple of weeks I can fly out again."

"Thank you." She paused. "Have you talked with any of the others?"

"No. It was your place to let them know what was happening if you wanted them to know."

"I think, for now, just you knowing is enough."

They talked a little bit longer and by the end of the conversation, Melanie felt like a weight she hadn't even know she carried had been lifted from her shoulders. Hopefully, this was a turning point that would stick with Jenni.

She stared down at her phone trying to decide if she was surprised or not that her first instinct after hanging up with Jenni was to call Tyler and let him know about the conversation she'd just had with her friend. Unfortunately, she hadn't seen or heard from Tyler since that conversation she'd had with him on Sunday afternoon. She'd been tempted to stop by his office after the meeting earlier that day but given the rumor that had already been going around, she decided that might not be wise.

It wasn't unusual for them to go a few days without contact, but this time it felt awkward. Had Tyler been jealous? They'd been friends for so long. Was it possible for things between them to change into something more? And was she ready for that?

If she did choose to go out with him, it would be because she felt there was a future for them. She had never been one to date casually, and she wasn't going to start now. Oh, who was she kidding? She didn't date, period. Casual or otherwise.

With a sigh, she set her phone back on the desk beside her. She'd give it another day. If she didn't hear from him by tomorrow night, she'd phone and tell him about Jenni's call and ask how it went with Simon at church. And maybe, in the meantime, she'd pray about it.

Maybe.

Tyler slipped his phone into its case on his belt and reached for his suit coat from the back of his chair. He was already walking out the door of his office as he shoved his arms into the sleeves, lifting it into place on his shoulders. Simon hadn't said what was wrong when he'd asked for Tyler to come see him as soon as possible, but he'd heard the distress in the man's voice.

He told the receptionist that he was on his way to the Wellness Center and could be reached on his phone if anyone needed him. Thankfully, it didn't take long to reach the Center since the midday traffic wasn't as bad as rush hour might have been. He got through security then went up to Simon's room instead of the physio room where they usually met.

"Hey, Simon," Tyler said when the man opened his door to Tyler's knock. He looked pale, and his lips were drawn tight. "What's going on?"

"Can we go down to the garden to talk?" Simon asked.

Tyler was totally on board with that since the serene setting was intended for exactly this type of situation. He walked beside the man's wheelchair as they made their way to the elevator that would take them to the main floor. Once in the brightly lit indoor garden area, Tyler led them to a spot where the sound of the waterfall would mask their conversation if it was anything sensitive.

He sat down on a bench next to where Simon stopped his wheelchair. Leaning forward, he braced his forearms on his thighs and looked at Simon. He'd come to consider the man a friend, and the strain on his features was a concern considering the progress the man had made of late. "What's going on, buddy?"

Simon's elbows rested on the armrests of the wheelchair, but his hands were clasped tightly in front of him. "I don't know if I told you that I had a fiancée."

Tyler felt a knot tighten in his gut. He had really hoped this was one experience he didn't share with Simon. "No, you never mentioned it."

Simon nodded as if he figured that was the case. "We were supposed to get married after I got back from that last tour. But then this happened." He gestured to his leg. "And everything kinda went south."

That would explain some of his attitude when he'd first arrived at the Center. Tyler could certainly understand that pain. "Have you been in contact with her?"

"No." After a moment, Simon tipped his head enough so their gazes met. "She sent me letters, but I sent them back."

Suddenly, Tyler got the feeling that maybe their situations weren't quite as alike as he'd thought. "Were you the one to call off the wedding, Simon?"

The man's gaze dropped as he nodded. "I thought it was the best thing for her."

"Did she agree?"

"No. And she phoned me today."

"She hasn't phoned you before."

Simon gave a single shake of his head. "I disconnected my cell number and when I got a new number I asked my family not to give it to her."

"So what did she want?"

"She said she's coming to see me." Simon rubbed a hand down the thigh that ended in a stump. "Said she didn't care if I had two legs or none, she loves me and refuses to take no for an answer."

Tyler stared at the man. "Is this about you really feeling that you can't be a good husband to her with just one leg? Or are you feeling that this is another instance where you can't embrace happiness because of those who lost their lives in your accident?"

Simon sighed and shrugged. "Probably a bit of both."

"You know what I'm going to tell you, man. Did you ask me to come just to hear me say it to you?"

Simon lifted his head enough that Tyler could see the smile tilt the corners of the man's mouth. "She said I had ten days to get used to the idea, that she was going to be here next Friday come rain or shine."

"Sounds like one determined woman. One who loves you very much. How do you feel about her? Do you love her?"

Simon's head snapped up. "Of course I do. She's the most wonderful woman in the world, and I let her go because I thought she deserved so much better than me."

"I get the feeling she didn't want to be let go. If you love her as much as she loves you, it would be a shame to not be together. For better or for worse. That's what the wedding vows say. Sounds like you've got someone who is more than willing to go through the worst with you." Tyler reached out to lay his hand on the man's shoulder. "That type of love and commitment is something to hang on to. Some of us aren't so fortunate."

Simon's brows drew together. "Did your girl leave you after you lost your legs?"

"She was my wife, and she hung around for a little while but then decided it wasn't the life she wanted. She didn't love me enough to want to go through the worst." Tyler was surprised that he was able to say that without the pang of regret it usually brought.

"I'm sorry to hear that, man."

"What's done is done. But it does give me enough experience to tell you to grab onto this girl and don't let her go."

Simon sat straighter in his chair. "Can you help me get ready for her?"

"Sure thing, buddy. What do you need?"

"I'm going to talk to physio about working more with crutches. I'd like to be out of this," he thumped the wheelchair, "when she comes. Also, I could use a haircut and maybe some new clothes."

"Well, I don't know why you think I know anything about haircuts," Tyler said with a laugh as he dragged his hand through his own unruly curls. "But I'll take you somewhere and then we can do some shopping."

"Thank you." Simon's expression turned serious. "That really doesn't seem enough. But thank you. Not just for this, but for spending time with me. For understanding. For sharing your life with me. For kicking me in the butt when I needed it. I'm a better man for having met you. Definitely a man more worthy of Tanya. Thank you."

Tyler smiled. "Seeing you smile and looking toward the future is thanks enough. And I'm coming out of all this with a new friend."

Simon held his hand out but instead of shaking it, Tyler slid his hand so his fingers clasped Simon's thumb. The man returned the grasp and squeezed hard. "The day Melanie brought you to see me was a day I'll never forget."

"Me, too." Tyler released his grip. "So when do you want to do this?"

"Are you free on Saturday afternoon? Maybe before we go play basketball?"

Tyler nodded. "Sounds good to me. If something comes up, I'll give you a call, but otherwise I'll be here around three."

Tyler walked with him back to the elevator and returned to the second floor. Simon took off to find his counselor while Tyler made his way to Melanie's office, hoping she would be free for a chat.

He could see right away that her office door was closed. Heather smiled at him as he stopped next to her desk. Something about her smile made him think she had also been privy to the rumor floating around.

"She's just on a phone call if you want to wait. It shouldn't be too much longer." Heather glanced down at the phone on her desk. "Yep. She's just finished."

The young woman turned to her computer and typed out a quick message. She waited a moment then swung back toward him with a smile. "She said for you to go on in."

"Thanks," Tyler said with a nod of his head.

He opened the door with one hand while he knocked on it with the other. Melanie looked up as he poked his head in.

"Heather said to come in," he said, suddenly hoping that Heather wasn't trying to create situations that would turn the rumor into reality.

"Yep. Perfect timing." Her smile warmed Tyler as he sank down into the chair across from her. "What brings you out my way?"

"Got an SOS call from Simon, so I came out to talk with him."

Her brows drew together, concern in her gaze. "Is he alright?"

"Actually, I'd say he's more than alright." Tyler described the conversation he'd had with Simon.

"That's wonderful," Melanie said, her brown eyes sparkling. "Although his girlfriend might be the impetus for taking bigger strides toward getting to a healthier place, I would say that you played a huge role in getting him to the point where he could actually be receptive to a reconciliation with her."

Tyler rubbed a hand along the back of his neck. "I'm just glad that it's working out for him. He still has some hard work to do, but at least he's got the motivation. He asked me to take him for a haircut and clothes shopping."

Melanie laughed. "He *has* seen your hair, right?"

"Hey!" Tyler ran a hand through his hair. "Are you saying there's something wrong with my hair?"

"Not a thing." Melanie's cheeks flushed at her words. "You have curls that a lot of women would give anything to get their hands on." Her brows snapped together. "No, wait. I mean, give anything to have. On their own head."

"And if I told you that I get this look by using a curling iron every morning?"

Laughter erupted from Melanie, and she clapped a hand over her mouth. When she could talk again, she said, "No way I'd ever believe that. Just the thought of you standing in front of a mirror trying to get your curls to hang just right..." Her words trailed off into laughter again.

Tyler chuckled. "My mom tells me that women have loved my curls since I was a toddler. And she didn't like to cut them, so she always made sure I was dressed in boy clothes so no one thought I was a girl. Strangely enough, some still did."

As he sat there watching the flush fade from Melanie's cheeks, Tyler knew it was now or never. "Hey. You want to go to a Timberwolves game with me tomorrow night?"

Melanie's eyes widened. "Tomorrow night? Ryan isn't available to go with you?"

"He probably is," Tyler said with a shrug. "I'd rather go with you."

She seemed to consider his words. At that moment, he probably would have given just about anything to be able to read her mind. It was clear she was considering things. Tyler fought the urge to give her an out. But if she didn't want to go with him, she'd have to say the words.

15

MELANIE'S FACE relaxed into a smile. "Sure. Sounds like fun."

"Do you want to do dinner ahead of time? It might be kind of rushed since the game starts at seven. We could grab something afterward. Or during, for that matter."

"I think I could handle something during the game. Even if it is on the unhealthy side." She settled back in her chair. "I was going to call you later."

"Really? What's up?"

"I wanted to tell you that Jenni called me the other night."

"That's great. How is she doing?"

"Much better. She wanted me to know that she didn't hate me. And to thank me for what I did in getting her help."

"Well, that's definitely an answer to prayer," Tyler said.

His response seemed to catch Melanie off-guard. She stared at him for a moment, her head tilted to the side. "Did you pray for her?"

"Sure. It sounded like she was really struggling, so I prayed that she'd come to a place of accepting the help she needed. And I prayed that you would be at peace about your role in what happened with her."

"Thank you," Melanie said, blinking rapidly as if holding back tears. "For praying for her and me. I guess I didn't expect that."

"Why not?" Tyler crossed his arms over his chest. "You're important to me. You were in pain over what had happened with Jenni. Of course I would want to pray for you and for her."

Melanie caught her lower lip between her teeth, her brow furrowed. "I guess I got used to God not listening to my prayers a long time ago."

Tyler's heart clenched at her words. Over the years, she'd mentioned going to church and he'd just assumed she had some sort of faith. "Well, here's the thing. God hears our prayers, but sometimes the answer He gives us is not what we want to hear."

"But sometimes He does give us the one we want to hear." Melanie's words were so soft that Tyler almost couldn't hear them. "At least this time."

"I've learned that even when He says no when we want Him to say yes, that looking back, the answer He gave was the right one. I may have wanted the *yes*, but *no* was really what I needed."

She didn't look completely convinced. "At one time I believed that. I accepted Jesus into my heart like they said to do in our Sunday school class. Just stuff kinda...went wrong, and I lost faith in God hearing my prayers."

The uncertain look on her face made Tyler want to take her into his arms and assure her that God was still there for her. And so was he. So many things were flooding him right then. Emotions. Realizations. Desires.

Melanie had always had a quiet confidence about her, as far back as when she'd still been a student. Tyler had seen how her presence had soothed people—even him during the earliest days of his time at the Wellness Center. And when Kelly had dumped him, she'd never patronized him with platitudes about how he was better off without her. She'd just offered her quiet encouragement to him each time she'd seen him.

But lately, he'd become much more aware of a vulnerability within her. And he'd be lying to himself if he denied that he wanted very much to protect her. To keep her safe from whatever was making her feel that way.

Tyler leaned forward, propping his arms on his thighs. "It's never too late to rekindle that faith."

Melanie nodded. "I went to Alex's church on Sunday instead of my parents'. Not that anything is wrong with theirs, but the pastor at the church Alex attends had a sermon that made me think."

"Those are always the best ones," Tyler said. "God wants us to seek after Him. It's like any relationship—you need to get to know the other person. That's true with God too. Study His word. Spend time in prayer. Listen to sermons that feed your knowledge of Him.

"But don't think for a minute that I haven't questioned God on occasion too. I mean, I didn't have much else to do while lying in that hospital bed in Germany with my legs gone. I questioned Him a lot. And then when Kelly left me, I questioned Him some more. Just don't let your questioning drive you away from Him."

"Yeah. I think that's what I did."

Before Tyler could respond to that, the intercom on the phone on Melanie's desk went. "Sorry to interrupt, Melanie, but Marcus is on the line for you. Do you want me to take a message?"

"No. Just tell him I'll be one minute." Melanie gave him an apologetic look as Tyler got to his feet. "Sorry about that."

"No worries." He headed for the door then turned back. "So we're on for tomorrow night?"

"As long as you don't care that it might feed the rumor mill."

Tyler smiled. "I'm counting on it and hoping that maybe it won't be just a rumor."

Before Melanie could say anything, Tyler winked at her and stepped out of her office. Heather sat at her desk, a wide grin on her face. She gave a fist pump and fake-whispered, "Go, Tyler!"

Feeling buoyed by the conversation they'd shared, Tyler headed out of the building toward his vehicle.

Melanie hung up the phone after a brief conversation with Marcus about how his sister was doing with her dog. She stared at the now-empty seat on the other side of her desk.

I'm going on a date.

Or at least she thought she was. She had little-to-no experience with this, but surely his parting comment supported her supposition. A squeal from the doorway drew her attention, and she spotted Heather peeking into the office, a huge smile on her face.

Melanie waved her in. Heather lost no time at all scooting into the room and dropping down into the seat that Tyler had vacated.

"Oh my goodness! He asked you out!" Heather's light gray eyes sparkled like polished silver. Melanie wasn't sure she'd ever seen her assistant so excited.

"I guess so?" It came out more a question than a statement.

"Of course, he did. You are so lucky. There are a lot of ladies in the company who are going to be jealous of you. They've tried to get his attention, but he never seemed to notice them." Heather clasped her hands to her chest. "Maybe this is why. He's only had eyes for you."

Melanie frowned. "I don't think so. We're friends. We've only ever been friends."

"Starting out that way is the best. You already know so much about the other person that you don't have to wonder if you're going to find out something unexpected about them."

That comment caused a spark of unease in Melanie. There was something major Tyler didn't know about her. She had seen the revulsion in his eyes when she'd explained what had happened to Jenni. At the time, she'd known it was a reaction to the actions of the abductors, but how would he feel knowing she'd endured the same thing as Jenni? Would that revulsion then be towards her?

"Hey now," Heather said, pulling her back from her dark thoughts. "You look pale as a ghost. I promise that it's nothing to be worried about. Tyler clearly adores you and is finally making a move. And there are going to be a few very happy people."

Melanie frowned, remembering the bet they had going about who was going to fall in love next. She knew it was all in good fun, but part of her hated having people know about her relationship...or what she hoped might become one.

The next day as soon as it was five o'clock, Melanie dashed out of the building to head for home. Tyler was picking her up at six so she'd barely have time to get changed. Thankfully, she'd decided on her outfit the night before. Or at least she thought she had...as she drove along the highway headed into the cities, she was second guessing what she'd chosen.

There was no one else home when she got there. Alex had said something about a dinner meeting with Eli Bennet. Melanie had no idea of Adrianne's plans, but she hoped to be gone by the time her sister got home. She took the stairs to her room, two at a time and slammed the door behind her when she reached them.

With quick movements, she stripped off her office clothes. She grabbed the dark green long sleeve bodysuit with a sweetheart neckline she'd laid out earlier and pulled it on. Normally, a bodysuit wasn't something she really liked to wear, but the black jeans she wanted to wear were on the low riding side, and she didn't want to constantly be worrying about her shirt coming untucked. She took a quick trip to the bathroom to refresh her makeup and make sure her hair still looked okay. After a moment's consideration, she switched out her jewelry, changing the more conservative stuff she wore at the office for a pair of long dangling silver earrings and a necklace with a silver pendant on a black cord.

After a quick spritz of perfume, she returned to her room to pull on her favorite boots, taking a moment to slip her driver's license, some cash, and her bank card into the hidden pockets along the calf before zipping them up. Lastly, she picked up her black leather jacket.

Knowing that Tyler would be there soon, she went ahead and shrugged into it. She zipped it halfway up then tugged it into place. It was fitted but also flared a bit in the hips so it came right to the top of her jeans. She knew the outfit gave her a kind of biker chick appearance, but if she was going to be unarmed, she wanted to know that her outfit wouldn't hinder her if she needed to fend someone off.

And she knew it wouldn't because she'd practiced in this very outfit on more than one occasion.

A buzz alerted her to the fact that someone was approaching the gate. She went to the control panel on the wall by the door to her room and pushed the button once she recognized Tyler's car. After taking a quick breath, she grabbed her cellphone from the bed where her purse's contents were spilled. She slipped it into a zippered pocket on the side of her jacket and left her room.

By the time she walked out the front door, Tyler was just getting out of the car. The way his eyes widened when he saw her brought a flush to her cheeks. Now that they had kinda moved into a new area of their friendship, Melanie was more aware of wanting him to find her appearance attractive. Right or wrong, it was there.

"Well, we may have selected similar outfits, but yours definitely looks better," Tyler said as he rounded the hood of his car.

Melanie smiled as she saw that he too wore jeans with a T-shirt and leather jacket. And as far as she was concerned, he looked just fine. Better than fine, actually.

He opened the door for her then waited until she was settled before closing it. As he slid behind the wheel, he glanced over and said, "You don't have a purse or bag?"

Melanie shook her head. "When I'm dealing with crowds, I find it easier to not have to fuss with one. I have my ID and money in a hidden pocket in my boot."

As Tyler guided the car around the driveway, he looked over at her, an eyebrow arched. "But no weapons, right?"

"No weapons," she confirmed with a grin.

Because this had gone from two friends going to a basketball game to a date, Melanie had anticipated that things might be a bit awkward, but that was not the case. They chatted about work and then Tyler talked a little about how his mom and Hank were doing.

Melanie wondered if Tyler expected to meet her parents if they were dating now. She cringed at the thought. The only benefit would be if it would make her mom back off Adrianne, although realistically, it could also make it worse for her. *Your little sister has a boyfriend. Why don't you?*

Tyler seemed to know the best place to park because it wasn't long before they were climbing out of the car. Since it was fall already, the days were starting to shorten, so it was nearly dark as they joined the streams of people heading into the Target Center. Unlike last time, Tyler didn't offer her his arm. Instead, he reached out and grabbed her hand.

Melanie had never really thought about holding hands with someone, but as soon as her smaller softer hand was engulfed in his larger calloused one, the connection sent a shot of warmth up her arm. He didn't release her hand at all as they went through the process of showing their tickets and then making their way to the seats. They once again had the two at the end of the row. Tyler let go of her hand, and she went ahead of him into the row.

Melanie looked down at the court, watching the activity there as the minutes ticked down on the big screen. "Are these your usual seats?"

"Yep. So unless they've given their tickets away for the game, you shouldn't have to worry about the other people in this row. They've been cool so far this year."

Melanie settled into her seat, a sense of rightness filling her as Tyler sat down beside her. "Was Ryan disappointed he couldn't come tonight?"

"Not really. We'll be going to a hockey game next week so he's happy about that."

"Do you have season tickets for that too?"

Tyler looked over at her, a flush rising in his cheeks. "Yeah. Hank buys me two season tickets for hockey, basketball, and football."

"Really? That's so nice of him."

"I try to tell them that the tickets can be my birthday and Christmas presents, but Momma still insists on getting me something practical, too."

Melanie laughed at that because she could totally see Shauna doing that. "Did you play sports in high school? Is that why you're such a fan now?"

"Yeah. I played basketball all through my high school years, but I enjoyed dabbling in all sports. Anything active, actually. Rock climbing. Skydiving. White water rafting. Hiking. Skiing. I enjoyed all of that."

Melanie didn't miss his use of the past tense. "Do you not do any of those now?"

Tyler leaned forward, resting his elbows on his thighs, and stared down at the court, but before he could reply, the noise amped up considerably as the team introductions began.

Melanie felt bad for introducing a sensitive subject. There were times she didn't even remember he had prosthetic legs. And part of that was because of how active he still was. She knew he played basketball at least once a week and that he hung out with the youth of his church on Friday nights. Plus, she'd seen the workout equipment in the basement of the house that he shared with Ryan. He was far from being inactive.

He sat back in his seat and leaned toward her. "Do you need me to refresh you on anything about the game?"

Melanie shook her head and grinned. "I think I remember the important parts."

The tension she'd sensed a few minutes earlier seemed to melt from Tyler as he smiled back. "Well, if you have any questions..."

The game quickly got underway, and Melanie found she enjoyed watching Tyler more than the action on the court. He got so into the plays, jumping to his feet to cheer when the Timberwolves scored. And he even had a few words for the refs on a couple of different calls.

When half-time rolled around, he stood up. "Want to come with me to get something to eat?"

She was hungry since her last meal had been almost eight hours earlier, but she wasn't sure if she'd be able to find any healthy food at the concession stands. However, she wasn't going to sit by herself waiting for him to come back, so she got to her feet and took the hand he held out to her.

Once again, he kept a tight grip on her hand as they moved around the concourse area looking at the concessions. Deciding she'd splurge this one time and pay the price later, Melanie let Tyler talk her into trying some of his decidedly unhealthy favorites. She did hold off on the sugary drinks and stuck with water as her beverage. Food wasn't something she usually ate for pleasure. Sure, she appreciated food that tasted good, but she'd long thought of it as a way to fuel her body.

When they got back to their seats, Tyler offered to finish off anything she didn't want, so Melanie didn't feel bad taking just a few bites of the items that didn't really appeal to her. It seemed strangely intimate to share food with someone. And surprisingly, she found that she liked it.

After what had happened to her, she'd wondered if she'd ever find herself wanting that type of physical closeness with a man. Something told her it was the fact that she was with Tyler that made it something she not only tolerated but actually enjoyed. Believing he was who he said he was wasn't an issue since she'd known him for so long, had been there through the ups and downs of his life. Now she just had to work up the nerve to tell him that the story she'd shared about Jenni was also *her* story. And then she had to hope he wouldn't back off after hearing that.

Tyler could honestly say he'd never enjoyed a basketball with Ryan as much as he had with Melanie. He was glad she seemed to be enjoying the game as well. Next date they'd have to do something that she wanted. He couldn't expect her to be as avid a sports fan as he was, but he did hope she'd come with him every once in a while.

She shouted as loud as he did when they all stood up to cheer the Timberwolves through the last minutes of the game that they ended up winning. After the game was over, he took her hand again and walked with her out of the arena. Once they were free of the press of the crowds, he didn't rush to get to his car. He wanted to make the evening last longer, but they both had work the next day and even if it had to end right then, it had been a great first date. At least he thought so.

He opened the passenger door for her before going around to the driver's side. As soon as he'd settled behind the wheel and started the slow process of leaving the parking lot, Melanie said, "Thank you so much for taking me to the game, Tyler. I never realized that I was a sport's fan. Alex played football in high school, but I was five years younger than him so not that interested in watching him play."

"I'm glad you had fun. Anytime you want to come, let me know."

"I don't want to take Ryan's ticket if he wants to go to the games."

"You don't have to worry about that. Ryan is willing to make a sacrifice for the cause."

"The cause?"

Tyler glanced over at Melanie but couldn't see her well because of the darkened interior of the car. "Yeah. He's been after me to ask you out."

There was a beat of silence before Melanie spoke. "He has?"

"Yep. Since before our birthday dinner."

"So why did you finally give in?"

Tyler wasn't sure how honest he should be about that. "Well, I'm not one to rush into things, and I really didn't want to lose your friendship if you decided you didn't want to date. I didn't want you to be uncomfortable around me after turning me down." He cleared his throat. "Actually, I heard that guy on the phone that day I called you when you were at the shooting range."

"Ugh," Melanie said, disgust clear in her tone. "That guy was not someone I was even remotely interested in going out with. He didn't want to take no for an answer. I finally threatened him..sort of...with my gun."

Tyler laughed before he could stop himself. "Seriously? Man, I wish I'd been there to see that."

"Eli Bennett apparently thinks he's God's gift to women, but he's nothing of the sort to this woman. However," Melanie said with a teasing lilt, "if that's what got you to ask me out, I'm not going to wish it hadn't happened."

Relief mixed with humor when Tyler realized she wasn't going to get upset that hearing another guy ask her out had been what had spurred him on. "Eli Bennett though? Isn't he one of our clients?"

"Yeah. Apparently an important one. Alex wasn't thrilled to hear about my encounter with him, but seriously, the guy needs sensitivity training. Some woman is going to knock him on his butt. I thought that was going to be me, but I managed to restrain myself."

"Wow, he was really that bad?"

"Let's just say that when I got done with...threatening him, the guy that was with him, gave me a thumbs up. I would guess he's not a nice guy to more than just me."

"Aren't there cameras in the shooting range? I'd love to see the tape of that encounter."

Melanie groaned. "I just want to forget all about it. If I never see him again, it will be too soon."

"Were you really worried about your safety?" Tyler asked, suddenly realizing that perhaps under the joking, she really had been afraid of the guy.

Her pause told him enough and his gut clenched.

16

Melanie shifted in her seat, her elbow rubbing against his. "If I had to, I could have taken him down. Even without a gun. And I knew that Justin was there. I had talked to him before I started shooting. If all else failed, I would have called him."

"That's good." Tyler wondered how he felt about Melanie talking confidently about Justin helping her out in a situation like that. He knew the other man was all about working out, weapons training and self-defense. Would Melanie consider Tyler as someone who could protect her if she needed it? Even with two prosthetic legs?

"Justin is big on women learning self-defense. I have always been into working out and learning how to use my weapons, but after that first course Justin put on for self-defense I pursued it on my own. I have trained in martial arts along with more extensive self-defense."

They'd touched on this before, but Tyler once again was getting the feeling that her fascination with weapons and self-defense went deeper than the average person. "That's something you enjoy?"

"I guess you could say that. I like the idea of not being defenseless. I never wanted to have to rely on a man to keep me safe. And I wanted to make sure that if I ever had to defend myself against a bigger, stronger person, I could."

"How often do you work out?"

"Every night. I usually run ten miles and then do weights."

Okay...so she clearly took the working out more seriously than he did. "That's great. I'm not into running as much as I used to be though I do have the prosthetics to do it. I spend more time with the weights than anything else."

As they continued to discuss workouts and the practicing she did with her weapons, Tyler began to wonder if maybe it was more of an obsession than a fascination. He supposed everyone had to have a hobby and in this day and age, self-defense wasn't a bad one to have.

Tyler hated to see the turn for the Thorpe mansion come into view. He wasn't ready for their time together to end, but he didn't have any choice.

"Ah man," Melanie murmured as the gates began to swing open.

Tyler glanced over at her. "What's wrong?"

"I didn't open the gates, which means that Alex or Adrianne saw your car approaching and opened them for you."

"Do they know you're out with me?"

"Nope. Well, I suppose they do now. Or will know soon enough."

As he pulled the car to a stop in front of the large house, Tyler asked, "Did you want to keep it a secret?"

"Not really, but they're family and they are ecstatic over any excuse to tease me." She paused. "Have you told your mom?"

"I see your point," Tyler said with a chuckle. "Want me to come in with you?"

"I think I'll be okay. Maybe next time."

Tyler pulled on the handle on his door to open it then felt a light touch on his arm. He turned back to Melanie, the overhead light allowing him to see the expression on her face.

She left her hand on his arm as her brows drew together. "I was wondering..."

Tyler turned to face her, laying his hand over hers. The cool evening air was drifting in his open door, but he wanted to see her face so he didn't shut it. He stayed quiet, just waited for her to finish her thought.

Her gaze met his as she tilted her head. "I was wondering if you'd be okay with me coming to your church."

Of all the thoughts that had gone through his mind while he waited, that hadn't been one of them. "Well, sure. That would be great."

A smile lit her eyes. "Really? I just don't feel like my parents' church has what I need right now. And I know I need some help in my growth so I thought maybe this way if I had questions about things, you could...I don't know...help me to understand?"

"I would love to do that." Tyler reached a hand out to cup her cheek. "You don't know how happy that makes me."

Her cheek moved under his touch as she smiled. "Will you send me the address so I know where I'm going on Sunday?"

"Sure. I'd offer to pick you up, but I teach a teenage boys' Sunday school class and you probably don't want to be there that early. At least not yet. I'll meet you after Sunday school is done so we can sit together."

"That sounds great."

Tyler was tempted...oh so tempted...to kiss her, but he didn't. They'd been friends for so long it felt like they shouldn't need to wait, but he knew in his heart that he did. With a smile, he pulled away from her and got out of the car.

He came around and opened her door, taking her hand to help her out.

"Thanks again for a great night," Melanie said as they stood holding hands. "Hope the rest of your week goes well."

"Yours too." Tyler glanced over his shoulder, wondering if he should walk her to the imposing front door.

The decision was taken from him when she squeezed his hand then let go. "I'll see you on Sunday."

Tyler closed the passenger door as he turned to watch as she climbed the steps and opened the massive front door. She waved to him and then stepped into the house. With a sigh, Tyler rounded the car and slid behind the wheel. He circled around the driveway and then headed through the still-open gates which started to close almost immediately after he was through them.

Melanie knew she shouldn't march into the house with a big grin on her face, but she'd had such a good time with Tyler—better than she had even hoped—that it was hard to keep it from showing.

"You look like you enjoyed your evening," Alex said when she walked into the kitchen. He was wearing a T-shirt and sweats so he'd probably been home for a little while.

"It was pretty good. I went to another basketball game with Tyler." She grabbed a glass from the cupboard and went to the water dispenser to fill it. "How was your dinner with Mr. Bennett?"

Alex grimaced as he leaned back against the counter, his arms crossed. "He's taken a liking to you."

"Well, I hope you told him I wasn't interested."

"Like you said, the man doesn't like to take no for an answer."

"In that case, just tell him I'm now unavailable." Melanie smiled when Alex lifted a brow at her comment.

"Something you want to share? Is the rumor floating around actually true?"

She took a sip of her water. "It is now. We went on our first date tonight, and I look forward to more."

"Never thought I'd see the day," Alex said, a corner of his mouth lifting. "And Tyler, eh? Guess we don't really have a policy about employees dating as long as you're not his supervisor."

"Which I'm most definitely not."

"He's a good guy. I hope it works out for you."

"Thanks." Melanie looked at her brother, noticing the strain there for the first time. "Was the dinner with Eli that bad?"

"It was fine once I got him on track. He is a piece of work and I swear, if we didn't need the contract, I would have punched him out for what he said to you." Alex sighed. "Marcus is just getting more and more stressed out that we haven't managed to figure out who is targeting BlackThorpe. Every day that goes by without another assault puts him more on edge. Given the timing of the other attacks, it could be any day."

"He doesn't think the increased security will help to prevent something from happening?"

"From day one, he's been convinced it's someone inside the company. He's been having Tyler look through phone records of anyone who started at BlackThorpe during the year before the first attack and everyone since."

"That isn't legal, is it?" Melanie frowned. "Tyler couldn't get in trouble for working on them, could he?"

"Marcus is the one getting the data—I don't ask him how—and then he gives it to Tyler. No doubt he's putting the company at risk. He says that pulling their phone records falls under the background check they all agreed to when they were hired."

"That's weak." Melanie's experience wasn't in legalities, but even she could see that Marcus was walking a fine line.

Alex shrugged. "I can't talk him down from this. Believe me, I've tried."

"I just hope that whoever he has getting the records is good enough they don't get caught."

"You and me both. All I can do is pray that the next attack doesn't end with someone's death."

Melanie swallowed hard at the thought. She had sensed tension in Marcus the last couple of times they'd talked about his sister and her dog, but she hadn't realized how far gone he was. And if even Alex couldn't rein him in? Yeah, that wasn't good.

"Well, I'm going to work out a bit then call it a night," Melanie said. She gave Alex a quick hug and headed out of the kitchen but turned around before she got too far. "Where's Adrianne?"

"Not sure. Probably out with one of her friends."

Melanie nodded though she wasn't as convinced as Alex appeared to be. Given the conversation they'd had regarding Adrianne's friends rarely being available to go out anymore, she would be surprised if that was who she was with.

Upstairs, she changed into her workout clothes and started her run. Though music flowed from the speakers she'd attached to the phone, two words kept repeating in time with her steps.

Tell him.

Tell him.

Tell him.

Tell him.

Did he really need to know? Surely there were things he wouldn't tell her about his past. Like things involving his ex-wife. Becoming a couple now didn't mean they had to share everything, did it? Her past had already tainted her life in so many ways. She didn't want it to tarnish what she was building with Tyler. It would be different if it affected her like it did Jenni, but while she obviously had things in place in her life because of the abduction, she didn't have the emotional ups and downs her friend did.

Tell him.
Tell him.
Tell him.
Tell him.

Melanie upped her pace, her feet pounding on the treadmill. *No.* She wasn't going to tell him. Most days she didn't even think about it anymore. It wasn't important enough to mention. Besides, she couldn't forget the expression on Tyler's face when she'd told him about Jenni. She never wanted him to look at her that way.

She just wanted to be with him like a normal person. She didn't want him to worry about her having a meltdown like Jenni at some point. Maybe just the possibility of that would send him running. *She* knew that would never happen, but would he believe her if she told him that?

Blocking out the thoughts that kept telling her she was making a bad decision, Melanie managed to finish up her workout. She took a shower and then crawled into bed. Though it was late, she tapped out a quick message to Tyler.

Thank you again for a great evening! Hope the rest of your week goes well. Have a good night.

She didn't get an immediate reply, but she wasn't really expecting it since it was already late. However, the next morning there was a text waiting when she woke up. His sweet, good morning message helped start her day with a smile. And that night when she texted him *good night,* he replied right away so they ended up sending a few messages back and forth about their day before ending the conversation.

It took Melanie awhile to decide what to wear on Sunday morning. She usually just picked out one of her work outfits when she went to her parents' church. Hopefully, that would be appropriate for Tyler's as well.

She input the address for the church into her truck's GPS then headed off, trying to fight the nerves that insisted on taking up residence in her stomach. When she finally found the church, she discovered that it was much larger than she had anticipated.

Thankfully, she'd arrived a little sooner than she'd planned, so after she found a parking spot a ways from the church, Melanie sat in her truck for a few minutes. She hoped she was ready for this. Though she had attended church sporadically over the years, it wasn't until recently that she had thought much about how it applied to her day-to-day life.

Her life basically fell in line with the "rules" the church her parents attended had seemed to set out for its members, but it had nothing to do with wanting to please God. She didn't do stuff like drink, do drugs or smoke because any of those things could impair her body's ability to react as she needed it to.

And sex? Well, that had been a non-issue since she hadn't been dating. And even though she found Tyler physically attractive, the talks her youth group had had with the young people before her abduction had emphasized the lines that shouldn't be crossed when in a boy-girl relationship. She was fairly certain Tyler was aware of those lines. The fact that he hadn't kissed her when he'd dropped her off after their date told her that he wasn't going to be pushing the physical side of things. Just one more reason why she...

Her phone's text alert went, interrupting her thoughts. She glanced at the screen and saw a message from Tyler.

You here?

She let out a quick breath and sent a message back to let him know she was just on her way inside. After turning off the ringer on her phone, Melanie grabbed her purse and got out of the truck into the gray, dreary fall day that seemed to promise rain but had not, as yet, delivered. However, a sudden gust of wind sent a shiver down her spine.

Keeping her eyes on the uneven asphalt surface of the parking lot, she made her way toward the entrance of the church. Before she reached the door, a pair of black loafers came into view, and she lifted her head to see Tyler standing there waiting for her. When their gazes met, he smiled.

Melanie couldn't keep from smiling in return. "Good morning."

"It definitely is now," Tyler said as he took a step toward her and took her hand. "Did you have any trouble finding the church?"

"Nope. Ms. GPS led me straight here."

He looked down at her, his smile crinkling the skin at the corners of his eyes. "I'm glad."

They walked up the steps together then he reached for the door and held it so she could precede him inside. He continued to hold it for two older women who thanked him with appreciative smiles.

"Your mom raised you right," Melanie said when he joined her.

"She tried," he said with a grin as he reached for her hand again. "Most of it stuck."

They weaved their way through clusters of people in the foyer then walked through open doors into the sanctuary where greeters waited to give them a bulletin. There was music playing though she could still hear murmurs of conversation as Tyler led her to a pew midway down the sanctuary on the right side.

When they reached the pew, he stepped aside to let her go first. Her gaze fell on a familiar face and she smiled as some of her nervousness faded.

"Good morning, Ryan," Melanie said as she scooted toward him on the seat. "Fancy meeting you here."

He quirked an eyebrow. "You can't truly be surprised to see me."

She chuckled. "No, not really. And it gives me a chance to thank you for giving up your ticket to the game last Thursday night."

Ryan shrugged. "Well, to be honest, I'm more of a hockey man so it wasn't that big of a sacrifice."

Tyler's arm slid along the pew as he leaned toward her. "See, I told you he was fine with it."

"Makes sense he's more into hockey since he's from that place where it's winter all the time."

Ryan laughed. "It's really not that different from here. But hockey was a big thing in our family, even before Kenton went pro. My dad—Kenton and Gabe's dad—used to flood a piece of the land around our house in winter so we'd have our own ice rink. There were six of us boys so we had three on three games a lot."

"But Kenton was the only one who went professional?" Melanie still had a hard time wrapping her mind around the fact that Ryan was related to a major league hockey player.

"Yeah. He was the most passionate about it. And you always wanted to be on his team because if you weren't, he would mow you down without a second thought."

"Your mother must have loved that."

Ryan grinned. "Mom stayed far away when we had those games, but she'd take care of any injuries that came about because of our roughhousing. Of course, she did mutter threats under her breath."

Melanie found herself smiling at the image. It sounded like Ryan had great parents who had been involved in his childhood the way Tyler's mom had with him.

"Hey, Ryan. Tyler."

Melanie looked beyond Ryan as he turned around to greet the group of people who were filing into their pew from the end. She felt Tyler's chest press against her shoulder as he leaned forward to talk to the man seated beside Ryan. The guy looked at her with curiosity in his eyes, but before Tyler could introduce her, the service began.

Though the service was similar in many ways to her parents' church, there were differences too. The most noticeable one was the pastor. He appeared to be a little younger than the man who had been pastor at her old church for as long as Melanie could remember. Sometimes she'd felt as if the man was a little out of touch with the issues faced by the younger generation.

This pastor, however, seemed very tuned into current-day issues even though he wouldn't be considered politically correct. He touched on the topic of bad things happening to good people. Timely for her as it was something that had once again been brought to the forefront because of Jenni's meltdown.

"People want free will to do as they please, but then they get upset when someone else's free will interferes with their life or hurts them. It wasn't God's will for evil to prevail, but once sin came into the world, people wanted the right to choose. And now we have sinful choices wreaking havoc on our world. Innocents are dying because religious extremists are exercising their free will to attack those who believe differently from them. Unborn babies are dying because people are exercising their free will and saying it's their right to do as they please with the child in their womb.

"Yes, the innocent will suffer in a way God never intended. But instead of washing His hands of us, God still offers us His peace as we deal with these consequences of choosing our own will over His. I'm sure I'm not the only one who has been amazed and moved by people extending their forgiveness to the person who has wronged their family. Why would they do that? Why would someone forgive their attacker? Why would a family forgive someone who murdered their loved one?

"They would do it because they know that peace cannot co-exist with anger, hatred or unforgiveness. Anger and bitterness will eat at your soul. God wants you to have peace. His peace. This means being willing to forgive."

Melanie shifted on her seat. She had peace in her life. Didn't she? Her thoughts went to her obsessive exercise and only slightly less obsessive focus on healthy eating. And then there was no denying the excessive focus she had on weapons and self-defense. Her life revolved around all those things because of someone's act of free will almost fourteen years ago. Did that mean she didn't have peace in her life?

She'd come to Tyler's church because she'd wanted to be able to discuss things with him, but there was no way she could discuss how personal this particular sermon was for her. Holding herself rigid, she listened as the pastor closed the service, challenging the people in the pews to search their hearts for any unforgiveness they might be harboring toward another—big or small.

Melanie bowed her head when everyone else did, but her eyes remained opened as she stared down at her clenched hands. Knowing she needed to put this aside for now, Melanie concentrated on Tyler sitting next to her, his hands dangling clasped between his knees, his head bent. Had he forgiven whoever it was that had planted the bomb that had taken his legs? Had he forgiven his ex-wife for walking out on him?

She gave herself a mental shake. That was not helping her to push aside the thoughts of the sermon for now. She could think more about it later. When she was alone and didn't need to hide how she was feeling.

Once the service had ended, people surged to their feet all around them. Tyler, however, remained seated, so Melanie did as well. She watched as people headed toward the back of the sanctuary, not too many lingering behind to talk.

"You going to join us at the buffet, Ty?"

Melanie looked over to see that the guy sitting next to Ryan was turned in their direction, his arm braced on the pew in front of them.

"I'll see what Melanie feels like doing," Tyler responded as he gave her a quick look with a smile.

"We'd love to have you both there," the man said. The statuesque woman standing behind him nodded her agreement. "You coming, Ryan?"

"Yep. I'll be there."

Melanie wasn't sure what kind of answer to give Tyler. On one hand, it would be nice to get to know his friends. But on the other, she didn't want to intrude on Tyler's time with his friends. They'd only had one official date, after all.

When Tyler got to his feet, Melanie stood as well. The rush of people had thinned so they had no problem exiting the pew. Tyler kept his hand on her lower back as they made their way out of the sanctuary. Once in the foyer, Tyler guided her off to the side where they were out of the way of people still milling around.

"Do you want to go for lunch with my friends? There's a group of about ten of us that get together after church on Sunday." He paused. "But if you don't want to go, that's fine."

"I had planned to just go home," Melanie said, feeling a bit uncertain about how this kind of thing was supposed to work.

She didn't want Tyler to feel like she was trying to barge into every part of his life. It had never crossed her mind that he might have a group of friends he did stuff with after church like this. Oh, she knew about the basketball games on Saturday nights and the Bible study on Sunday evenings, but stupidly it had never occurred to her that it might be more than that.

"If that's really what you want to do, I won't pressure you to come with us, but I'd really like it if you would."

She stared at him for a moment and realized there was no way she could resist the expectant look on his face. "Okay. I'd like that."

A smile spread across his face. "That's great. Let me just tell Ryan I'll be riding with you."

17

TYLER PULLED out his phone and quickly sent a text before sliding it back into the pocket of his jacket. When he reached for her hand, Melanie once again relished the strength and firmness of his grasp. He greeted a few people as he led them through the doors and out into the chilly day.

"By the way," Tyler began as they made their way through the parking lot to where her truck was parked, "you look beautiful."

Melanie felt a rush of heat in her cheeks as she looked down at herself then up at Tyler. "Thank you."

In the past, she'd never considered what a man might think when she was deciding what to wear, but she had to admit that she had thought of Tyler when she'd been trying to choose her outfit for church.

"You always look beautiful. I just haven't felt comfortable saying it until now."

Yes, that might have made things awkward or perhaps it would have been the catalyst to move things to this point more quickly. Too late now to entertain that notion.

She pulled her keys from her purse and held them out to Tyler. "Probably easier if you drive since you know where we're going."

"Sure thing." He took the keys and unlocked the truck as they approached it.

As he drove the short distance to the restaurant, Tyler talked about the time he'd spent with Simon the previous day.

"It appears you let them take the scissors to your hair as well," Melanie commented with a smile.

Tyler grinned as he shrugged. "Yeah. I figured I was there anyway, and it had been awhile."

"Well, I'm glad you didn't let them cut too much. I like your curls though it is a bit odd to think that your hair is longer than mine."

"Have you ever had long hair?" Tyler asked.

"A long time ago. When I was a teenager." She paused, aware this was treading into territory she'd rather avoid. "With my busy schedule of school and work at the Center, it was easier to keep it short. Growing it out would be a pain, so I've just kept it that way."

"It suits you like this," Tyler said. "Of course, I've not known you any other way."

She, on the other hand, had known him with much shorter hair. When he'd first come to the Center, his hair had been recently shaved off. He'd told her it was at his request since he didn't want to have to fuss with it while going through physical therapy.

Tyler turned the truck into the parking lot of a strip mall and quickly found an empty space. "Um, just one thing before we go into the restaurant..."

Melanie looked at him as he killed the engine and turned toward her. She undid her seatbelt but made no move to get out, waiting for him to speak.

"There's a woman—her name is Betsy—and she might make some comments or be a bit standoff-ish with you. I'm hoping not, but..." He shrugged one shoulder.

"She someone who wanted you for herself?" Melanie said as she lifted an eyebrow.

"Pretty much." Tyler's tanned cheeks turned slightly pink. "I have no idea how she'll really react since I've never brought a woman around. I've never encouraged her, but she's really not the sort to need encouragement. Anyway, just wanted to warn you. Hopefully, she'll just turn her attention to one of the other single guys in the group."

"I'm sure it will be fine, but thanks for giving me a heads-up."

Tyler got out of the truck and came around to open her door. Once again, he offered her his hand as she slid from the truck then kept it in his as they walked to the restaurant.

They got in line and paid for their meal and then found where the rest of the group were sitting. Ryan stood as they approached and motioned to the chairs next to him. "Saved 'em for you."

Grateful for one familiar face, Melanie sat down next to him. "You got here fast."

Ryan grinned. "I have a feeling Tyler took you the scenic route so he had you to himself for a few extra minutes."

Melanie looked over at Tyler as he relaxed into his seat, his hand resting on the back of her chair. He didn't deny what Ryan said as he smiled at her. She couldn't figure out why the truth of Ryan's words warmed her so much, but she couldn't keep from smiling back at him.

"You going to introduce us, Ty?" The man who had spoken with Tyler and Ryan at the church held a chair for the woman he was with, only settling into the seat beside her when she was seated.

Tyler straightened and said, "Melanie, this is my friend, Jeff and his lovely wife, Rena." He rested his hand on her back, just below her neck. "This is Melanie Thorpe."

Though he didn't add anything about them being in a relationship, no doubt the way he touched her spoke that loud and clear.

Rena tilted her head, her thin dark brows drawing together. "Thorpe? As in BlackThorpe?"

Melanie nodded. "My brother, Alex, is one of the founders of the company."

"And you work there, too?" Rena asked. Her blue gaze was friendly and curious.

"Yes. I work for the BlackThorpe Wellness Center."

Tyler leaned forward, bracing an arm on the table, his other hand still on her back. "Melanie is in charge of the Center. That's where we met. She wasn't running the place back then, but she is the driving force behind the success of the Center now."

Warmth spread through her at the pride she heard in his voice. "It's my privilege to be able to help provide a place for people who need the services we offer. Tyler is definitely one of the Center's success stories."

"So you guys have known each other for a while?" Though Rena was the one asking the question, Melanie could see that others at the table were listening.

"Almost seven years," Tyler said. "Before I even left the Center, Marcus Black offered me a position at the company."

Rena's gaze moved between Melanie and Tyler. "And it's only now that you've started dating?"

"Hey, ya'll."

A woman approached the table, a wide smile on her face. She had long blonde hair that curled over her shoulders and her eyes were a light shade of blue. Though she looked to be about Melanie's height, her figure had more curves. The greetings that were called out to the woman quickly clued Melanie into the fact that this was Betsy.

Her gaze swept the table, moving past Melanie to Tyler only to jerk back to her. Betsy's eyes narrowed, and Melanie was sure she was seeing where Tyler had his hand on her. Betsy moved toward the end of the table where there was a vacant chair between Tyler and Jeff. Melanie felt a tightening in her stomach, and it had nothing to do with the way the woman looked at Tyler.

It had everything to do with the woman's appearance. Melanie felt like she was seeing what she would have looked like if she hadn't worked so hard to change her appearance. Without the dye, colored contacts and leaner body because of her excessive workouts and strict eating, she would have looked very similar to the woman.

Betsy held out her hand toward Melanie. "Hello. I'm Betsy St. John. I don't believe we've met."

"Melanie Thorpe." Melanie took her hand in a firm shake. "Nice to meet you."

She could feel Tyler's hand tense on her back, but until the woman said or did something to provoke her, she would be friendly.

Before Betsy could ask any more questions, Rena quickly filled in the details she'd managed to gather already.

"Why don't we say grace and then we can go get our food," Jeff suggested when his wife finished talking.

Melanie was just bowing her head when she saw Tyler flip his hand palm up on the table where it rested. Remembering that they'd held hands during the prayer for the food with his parents, she reached out and pressed her palm to his. As his fingers closed around hers, she felt the brush of his thumb on the skin just above the neck of her jacket.

Jeff's prayer was way too short, Melanie thought as it ended, but Tyler didn't let go of her hand as he stood, drawing her up with him.

"Ready to go get some food?"

She nodded, though the thought of food wasn't the most appealing thing at the moment. Thankfully, there were lots of choices at the buffet so Melanie was able to find enough acceptable food to fill her plate. Back at the table, she concentrated on taking small bites and chewing so it looked like she was eating even though she was still on her first plate when others were going up for seconds.

Every time she looked at Betsy all she could see was what might have been. And despite what she thought the woman might be like, given Tyler's warning about her, Betsy was actually a friendly and funny woman. Would she have been more like that if she hadn't had the experiences she'd had? There were also some other similarities between them in addition to the physical. Betsy was in the medical profession as well and she had just started up her own pediatrics practice.

Why had Tyler not been interested in her? Was dark hair and eyes his type? Melanie thought back to when she'd met his ex, Kelly. Though she couldn't recall her eye color, she definitely had had dark hair. Her gut clenched. If things got serious between them, eventually she'd have to at least reveal that her eyes were blue. Was it false advertising for her to let Tyler think this was how she looked when it was all fake?

And now she had more thoughts to shove to the side for the moment. Before this got too much more serious, she needed to make some decisions.

Although, according to her heart, it was already serious.

Tyler was surprised at how accepting Betsy was being of Melanie. Given her dogged pursuit of him in the past, he was sure she'd have an issue with it. Of course, he was thankful that she was being nice. He'd seen the way she'd been studying Melanie as she had interacted with Rena and Jeff and others at the table. He sensed she was curious about what it was Melanie had that had finally managed to get him to start dating again.

After he had finished the food on his plate, he glanced over to see that Melanie still had over half of the food she'd taken, left on hers. And even what she'd taken had been the healthiest out of the selections. Fish. Salad. Baked chicken. No potatoes, pasta or any of the bread they had. He admired her for sticking to her healthy way of eating, but she still needed to actually eat it.

"I'm heading up for more," he said, leaning close to her. "Do you want me to grab you anything?"

She smiled at him. "No, I'm good."

Ryan stood when he did and walked with him back to the food. "Melanie seems to be fitting in."

Tyler stopped near the part of the buffet with the roast beef. "Do you think so? She's hardly eating and seems tense."

"Well, I didn't say she wasn't nervous, but she's engaging in conversation and seems to be connecting with Rena and—surprisingly enough—Betsy."

"I'm just...worried." Tyler glanced over to see Melanie leaning forward, her gaze on Rena and Jeff.

Ryan took a step closer as people passed by him. "What's the deal?"

Tyler thought through all the little things, wondering if he was adding one and one and getting five. "Did you know she runs ten miles a day? And then still does weights on top of that?"

Ryan's eyebrows rose at that revelation. "Ten miles?"

"Yeah. And you can see what she had on her plate here, and she's hardly eating it. I worry that she's got an issue with food and exercise."

"Or maybe she's just super health conscious. I mean, she looks healthy. Not overly thin like you'd expect from someone who hardly ate and exercised excessively."

Ryan was right about that. "I'm probably making a mountain out of a molehill. It's just now that I've finally got her, I don't want anything to happen to take her from me."

His friend clasped a firm hand on his shoulder. "I hear you. Not saying ignore it, but take circumstances into account. I'm sure that today she's just not eating much because this is all a new thing to her."

"You're right." He motioned to the food. "I'm eating enough for the both of us."

Ryan laughed as they proceeded to fill up their plates for the second time.

Back at the table, Melanie still hadn't made much of a dent in her food, but Tyler was going to assume that Ryan was right and it was just nerves.

It wasn't too long before people began to get up to leave. Tyler, however, wasn't in a rush for their time to be over since it would mean Melanie would be headed home.

"You'll have to come to our next monthly get-together," Rena said to Melanie.

"Get-together?"

"Yeah. We all go to someone's house for a night of games and food. It's usually a lot of fun."

"Usually?" Melanie asked as she lifted her glass.

Rena laughed. "Well, depending on the games we choose to play, a few people can get a bit more competitive than necessary."

"That sounds like fun."

Tyler couldn't tell if she was being serious or polite, but he nodded when Rena instructed him to bring her to the next one. He hoped she would agree. This group of people was important to him. Some of the guys were ones who played basketball with him on Saturday nights, and others were part of the Sunday night Bible study. Though he was closest to Ryan, he considered Jeff and a couple of the other guys as close friends as well.

"Ready to go, babe?" Jeff asked as he leaned in and pressed a kiss to Rena's temple.

"Yep." Rena reached up and rested her hand on his cheek briefly. "It was so great to meet you, Melanie. Hope to see you again soon."

Melanie glanced at Tyler as if asking him if that was possible. Did she think he didn't want her to be part of this group? "It's been a pleasure getting to know you."

Betsy stood when Rena and Jeff did and after saying goodbye, she walked out of the restaurant with them. Melanie laid her knife and fork across her plate and took another drink of water.

"Are you ready to go?" Tyler asked.

Melanie nodded. "It's been fun, but I do need to get home."

Ryan left with them then waited at his car while Tyler walked Melanie to her truck. After she'd climbed behind the wheel, Tyler stepped close. "It was great to see you today. Do you think you'll come back to the church again?"

Melanie seemed to consider it before nodding her head. "It was good. Made me think."

"If you want to talk about the service or the sermon, give me a call. I'll be at the Bible study from seven until nine, but you can call me before or after."

"Thank you for introducing me to your friends. They seem really nice." The corners of her mouth turned up. "Even Betsy."

"Yeah, that blew me away. And my friends are your friends. I think they liked you too."

When silence fell between them, he said, "Guess I'd better go."

Melanie nodded. "Hope the rest of your day goes well."

"Yours too." He was reluctant to leave her but loitering around in a parking lot while his friend waited on him wasn't exactly the place to hold a long conversation. "I'll talk to you later."

He fought the urge to stand to watch as she drove away. Instead, he made his way back to where Ryan waited. He sat behind the wheel, studying his phone, and glanced over when Tyler opened the door and slid onto the passenger seat. "Thought you'd be a bit longer."

Tyler shook his head. "Standing in the cold in a parking lot doesn't really work. Plus, we're not teenagers. We don't need to spend every moment of every day together."

Ryan chuckled as he started up the car. "But you sure want to."

"Yeah," he agreed. "But I'm trying to take my cues from her, and I think she was ready to go home."

"Maybe I'd better give you some pointers on reading body language."

"Yeah. You probably should."

Tyler was wishing for those pointers when he happened upon Melanie on Tuesday morning. Marcus had asked him to come to the boardroom to meet with him and Alex before their management meeting. As he left the boardroom, he'd immediately spotted Melanie standing a little ways down the hallway with Justin. They were standing fairly close together, and Justin had his head bent as if to hear what she was saying.

Jealousy wasn't something he'd dealt with often but now within the space of a couple of weeks, he'd experienced it twice. He didn't like the feeling. The churning in his gut. The thoughts going through his head. Especially since he knew that Melanie had been friends with Justin nearly as long as they'd been friends, and Justin was engaged to someone else.

Not feeling comfortable with interrupting their conversation, Tyler turned to go down another hallway which would eventually take him to the elevators even though it was a more roundabout way. Maybe if they'd been together in a relationship a little longer, he would have felt comfortable approaching them. Though, as he thought about it, if they were still *just* friends, he probably would have approached them. Instead, he felt like he was in limbo. No longer just a friend, but not feeling quite a boyfriend.

He pushed the button to call the elevator then stood waiting for it to come, his hands shoved into his pockets, head bent as he stared at his shoes. When he heard the ding, he looked up and waited for the doors to slide open.

Adrianne walked out, surprise on her face when she spotted him. "Hey, Tyler. Fancy meeting you here."

"Yeah, I had an early meeting with Alex and Marcus. Now they're all yours," Tyler replied as he put out a hand to hold the doors open. He stepped into the elevator and gave her a smile—at least he hoped it looked a smile. "Hope your meeting goes well."

Adrianne glanced down the hallway to her right and then back at Tyler. "Yeah, me too."

He moved his hand from the door and pressed the button for his floor. "See you later."

She smiled at him just before the door slid shut. He leaned against the wall and tilted his head back. This was crazy. She was Melanie. His friend. First and foremost, his friend. And yet, his greatest fear was that she still viewed him as just a friend, in spite of agreeing to something more.

Worst of all, what if she didn't feel about him the way he was already feeling about her?

"Hey." Melanie looked over to see Adrianne sink into the seat next to her. She leaned toward her. "Did you and Tyler already have an argument?"

Melanie frowned and, keeping her voice low, she asked, "What are you talking about?"

"He was waiting for the elevator when I got off. He seemed upset or maybe it was more that he didn't look like his usual friendly self."

"Tyler was on this floor?"

"He said he had an early meeting with Alex and Marcus." Adrianne tilted her head. "You didn't see him?"

Melanie shook her head. "I rode up with Justin and then we were talking in the hallway. He would have had to walk past us to get to the elevator."

"Unless he went the long way."

Marcus called the meeting to order, but Melanie's thoughts were not focused on the agenda. Had he intentionally gone the other way to the elevator? Had he seen her with Justin and assumed she wouldn't have wanted him to interrupt them? A sick feeling tightened her stomach.

If that was the case, how was she supposed to deal with this? She chewed the inside of her cheek. Was she not supposed to have any male friends now that she and Tyler were dating? *Ugh!* This is what happened when she waited until the ripe old age of thirty to seriously date. And maybe Tyler had been right to be concerned about losing a friendship if things didn't work out. Already their friendship was suffering because she didn't know how to do this kind of stuff.

The irony was that she'd been talking to Justin about Tyler. She was letting him know that she'd taken his advice about taking the step and praying it would work out if it was God's will. But now what did she do? They hadn't made any plans to meet today since Melanie hadn't been sure if she'd have to return to the Center to meet with a potential new resident. As it turned out, they weren't going to be at the Center until two o'clock, so now there was no rush to get back.

Keeping an eye on Marcus and half listening to what he was saying, Melanie pulled her phone out and sent a quick text to Kelsey, the receptionist on the management floor.

Can you get a roast beef sandwich and a chef's salad sent up from the deli? Pretty please? I'll swing by your desk and grab it after the meeting. Oh, and a bottle of water and an iced tea. Have them put it on my account.

Melanie turned her attention back to the meeting, listening as each department head reported on their area with a special focus on the increased security. She spoke when it was her turn. Thankfully, she'd known she would need to give this update so she was prepared.

Adrianne didn't have a department to report on security-wise, but she did give an update on the big dinner/fundraiser that would happen at the end of November. Though they had smaller ones throughout the year—usually with a special focus—this big one was a chance to meet potential clients as well as thank current and previous ones all while raising money for the BlackThorpe Wellness Center.

This year, she might have a date for the first time. No, she *would* have a date. Whatever was going on with Tyler right then, she planned to get them over it. When her phone vibrated, she flipped it over in her lap and read the message.

It's all here whenever you're ready. :)

Feeling a bit nervous about her plan, Melanie tried to keep her focus on the meeting and not on what might happen when she went to see Tyler. When Marcus dismissed them, she didn't linger to chat. She just assured Adrianne that everything was fine—boy, she hoped she was right—and that she'd talk to her later.

Kelsey smiled when she got off the elevator. "Your order is all ready to go."

"Thanks so much, Kels. Last minute planning is not my thing." Melanie picked up the two bags that sat on the corner of her desk.

"Is this for you and a certain curly-haired someone?"

Melanie decided she wasn't going to try to hide her relationship with Tyler even though it was still rather new. "Yep. Gonna try to grab a quick bite with him before I have to head back to the Center."

Kelsey's smile grew. "I'm so happy for you two. You're perfect for each other."

"Well, I don't know about perfect," Melanie said with a laugh. "But I think we suit pretty good. We know each other fairly well since we've been friends for so long."

"I've always heard that friendship is a great basis for a relationship."

"Here's hoping they're right." She glanced at the elevator as it dinged and the doors opened. "I'd better get down there. Thanks again."

Than and Alex stepped out of the elevator, both of them looking surprised to see her there.

"What's up?" Alex asked as his gaze dropped to the bags in her hand.

Melanie lifted them. "Just had Kelsey order some lunch from the deli for Tyler and me."

Than grinned. "So, it's a go then?"

"We'll see." Melanie returned his smile. She stepped around them to push the button to call the elevator which had once again gone to a lower floor.

"With the way we're all dropping like flies, you're gonna be next, big guy," Than said as he poked Alex in the side with his elbow.

Alex frowned. "Not gonna happen."

"I think we've all said that on occasion and yet here we are." Than spread his arms out. "Me and Justin planning weddings. Who would ever have thought that?"

Thankfully, the elevator arrived, this time empty. Melanie stepped in and pressed the button for Tyler's floor. "See you guys later."

"Have fun," Than said with a wink.

Melanie wasn't looking for fun, but she did want to show Tyler she was serious about them and to maybe talk about what had happened. *If* it had happened. She still wasn't sure that anything had.

When she stepped out of the elevator on Tyler's floor, the receptionist gave her a knowing smile as she walked past. Yeah, this building had a ton of gossipers. She headed down the hallway to Tyler's office. As she approached his open door, she lifted her hand to knock only to see the office was empty.

Disappointment filled her, but she knew it had been a risk. He was as busy as she was, so it wasn't too surprising he was out of his office. With a sigh, she put the bags on his desk and took out the plastic container holding his sandwich and put it beside his keyboard. She put the bottle of iced tea next to the sandwich, setting it on a napkin the deli had included.

She toyed with the idea of texting him, but if he was in the middle of a meeting, she didn't want to interrupt. After all, eleven o'clock was still a little early for lunch. Instead, she looked for something to write on. Not seeing anything that was clearly a piece of scrap paper, Melanie took another one of the napkins and used a pen from her purse.

Sorry to have missed you. ~M

She knew it was short but had no idea what else to write. Trying not to let the disappointment drag her down, Melanie left his office and headed back to the elevator. Thankfully, the receptionist was busy on the phone and didn't make any comment when Melanie walked back past her desk.

In the basement garage, she unlocked her car, slid behind the wheel, and dropped her purse and the bag with her salad and water in them onto the passenger seat. She sat there for a moment, not anxious to return to the Center without seeing Tyler. They hadn't made arrangements for a future date yet, and she found she wanted the assurance that she was going to be seeing him again.

Soon.

18

WITH A SIGH, Melanie reached out and started her car. Her cell phone rang, connecting with the Bluetooth in the vehicle. She stared at the display, smiling when she recognized Tyler's number. Without delay, she tapped the screen to accept the call.

"Hello?"

"Hey!" Tyler's voice filled the interior of the car. "Where are you?"

"In my car in the garage."

"Here at BlackThorpe?"

"Yep. Just getting ready to head back to the Center." She wasn't sure if he'd seen the food on his desk or was just calling out of the blue.

"Come back and eat with me," he said, his tone warm. "You did get something for yourself, right?"

Melanie glanced at the bags on the other seat. "Yes, I did."

"Will you come back? Please?"

Even if she'd wanted to, she couldn't resist his request. "I'll be right there."

This time when the elevator doors slid open, Tyler stood waiting for her. She smiled and took the hand he offered her. "Thanks for coming back."

Melanie heard an *ahhhh* from the receptionist as they walked by her. She wondered if this would be enough to win the bet for whoever had said she'd be the next victim love would claim.

When they got to Tyler's office, he waited for her to go in first then followed her. He pushed some files from the edge of the desk to make room for her salad then, instead of taking his seat behind the desk, he picked up the sandwich container and sat down in the chair next to hers.

"Sorry I wasn't here when you stopped by. I'd gone to see someone about a file. We must have just missed each other. I swear I wasn't gone but a couple of minutes."

Melanie smiled. "It's okay. You caught me before I'd gone too far."

"I'm glad." When he smiled at her, Melanie wondered if perhaps the thoughts Adrianne had put into her head were off base. Maybe he hadn't seen her with Justin and assumed the wrong thing.

"I saw you earlier—I was at a meeting with Alex and Marcus—but you were talking with Justin, and I didn't want to interrupt," he said casually as he opened the container holding his sandwich.

Melanie's eyes widened. Well, Adrianne had gotten it half right. "I wish you had."

Tyler looked at her in surprise, his movements stilling. "Oh. Well, next time, I will."

Before he returned his attention to his sandwich, he held out his hand. Melanie took it and, knowing what was to come, she bowed her head. In a way she was coming to appreciate, Tyler's fingers tightened around hers as he said a blessing for the food.

If someone had asked her six months ago if she'd admire a man for his faith, she probably would have said that it wasn't something she necessarily looked for in a man. However, having seen this side of him, she knew it was an integral part of Tyler and just one more thing that drew her to him.

"This looks good," Tyler said as he lifted half of his sandwich from the container. "How was the meeting?"

"It was good." She paused. "Adrianne updated us on the annual BlackThorpe banquet coming up. Were you planning to go this year?"

Tyler nodded. "I've gone to every one since I was able. Won't be missing this year."

"Yeah, it's quite the shindig. Adrianne manages to outdo herself every year. I'm sure this year won't be any different." Melanie wondered if it would be okay for her to ask him to accompany her. Before she could make up her mind what to do, he spoke again.

"I know you always go," he said, glancing over at her. "Would you like to go with me this year?"

"Are you asking me on a date?" Melanie asked, injecting a playful tone into her words.

"Well, yes, I guess I am." His blue eyes were so serious, almost as if he really thought there was a possibility she'd say no.

She dropped her gaze and stabbed at the lettuce in her salad. "Well, I suppose since you ask so nicely."

When he didn't respond, she peeked at him and saw him watching her, a smile playing around the corners of his mouth. "So that's a yes then?"

Melanie sat back in her chair. "I guess there's a first time for everything. So yes, I'd love to be your date for the dinner."

"It's the one time of year I'm guaranteed to see you in a dress," Tyler said as he lifted his sandwich then took a bite.

"Yeah, it's pretty much the only time I get that dressed up." She took a drink of her water. "Will your mom and Hank come?"

"I think they might this year. It's close to Thanksgiving so they could kill two birds with one stone."

"It will be nice to see them again. I can't believe I'd never met them after all these years."

"The timing must have been off. Also, there were a couple of years where they didn't come here at all. I went to them."

"What's London like?" Melanie took another bite of her salad as she waited for Tyler to answer.

"It's nice, but I preferred when Hank took us outside the city. It's beautiful countryside." He tilted his head. "You've never traveled over there?"

More stabbing at her lettuce. "I've...uh...never been one for traveling much outside the US." Or in it either, for that matter, but she wasn't going to tell him that.

"I like traveling, but I always enjoy coming home more. This is where my friends are. Where my life is." One corner of his mouth lifted. "Where you are."

Melanie didn't know how to respond. He'd done this before. His marriage proved he'd been in at least one serious relationship before, so he knew how to do this flirty stuff better than she did. "Thank you for sharing parts of that life with me. I enjoyed meeting your friends."

"You made quite an impression on them."

"Hopefully a good one."

"Definitely." He laughed. "I got several texts Sunday afternoon and the guys at the Bible study all wanted to know how I'd managed to land you since you were so obviously out of my league."

"Oh." Melanie frowned. "You don't think that, do you?"

"That you're out of my league?"

She nodded. "I would never want you to think that."

Tyler reached out and took her hand. "I never really thought that, but I have always thought I was fortunate to have you as a friend. And now I feel doubly fortunate that we are...more."

More. Yes, they were most definitely more. "I think I'm the fortunate one."

"My mom thinks we're both fortunate," Tyler said with a smile.

Melanie gripped his hand a little tighter. "You told your mom?"

"Yes. After she met you, she asked if there was something between us. When I told her there wasn't, I think she was disappointed."

"Wait. You didn't ask me out because your mom wanted you to, did you?"

Tyler laughed. "I may do a lot of things to make my mom happy, but I can guarantee you that doesn't involve who I choose to date."

Melanie bent her head. "Well, I haven't mentioned anything to my parents yet."

"I realize it's still kind of new," Tyler said as he let go of her hand and picked up his sandwich.

"It's not that, so much. Alex and Adrianne know we've been spending time together. It's more my mom." Melanie toyed with her salad as she explained how things had been for Adrianne. "So it could go one of two ways. Knowing I'm dating could take the pressure off her, or it will just increase it since Adrianne is older than me. You know the *if your sister has a boyfriend, why don't you* type of thing."

"Maybe it's a good thing I never had siblings." Tyler wiped his hands on a napkin after finishing his sandwich.

Melanie laid her fork on the top of the salad and closed the container. She saw Tyler glance at her food and frown. She knew she hadn't eaten much, but she'd grab something later. The Center had a good cafeteria since the people living there needed a place to eat.

"Just think," Tyler said as he gathered up their trash, "if you worked here, we could have lunch together whenever we wanted."

Melanie wiped down the edge of his desk with a napkin. "Or if you worked at the Center."

"On second thought, having you that close by might be a bit of a distraction." Tyler's smile warmed her and Melanie knew she'd never tire of seeing that look on his face.

"On that lovely note, I guess I'd better head back to work." She grabbed her purse and slipped the strap over her shoulder. "I really did enjoy having lunch with you."

"I'm just glad I caught you before you left." He grabbed her hand as she walked by him to the door. "Next time text or call me. I would have hated if I'd just missed you because I'd gone to get a drink or something."

"I'll be sure to do that," Melanie promised.

As they walked together to the elevator, Tyler kept hold of her hand and they made plans to go for dinner Thursday.

"I won't be out to the Center until Friday," Tyler said as he pressed the button for the elevator. "Simon wants me to meet his fiancée."

"I think that's so wonderful that they're reconnecting."

Tyler nodded. "It's nice to see that a relationship might survive a tragedy like his. And I'm glad Simon is in a place to accept that."

When the door of the elevator slid open, Tyler lifted her hand and pressed a kiss to the back of it. "Drive safely."

Melanie found herself smiling as she drove back to the Center. She could get used to having Tyler in her life like that. Thankfully, it seemed he was happy to have her in his life too.

After work, she headed for the gym to meet with her trainer. She hadn't made it in a few weeks, preferring to work out at home, but a few reminder texts from him had her heading there instead of home.

As she walked into the gym, Melanie realized that for the first time in forever—or maybe ever—she had a sense of anticipation and excitement for the future. Most the time her focus was on the future as it pertained to the Center, rarely was it on her personal life.

Tyler had changed all of that in the matter of a few days.

Taking Melanie home after their dinner on Thursday was a little easier for Tyler since he knew he'd be seeing her the next day. But still, even after he pulled up in front of the Thorpe home, she didn't get out of the car right away.

"Do you want to come in for a bit?" Melanie asked.

"Alex and Adrianne won't mind?"

"Nope."

"In that case, yes, I'd love to."

When they walked into the house, there didn't appear to be anyone else around, so when Melanie offered a tour, Tyler jumped on it.

"Alex bought this property when the market hit that slump a little while back. The first floor is basically the same, but he reworked the upstairs so there were three suites of rooms." Melanie gestured to the large staircase that ran up to the second floor and a balcony that looked out over the foyer where they stood. "Adrianne's is on the left. Alex's in the middle and mine on the right."

She turned to the right and led the way into a dining room. "We use this if we have company or a special dinner. Usually, we eat at the breakfast nook in the kitchen."

The large kitchen would be a gourmet chef's dream with its wide granite counter spaces and stainless steel appliances. The breakfast nook sat in front of large windows that ran along the back wall. He wondered what the view was like, but darkness kept it shrouded. Maybe he'd get a look at it during a future visit. He certainly hoped this wasn't his first and last visit to the Thorpe home.

"The living room is through there," Melanie said with a wave toward a darkened room on the other side of the house. "But my favorite spot on this floor—aside from the kitchen— is back here."

Tyler followed her as she led the way down a short hall to a set of wooden doors with glass panels. She smiled back at him as she pushed open one of the doors and walked into the darkness beyond. Almost immediately, lights turned on, obviously triggered by a sensor on the door. He heard the sound of running water as he stepped into the room.

Right away he could see why Melanie liked this place. The walls were lined with cedar and brass sconces cast a dim yellow glow around the room. A large pool with curved edges and underwater lights filled the middle of the space. There were windows on the wall, but no doubt the most stunning feature was the rock waterfall at the far end of the room.

"This is pretty incredible." Tyler turned to find Melanie watching him.

"It is, isn't it?" She reached for his hand. "Come see my spot."

She didn't need to ask twice. And if he thought the main part was incredible, when she led him into an alcove off to the side of the waterfall, Tyler was blown away. The circular room was made of rock and wood and had the same wall sconces that cast a soft light. The perimeter of the room was made up of one long curved, cushioned bench seat along with a ton of throw pillows. A large round wooden coffee table with glass panels sat in the middle of the room.

"Want to sit for a bit?"

Melanie dropped down amongst the pillows, still holding his hand, so Tyler settled beside her. It was like they were in their own little world and the sound of the nearby waterfall added to that perception. He leaned his head back against the cushions and closed his eyes. He could see why Melanie loved this spot.

He felt movement, but Melanie still didn't release his hand. Turning his head, he opened his eyes to see her sitting with her feet propped up on the edge of the coffee table.

"Thank you for showing me your special spot."

"I get so busy sometimes that I don't come here as often as I'd like to, but at least I know it's here when I need it."

When Tyler shifted and propped his feet up next to hers, their arms pressed together and their clasped hands were trapped between their legs. He would happily stay like that with her for as long as she wanted. "What do you think about when you come here?"

"To be honest, I try not to think about anything. I'll lie down and listen to the waterfall and imagine it washing away all my stress."

"Does your career help you deal with stress and stuff?"

She looked over at him, a corner of her mouth lifting. "Kind of like *physician heal thyself*, you mean?"

"Yeah. Something like that."

"Well, it gives me tools to cope, I suppose," she said with a slight shrug. "But it doesn't necessarily mean I don't still have issues. Hope you didn't assume that."

Tyler chuckled. "I would never have made that assumption. After all, I've yet to meet someone who is completely without issues of some kind."

"You have issues?" she asked, and from the expression on her face, it seemed she was actually serious about the question.

"No. I'm perfect," he said. "Obviously, I was talking about everyone else."

She laughed at that, her eyes sparkling. Without realizing what he was doing, Tyler turned slightly and lifted a hand to cup her cheek. He skimmed his thumb across her skin, so soft and silky beneath his touch.

Her lips parted, and he felt a puff of air across his hand. Was it too soon for a kiss? It didn't feel like it. It felt like he'd been waiting his whole life for this moment. Had she?

He moved slowly, giving her the chance to pull away, but her eyes closed, Tyler pressed hip lips to hers.

Melanie wondered if it was possible to pass out during a kiss. Her anxiety level was high, but she tried to focus on the feel of Tyler's hand in hers, of his other hand cupping her cheek. Tyler had given her the chance to back-off, but she hadn't. She wanted this.

He placed several soft kisses on her lips, not pressuring for anything more. She pressed her hand against his where it rested on her cheek. His touch was soft. Caring. This was the first kiss she'd experienced that she'd wanted.

His hand let go of hers, and he slid is arm around her waist, drawing her into his side. His embrace brought a sense of security, and she felt the tension in her chest ease. She moved her hand to his neck, sliding her fingers into his silky curls and returning his kisses as the rightness of being in his arms flooded her.

When Tyler finally left one last kiss on her lips and moved back a bit, Melanie rested her head on his shoulder. Both his arms went around her and held her tight to his side. She'd never thought that being close to another person would make her feel safe, but she did feel safe with Tyler. She slid her arms around his waist and pressed her face into his neck, inhaling the scent she would always associate with him.

The waterfall kept the silence from being awkward. Closing her eyes, Melanie let herself relax and enjoy the sensations of being physically close to someone for the first time. She thought it might be too overwhelming. That the closeness would trigger something in her, but she was secure in knowing this was Tyler. He'd been part of her life for so long that there was no fear in being close to him. She realized that was just one of the reasons this thing between them felt right.

"You falling asleep?" Tyler's voice rumbled under her cheek.

"No." Melanie shifted a bit. "Just enjoying...us."

His arms tightened briefly. "Me, too, but I should probably go."

This time, she tightened her arms. She didn't want their evening to end, but they both still had to work the next day. Tyler turned his head and pressed a kiss to her forehead.

Slowly, they disentangled themselves and got up from the seat. They kept their arms around each other as they wandered out of the pool area and through the house to the front door. Melanie was glad that no one was around. She didn't need her siblings interrupting what had been a perfect evening so far.

"Don't come out. It's cold," Tyler said as he opened the door. "Thanks again for sharing your spot with me."

Melanie leaned against the edge of the open door. "Thanks for a beautiful evening."

Tyler bent down and pressed a lingering kiss to her lips. "See you tomorrow."

As she watched him walk down the steps to his car, Melanie again found herself filled with hope. Maybe, just maybe, there was love in her future. She gave a wave when his car started to pull away then closed the door. After seeing his car pass through the gates on the monitor, she pressed the button to close them, realizing as she did that they hadn't closed the gates earlier. No doubt she'd get an earful from Alex later if he reviewed the security activity for the evening.

Smiling as she walked up to her room, Melanie couldn't find it in herself to really care. Nothing could spoil the evening she'd just shared with Tyler.

The next afternoon, Melanie was standing in front of Heather's desk talking about her weekend plans when Tyler appeared in the doorway. A rush of warmth flooded her at the smile he had just for her. Before she had a chance to say anything, he stepped to her side and slid his arm around her waist. In one quick movement, he brought them close and bent his head to press a quick kiss to her lips.

Melanie heard Heather's sigh but ignored it as she went up on her toes to give him a kiss of her own then smiled. "Hi."

"Hi." The emotion in his eyes and the feel of his arm once again filled Melanie with the sense of rightness. "I'm here to meet with Simon but had to see you first."

"I'm glad you stopped by."

"Me, too," Heather chimed in. "You guys are just too cute."

Tyler grinned at her words. "I'll stop by again after I'm done with Simon."

"I'll be here."

He gave her one last kiss before walking back into the hallway. Melanie stood staring at the empty doorway. Was this really her life?

"Seriously, you guys seem so right for each other."

Melanie agreed, but there were still some rough waters ahead. She knew she had to tell him about her past.

"Okay, back to work." With a quick smile for Heather and her dreamy expression, Melanie went to her desk.

She picked up her pen, but her thoughts were still on when would be the best time to tell him. There would never be a perfectly good time for him to hear what she had to say, but maybe if she waited a bit longer. Until things between them weren't so new. Hopefully, by then their emotional connection would be strong enough to withstand the impact of her past.

As Tyler watched Simon and his fiancée, he was somewhat surprised that his first thought wasn't that he wished that Kelly had been like that for him. Instead, he found himself hoping that at some point, that would be him and Melanie. His focus was definitely on the future. It was time to leave the past in the past.

"It was a pleasure to meet you, Tanya," Tyler said as he shook her hand. "Now I'll leave you two to spend some time together."

Tanya grasped his hand in both of hers. "I can't thank you enough for all you've done for Simon. He's told me how you've stuck by him even when he was being difficult."

"It has been my pleasure." Even as he said the words, Tyler recognized the truth in them. He would now count Simon as one of his friends and looked forward to continuing to keep in contact with him even after he left the Center. And from the strides the man had made in the past week, it appeared he was well on his way to that.

After a promise to see Simon the next week, Tyler headed up to Melanie's office again. He really needed to get back to work, but he wanted to see her one more time. Because of his weekend schedule, he wouldn't get a chance to see her until Sunday at church. He'd offered to bail on the Saturday night basketball game with his friends, but she'd insisted that he still hang out with them.

Heather wasn't at her desk when Tyler got there, but he found Melanie at hers. She looked up as soon as he walked into the office. The smile that spread across her face was different from what he'd seen from her before. It took a second for him to realize what it was, but then it struck him that this one went right into her eyes. The reserved smile she usually gave people was gone when she smiled at him. He'd always thought she was pretty, but in that moment, she took his breath away.

"How did your visit go?"

Before he could answer, his phone rang. Frowning, he pulled it out and glanced at the screen. "Marcus. Hang on a second."

"Tyler, I've sent you a new file I need you to review. One of the calls made from a number we've been keeping an eye on was to a Minnesota area code."

Knowing that Marcus had been concerned about another attack, Tyler understood the man's concern. "Okay. I'm just out at the Wellness Center, but I'll have a look at the file now before I head back to the office."

"Thank you."

The call ended abruptly before he could respond. Tyler let out a breath as he slid the phone into his pocket. "Is there a computer I can use for a few minutes?"

Melanie pushed back from her desk. "You can use mine."

"Thanks." As they passed each other to change seats, Tyler slid an arm around her waist and gave her another quick kiss. He knew it wasn't the most appropriate place for public displays of affection, but he couldn't help himself.

"Something happening?" Melanie asked as she sat down across from him.

"Marcus had something pop up that he's concerned about." It only took a few moments for him to click into his computer through the BlackThorpe network and pull up the file Marcus had sent him. "I go back and forth between wondering if Marcus is overreacting or not."

"I suppose considering the fact that he's still limping from the last run-in, it makes sense he'll err on the side of caution."

Tyler nodded. "And that's why I jump when he needs something from me on this."

"Melanie?"

Tyler glanced over at the door and saw one of the counselors standing there, her gaze going back and forth between them. Melanie stood up and went with them into Heather's office.

He took a deep breath and focused on the information on the screen. It was probably a good thing that he and Melanie worked in two different buildings. She was definitely a distraction when she was around even more than she used to be. Truth was, she'd always been a bit of a distraction to him, he just hadn't understood why. Or maybe he hadn't wanted to consider why.

Once the program had started to run the numbers Marcus had given him, Tyler logged out of his computer and stood up. He would have liked to hang around and chat with Melanie some more, but the program wouldn't take too long to finish the process.

"You gotta go?" Melanie asked when she came back into the room.

"Yep. I want to be back by the time this finishes. Marcus will be waiting for the results."

He smiled when she came to him and slid her arms around his waist. For some reason, her initiating the contact between them made him happy. It told him that she was comfortable with him. With them as a couple. Yes, that definitely made him happy.

They kissed a couple of times before she released her hold on him. "Hope the rest of your day isn't too stressful."

"Me, too. I'll give you a call later after I get home from youth group."

"I'll be waiting."

Her smile lingered with him as he left the Center and headed back to the office. His thoughts as he drove were filled with Melanie and the time they'd spent together over the past couple of weeks. When his mom called on Sunday, he was going to tell her about what had developed between him and Melanie. He knew she'd be thrilled, and it felt like it was the right time.

Melanie's confidence in their relationship was a turning point for him because now he could envision a real solid future for them. That meant it was time to share it with his mom.

19

"T HAT CALL WENT to a hotel in Rochester," Tyler told Marcus as he sat across from the man. "I looked at a few of the previous long distance calls made recently and several were made to someone in Florida. The name isn't one I've run across before though, so I'm not sure if it's relevant or not."

"What's the hotel?" Marcus asked.

Tyler gave him the information he'd uncovered, figuring as he did so that Marcus was going to be sending someone down there to check it out.

"And the name of the person in Florida?"

"Craig Ellis."

"And that name hasn't popped up in any of our previous searches?"

"Nope. I did a cross-reference with it, and there is no previous connection."

Marcus sighed. "Okay. We'll let that go for now and see what the Rochester link turns up."

"Let me know if you need me to do something more."

As he put his phone down on the desk, Tyler let his mind flip through possible options for an attack. The first one had been directed at a person—Marcus, except that Eric had taken his place on that trip—but since then, the attacks had been aimed at the organization, not an individual. Would whoever was behind the attacks move back to an individual attack? And if so, would that be focused on Marcus and Alex or was any employee fair game?

Tyler could understand Marcus's obsession with the safety of his company and employees, but without a clearly defined threat, it was hard not to wonder if they were grasping at straws and being paranoid for no reason.

Melanie flopped onto her bed and stared up at the ceiling. What a long day! It almost took more energy than she had left to get under the covers and turn out the light. She'd sent Tyler a text to let him know she was heading to bed early. It was rare she was in bed before ten, but when her day had started at four with an anxiety-ridden phone call from Jenni, an early bedtime was in order. Especially if she planned to go to church the next morning.

She'd taken her prescribed sleeping pills because she was sure that if she didn't, her mind wouldn't stop racing with thoughts of Jenni. And that was the worst when she was already so tired. Everything was worse when the control of her emotions was worn thin by exhaustion. All she wanted was about ten or eleven hours of solid sleep.

With a sigh, she got to her feet and pulled the blankets down far enough to slide under them. She touched the base of the lamp to turn it off and then slid her hand under the pillow next to hers. Making contact with the solid butt of her gun was the last thing she did before sleeping each night. Maybe there would be a time she didn't sleep with a gun so close at hand, but that night was not tonight.

She took a deep breath and let it out, exhaling the stresses of the day. *Dear God, please take care of Jenni.*

A hand landed on her shoulder, jerking her from a deep sleep. Reflexes had her grabbing her gun, thumbing off the safety as she hit the base of the lamp to turn it on. Just about the time she registered Alex's face in the light, his hand gripped her wrist and moved the gun away from him.

"Alex?"

His face was tight with anger. "You have two minutes to get up and get dressed. Justin's in the hospital. He was attacked and Alana was abducted." He paused then said, "We will be having a discussion in the near future on why you sleep with a loaded weapon."

Melanie's mind was scrambling, sluggish from the sleeping pills still affecting her. But as Alex headed out of the room, he called out, "Two minutes, Melanie. Move it."

Struggling to make her body work, she put the safety back on and dropped the gun on the bed as she tried to kick free of the blankets. Once she made it to the dresser, Melanie pulled off her pajamas and jerked on a pair of jeans and a sweatshirt. Socks, shoes, her gun and her purse, and she was running out of the room.

Alex and Adrianne were waiting out in Alex's truck. Melanie scrambled into the back seat, her heart pounding. As soon as she shut the door, the truck jerked into motion.

"Arm the house, Adrianne," Alex said as he approached the gate that stood open.

The light from Adrianne's phone illuminated her face as she remotely armed the security system of the house. As the gate closed behind them, Melanie took several deep breaths.

"What happened?"

"Not entirely sure. Daniel—Justin's brother-in-law—called me a few minutes ago to say Justin had managed to call him for help before passing out. He said they went over and had to call an ambulance for Justin and that Alana was gone."

Melanie pressed her knees together to try to stop the shaking that had started in her legs. "Did Justin say who did it?"

"He hasn't regained consciousness. They were doing some scans, but Daniel said it sounded like he'd be going into surgery right away."

"Justin?" How could it be Justin? If anyone was prepared to deal with an attack, it would have been Justin. They had to be wrong.

"Yes, Justin," Alex said. "What is wrong with you?"

What's wrong with me? The trembling had now moved to her core, and there was no way she could stop it from spreading.

This is a bad dream. It has to be.

"Melanie!" Adrianne's voice was sharp.

"Maybe we shouldn't have told her. I don't know what's going on."

I need my calm place.

She tried to take a deep breath, but emotion constricted her chest. When she couldn't get relief that way, Melanie tried again to picture her calm place in her mind.

The cabin. The crackle of the fire in the fireplace as it spreads its warmth into the room. The comfortable chair with a lamp next to it. The soft blanket covering my legs. There's a storm raging outside but inside I'm safe. It's peaceful. Secure.

It wasn't helping. She didn't feel safe. She didn't feel secure.

How could this happen to Justin? And Alana... She was trying so hard not to think about what she might be going through. *Abducted.* The past was rising up and overwhelming her with memories and fears she'd thought she'd moved beyond.

Suddenly the interior of the truck was filled with light. Strong hands grasped her arms. "Are you going to be able to handle this, Lanie?"

Alex.

She could do this. She had to do this for Justin. Be there for him.

"Maybe I should take her back home?" Adrianne said.

"No. No. I'll be okay." She didn't want to be alone at home. "Just a shock."

"Are you sure?" Alex asked.

"Yes." She tried another deep breath, and this time was able to pull the air into her lungs.

"Let's go."

She grabbed her purse—which held her gun—and slid out of the back of the truck. Alex kept his arm around her shoulders as they made their way into the hospital. He didn't let her go until they reached a waiting room. Justin's sister was there sitting close to her husband, her face pale and strained. Marcus was also there, pacing the small space with his limping gait.

Alex led Melanie to a chair in the corner. She sank down onto the cushioned surface, sliding her hands under her thighs so no one could see how they were shaking. Staring down at her feet, she realized that her socks didn't match. How had that happened? She always put her socks away in pairs.

"Are you okay?" Adrianne's soft question drifted through the fog of her mind.

"What time is it?"

"It's just after eleven."

She'd only been asleep for an hour or so. No wonder she was so out of it. That had to be why she was reacting the way she was.

"They said it looked like the person attacked Justin as soon as he opened the door. He was also shot twice." Daniel's voice carried to where they were sitting. "And at some point they got Alana."

And just like that, a sledgehammer hit the walls she carefully erected around herself. Everything she'd told herself over the past fourteen years. Everything she'd done to make sure she'd never again be a victim was for nothing. She would never be safe again. If this could happen to Justin—if he couldn't protect himself or Alana—what hope did she have?

"Dude, your phone's vibrating," Ryan said as he came out of the kitchen with it in his hand.

Tyler glanced away from the game he was playing with one of the guys who'd come back to his place after the basketball game. "Here, play for me."

He swapped the controller for the phone and shifted on the couch to make room for Ryan while he looked at the display on his phone.

Six missed calls.

Three from Marcus. Four from Alex. Plus a text from him.

What on earth was going on?

Call me as soon as you get this.

A knot formed in the pit of Tyler's stomach as he pushed up from the couch and went into his bedroom where it was quieter. Had something happened to Melanie?

Oh, please no.

He tapped the screen to call Alex and lifted the phone to his ear as he dragged a hand through his hair.

Alex didn't even bother with pleasantries when he answered the phone. "We need you to come to the hospital. Justin's been attacked, and Alana was abducted."

"Is Melanie okay?" Justin was her friend so it stood to reason she'd be upset by something like this.

Alex didn't respond right away then all he said was, "Just get here."

Tyler got the information on the hospital where they were and then hung up. He was still wearing his basketball stuff which included the prosthetics he used when he played. Trying to keep his thoughts from going to the worst possible scenarios, he sat down on his bed and took the time to swap his prosthetics then changed into a pair of jeans and a clean T-shirt.

Ryan looked at him as he walked out of the bedroom. "Everything okay."

"Nope. Justin's in the hospital. Alana's been abducted and though Alex didn't say anything specifically, it seems Melanie's not doing too well. They want me at the hospital."

"Do you want me to come with you?" Ryan set his controller down on the coffee table and got to his feet.

"We're out of here," one of his friends said. "We'll let you guys deal with this."

"Sorry," Tyler said with a shrug.

"No worries." The guy clapped him on the shoulder. "We'll be praying."

Within a couple of minutes, it was just him and Ryan left. "Meet you out front."

Tyler thought about telling him not to bother, but honestly, he wouldn't mind the company. He had no idea what he was walking into, so company sounded good. He grabbed his keys and a jacket and walked out his front door. Ryan came out his front door a few seconds later. And when he suggested he be the one to drive, Tyler didn't argue.

Once at the hospital, they followed Alex's directions to the waiting room. Tyler immediately looked for Melanie. His heart clenched when he saw her huddled on a seat in the corner. She had her legs pulled up with her arms wrapped around them. Adrianne sat beside her, worry on her face.

Tyler didn't care if they needed him there for something else, he walked across the room to where Melanie sat and sank onto the seat next to her. She didn't lift her head from where it rested on her knees so the first thing Tyler noticed was that her hair looked...different. It was unstyled which—given the text she'd sent earlier about going to bed—wasn't a surprise, but about a half inch or more of the hair at her roots was a surprisingly light color. It looked almost like the color of Adrianne's and stood in stark contrast to the rest of her dark brown hair.

"Melanie?"

At the sound of his voice, she lifted her head and Tyler stared at her, trying to figure out what was going on. Her face was drawn and pale, and she had dark circles under her eyes. Her bright blue eyes. The sight knocked him back, robbing him of thought and words.

What on earth was going on? Was this a dream where he was in an alternate universe or something?

Tyler looked around the room and then met Adrianne's gaze. She glanced at Melanie and then back to him, comprehension dawning.

"She didn't tell you?"

"Um...I'm guessing...no?"

Adrianne's lips tightened as she gazed at Melanie, who had laid her head back down. "I'm sorry, Tyler. I thought she would have told you."

Told him what?

He was lost. Totally and completely lost. Melanie didn't look like...Melanie. She also appeared to be out of it—like she was in a daze or something. It was like she wasn't the same person he'd just held in his arms and kissed the day before.

Taking a deep breath, he returned his gaze to Melanie. Appearance aside, her demeanor was also shaking him up a bit. Except for that one time in his office when she'd told him what Jenni had said to her, he'd never seen her so...shattered. Had the attack on Justin done this to her?

Tyler knew they were close, but had he underestimated exactly *how* close? A sick feeling gripped his stomach. Had there been something between the two of them at one time? It shouldn't matter—after all, he had a past relationship—but the image of Melanie and Justin standing together in that hallway flashed in high definition in his brain right then.

Okay. First and foremost, she was his friend. Clearly, she needed some help so he would help her and sort everything out afterward. And pray to God there was a reasonable explanation for this left turn he'd taken into weirdville.

"Should I take her home?" Tyler asked Adrianne. Part of him wanted to scoop her up and hold her close, but the woman sitting beside him curled in on herself wasn't the woman he'd held in his arms just the day before.

Adrianne looked back at Melanie as if waiting for her to give some sign of what she wanted. But there was nothing, just large blue eyes framed by long dark lashes that stared vacantly at the room they were in. Concern flooded the older sister's face as she reached out to brush her fingers through Melanie's hair.

"I think maybe you should."

Grasping onto the plan of action offered by Adrianne, Tyler nodded then looked to where Ryan stood beside him, his friend's expression a weird mixture of contemplation and confusion.

Ryan nodded. "You take care of Melanie. I can get myself back home."

Tyler got to his feet, trying to figure out how to do this. Could she walk or was he going to have to carry her?

"Tyler's going to take Melanie home." Adrianne's words drew his attention from his predicament and he saw that Alex had joined them. The man stood with his hands on his hips staring down at Melanie.

"Did you need me for something else here?" Tyler asked Alex, remembering that something had happened with a Black Thorpe employee and it wasn't just about the state Melanie was currently in.

Alex shook his head as he dragged a hand through his hair. "No. Take her home. Just keep your phone close in case we need you for something."

"C'mon, Lanie," Adrianne said as she helped Melanie get to her feet. "I'll walk down with you."

By the time he and Adrianne had Melanie upright, more people had come into the waiting room. Tyler saw Ryan standing with Eric while Than and Trent were talking with Marcus. Several women were grouped around Justin's sister. It warmed him to see the support they offered each other. They were more than just co-workers. They were family.

Adrianne came with him and Melanie. Once they got to his car and Melanie was secured in the front seat, Adrianne gave him instructions on how to get into the house.

"Text me when you get to the gate. I'll open it remotely and then will disarm the house so you can get in."

"I'll just stay there until one of you guys get home. Is that okay?"

Adrianne nodded. "Alex won't leave until Justin is out of surgery for sure, and he figures it's only a matter of time before the cops show up to ask more questions. Top priority is finding Alana. Justin is going to go ballistic when he wakes up from surgery and she's not around."

Tyler could only imagine. He looked in the car window to where Melanie sat. He knew that if he were in Justin's shoes and Melanie had been abducted he would have reacted the very same way. "Can you let me know any updates? I'm sure Melanie will want to know how Justin is and anything about Alana too."

Adrianne nodded. She stared at Melanie for a long moment then lifted her gaze to his. Though there were lights in the parking lot, Adrianne's face was still shadowed as she looked up at him.

"You're good for Melanie, Tyler. I haven't seen her this happy in...years. Please give her a second chance."

A second chance? Had she seen something in him that had led her to believe that he was going to end things with Melanie? While he hadn't actually thought those thoughts exactly, he was confused, and it wasn't a feeling he liked.

He gave a quick nod but didn't say anything. She seemed to understand that words on that particular subject were beyond him at that point. As he pulled out of the parking lot a few minutes later, Tyler had to admit that he was not sure where things were going to go with Melanie. Everything about tonight had completely thrown him off balance. He didn't even know where to begin to process everything.

So, instead of focusing on the confusing part, he took the time as he drove to the Thorpe home to pray for Justin and Alana and their families. If he remembered correctly, Alana had a young son who would no doubt be terrified to have both his mom and soon-to-be stepdad gone.

When he reached the gate of the home, Tyler stopped the car and texted Adrianne. It was barely a moment later when the gates began to open. As he drove toward the house, he looked in the rear view mirror and saw them close. He parked by the steps leading to the front door. Hopefully, Adrianne would have already disarmed and unlocked the door. He saw lights come on inside and realized she controlled more than the security of the home.

Slipping his arm around Melanie's waist, he helped her up the steps to the front door. The door opened at his touch and they were soon inside the large home. Tyler hesitated, not sure where to take Melanie, but then he recalled their last time there together and made his way to the pool room.

The warmth of the room enveloped them as they walked through the door, and the sound of the waterfall was immediately soothing. He had her sit down on the curved seat, but instead of leaning back against the cushions, she grabbed a loose pillow and laid down with her head on it. She curled up on her side and closed her eyes.

Tyler carefully removed her shoes and set them on the floor before taking a seat opposite her. He took his shoes off as well and propped his feet up on the table like they had done the last time they were there. As he took in her sleeping form, his thoughts kept going to that moment when she'd looked up at him earlier and he'd seen her eyes.

It wouldn't be bothering him so much if he hadn't asked her specifically about the difference in her appearance from Adrianne and Alex. It had nothing to do with her looking like another side of the family and everything to do with her making the choice to color her hair and wear contacts to hide her blue eyes.

She had intentionally misled him.

Trust was paramount in a relationship. Honesty, too. It wasn't fair to either of them if she was keeping secrets that could affect the future of their relationship. Not that he cared about the color of her hair or eyes, but between that revelation and what Adrianne had said, he had to wonder what else she was keeping from him.

He watched her sleep, her hands curled up under her chin. She looked so vulnerable, not at all like the weapon-toting, self-defense pro he'd come to realize she was. It was like there was a whole other side to her that she hadn't even hinted at having.

With a sigh, Tyler dropped his head back against the cushions, his phone clutched in his hand. He felt like he needed to brace himself for things to go horribly wrong. But even as the thought entered his head, Tyler gave himself a mental shake. Right then, there were more important things going on.

The situation with Melanie was confusing and potentially hurtful, but she was safe and alive. And so was he. Justin, on the other hand, was injured seriously enough to warrant immediate surgery. And Alana...who knew what was happening with her. If this was an escalation from previous attacks on BlackThorpe, she was definitely at risk.

For now, he needed to keep focused on that and deal with the situation with Melanie when the other things had been resolved.

20

MELANIE GROANED as she came awake. She straightened her legs and winced at the stiffness in her limbs. It felt like she'd slept a solid twelve hours without even moving. As the fog of sleep gradually left her brain, a few things registered.

She had no blanket. She wasn't in her bed. And the sound of running water was making her need to use the bathroom.

Opening her eyes, she pushed herself to a sitting position. What was she doing in the pool room? That was definitely not where she remembered going to sleep the night before. She looked down at herself, staring when she saw sweatshirt and jeans instead of her pajamas.

What was going on? Spotting her purse on the table, Melanie grabbed it and searched for her phone. The screen was blank. No calls. No texts. And the clock said it was 11:18.

Gripping her phone in one hand and her purse in the other, Melanie got to her feet and left the room. She heard noise in the kitchen and headed in that direction hoping to get some answers. Things were coming back to her, but she really hoped that it was all a bad dream. It had to be.

She found Alex standing with his hands braced on the counter, staring at the coffee maker. Sunlight was coming through the window so she knew it had to be morning and not night and if that was the case, they should have both been in church.

"Alex?"

Her brother looked over his shoulder at her before straightening. One look at his face told her that the memories were real, not her imagination or a dream.

"Justin?"

Alex pushed away from the counter and came to where she stood. He pulled her into a tight hug, causing her anxiety to spike. "He's going to be okay. They were able to remove the bullets and stop the internal bleeding. He's going to be in the hospital for a few days, though."

Melanie pushed back so she could see his face. "Alana?"

With a sigh, Alex released her and returned to the coffee pot. "We have no word on her yet. The police have been gathering what evidence they can, but there is no sign of her or her abductor."

She moved to the counter and laid her purse and phone on it. "Is this connected to the other attacks on BlackThorpe?"

Alex shrugged. "We can't discount that theory."

Melanie gripped the edge of the counter as some of the feelings from the previous night because to rise within her again. She took a moment to draw a couple of deep breaths in. Last night, the combination of her tiredness and the sleeping pills she'd taken along with the phone call from Jenni earlier in the day had left her defenseless against the news about Justin and Alana. Those fears were still there, but she was trying her best to keep them under control.

"Tyler brought you home last night and stayed with you until Adrianne and I got back."

Melanie's eyes slid shut briefly. This morning, that concerned her most of all. He'd taken care of her, but she'd heard and seen enough to know that he was bothered by the things he'd discovered about her the night before. "Why did you call him?"

Alex leaned a hip against the counter and crossed his arms. "When we got to the hospital and I saw the state you were in, I knew you needed him. Of course, I didn't realize you hadn't told him about your hair and eyes. You've been friends for so long I just assumed he knew." He paused, his brows drawing together. "Why haven't you told him? I mean, if you're in a relationship that's heading towards something serious, he was going to find out eventually. When were you planning to tell him?"

Melanie lifted her thumb and bit her nail, anxiety gnawing at her gut. "Soon. I guess. I don't know. I just didn't want to talk about that or my past."

"Well, I think you're going to need to do some repairing of your relationship with him. He needs to know everything."

Everything? She couldn't help but wince a bit at that. What if it changed how he felt about her? If he was upset because he realized she colored her hair and wore colored contacts, she could only imagine what he'd think when she revealed the rest.

"I'm going to go to my room," Melanie said as she picked up her purse and phone. "Let me know if anything develops with Justin and Alana, please."

Alex stared at her for a moment before nodding. "Talk to him, Melanie. He deserves to know the truth."

"I will." Melanie walked up the stairs to her room, her heart heavy. So many emotions were pulling at her, demanding her attention, but all she wanted to do was pull the covers over her head and go back to sleep.

Once in her room, she pulled off the clothes she'd slept in and grabbed her workout clothes. Sleep wouldn't be her escape because she'd slept off the pills, and now her mind would just whirl with everything going on. She might as well benefit from her restlessness.

As she reached for the button to turn on the treadmill, Melanie froze. Why was she doing this anymore? Her very reason for the exercise, food, and weapons training had been proven all for naught. Justin was stronger than she was and even more experienced with weapons and self-defense, yet he lay wounded in a hospital bed. He'd been unable to protect himself or Alana.

She grasped the handles of the treadmill as once again a trembling overtook her. It felt like she'd been cut adrift. The very foundation on which she'd built her life since that horrible time fourteen years ago had been shattered. As panic crept in, she suddenly had a clear understanding of why Jenni felt the way she did. She reached up and gripped handfuls of her hair. That was all she had left of her protection.

Her hair and her eyes. They would have to protect her now that everything else was gone. She couldn't let go of that. What if Tyler wanted her to? What if he didn't understand? What if he would only continue their relationship if she went back to her normal appearance?

She couldn't rely on him to keep her safe. He wasn't with her every hour of every day. She could only rely on *herself*. So she would have to let Tyler go if he insisted on her giving up the last way she was able to protect herself.

The thought made her already aching heart fragment into a million pieces. She sank down, her knees pressing against the end of the treadmill, and let the tears come. Tears for Justin. For Alana. For Tyler and what she'd lose because of her past. It was that last thought that pushed her over from just tears into wracking sobs.

Tyler ran a hand through his hair and sighed. Three days. It had been three days since he'd last seen Melanie. Every time he'd picked up his phone to call or text her, he'd been at a loss for words. And apparently she felt the same way as there had been nothing from her either.

It felt wrong to be so torn up about that when things with Justin and Alana were still so bad. Justin was out of control in the hospital. He'd torn stitches trying to get out of bed, insisting he needed to be part of the search for Alana. Even injured, the man was strong, and it had taken a nurse and two orderlies to get him back into bed and sedated so he couldn't do more damage to himself.

Rumor had it that the only people who could keep him calm in the hospital were Caden, his sister, and Melanie. He'd tried not to let that news hurt. He knew that Melanie was one to be there for her friends when they needed her—proof of that was his bout with that stomach bug. Still...it hurt.

The only good news—if one could call it that—was that they had a fairly good idea of who had Alana. On a whim, Tyler had suggested that Marcus run the name he'd come across for the phone number in Florida past Justin. If the attack was, in fact, associated with the previous ones on BlackThorpe, Tyler had thought Justin might recognize the name. And he had. They were now fairly convinced that the man who'd taken Alana was her ex-husband.

What remained a mystery was the connection between Craig Ellis and the mastermind behind the attacks, and Marcus's intense focus on it had reached an all-new level. He no longer apologized for phoning late at night. When he needed information or wanted an update, the man was demanding in a way he hadn't been before. Tyler's stress about that only added to what he was already feeling with regards to Melanie.

"You need to call her, Ty." The softly spoken words just twisted the knife in his gut.

Ryan sat on the other end of the couch, a serious look on his face. They'd just finished a pizza Ryan had picked up on his way home from another long day at work.

"I know. I will."

"The longer this goes on, the harder it will be to break the silence between the two of you."

Tyler leaned back on the couch and stared up at the ceiling. Ryan was absolutely right. But he just didn't want to hear the words from her. The ones that would kill off their relationship and make a return to a friendship impossible. Adrianne had said he was good for her sister, but he wasn't sure that Melanie felt the same way. Whatever she hadn't been able to trust him with was still there.

He lifted his head when he felt the couch shift as Ryan got to his feet.

"I'll keep praying for you guys," he said as he picked up their garbage.

Tyler nodded his thanks, words failing him. Once he was alone, he pulled out his phone and stared at it. Still no call. Still no message. Only the picture he used as his lock screen. The selfie he'd taken of the two of them at the last Timberwolves game they'd gone to. He'd had so much hope that night.

As the ache in his chest increased, Tyler sat forward, elbows on his thighs as he pressed his hands to his eyes. He wondered if Ryan had recognized what he was barely able to admit to himself. He loved Melanie. He supposed he'd been a little bit in love with her for a while now, but over the past month or so, it had gotten to the point where when he imagined his future, it had included her.

Now that future was all out of focus.

His head dropped forward. Ryan's words kept repeating in his head, and Tyler knew that for sure they'd have no future together if he wasn't willing to fight for it. He had wanted her to come to him to show she trusted him, but maybe she needed to know that he still cared.

He flipped his phone over and over in his hand. It was already almost eleven o'clock so maybe a text would be better than a call. Or maybe he should wait for just one more day in case she wasn't ready to talk to him yet.

The debate in his head continued as he got ready for bed, and finally, after crawling under the covers, he picked his phone up and tapped out a quick message and hit send before he could second-guess himself.

When her alarm went, Melanie reached to shut it off then rolled onto her back. In the past, she'd had no trouble getting out of bed when it was time. Most days she'd been eager to get her day underway. All of that had changed in the past few days. Now it took her far too long to prepare herself mentally to get up and face what the day held.

It was day four of this nightmare. It had been—and continued to be—devastating on so many levels. Her own emotions had already been so raw when Alex had asked her to spend more time with Justin. When she'd first agreed, she hadn't realized the sole-wrenching impact it would have on her.

Realistically, if she'd known how challenging it would be to deal with Justin's emotions on top of her own, she would have told Alex it wasn't a good idea. The strong, in-control man had wept in her arms when she'd gone to see him that first time. Out of sight of Caden and his sister, he'd unburdened himself on her. And when he voiced every fear and vulnerability that Melanie had been experiencing herself, it was all just magnified.

But beyond that, seeing his absolute anguish over Alana's abduction had just about done her in. If they weren't able to get Alana back safely, Melanie feared that Justin would live out the rest of his life just a shell of the man he'd become because of the love they'd shared.

And that always brought her back to Tyler. Already she was feeling the loss of his presence in her life, and it hurt so much more than she could ever have imagined. If this was what she was feeling and her relationship with Tyler was fairly new, she couldn't imagine what would happen if something happened to them later on down the road when their emotions were even more intertwined.

Pressing a hand to her heart, Melanie closed her eyes and let hot tears slip down her cheeks. *Please God, help them find Alana and bring her back to Justin safe and sound. Please give Justin peace through all of this. And help me to know what to do about Tyler. He deserves better than me, but I want Your will for us.*

She opened her eyes, blinking to clear away the moisture. Taking in several painful deep breaths, she began to prepare herself for what lay ahead. Fear continued to wrap its tendrils around her heart. No matter how much she prayed that God would take them away, they never left. It was all she could do to erect her temporary barriers before facing the world.

One more deep breath in and out.

Pushing up, Melanie swung her legs over the edge of the bed and sat up. Would this be the day that the nightmare ended? Or would it be just one more day to get through?

First up was a visit to Justin at the hospital. After that, she'd head out to the Wellness Center and try to get some work done. The whole atmosphere at all three BlackThorpe locations had taken on a somber tone. And Marcus was like a dark thundercloud moving ominously through the hallways of the company. Of course, his worry was compounded by the fact that Justin was his cousin.

With a sigh, Melanie grabbed her phone from the nightstand and checked to see how much time she'd wasted trying to mentally prepare herself.

Her heart skipped a couple of beats when she saw that she had a text.

Tyler Harris

I miss you.

A sob escaped before she could stop it. The band of tightness she hadn't even realized had encompassed her chest, snapped, and it was like she could breathe again. Bracing a hand on her leg, she bent forward and closed her eyes.

Thank you, God.

His text didn't automatically clear up their issues, but it did connect them again. She'd needed that to know that he hadn't completely written them off.

With trembling fingers, she tapped out a response. *I miss you too.*

She was tempted to sit and wait for a reply, but she still had to get ready for the day. At least her heart was a little lighter as she made her way into the bathroom. Maybe they would get more good news today.

There was no reply to her text, but she knew from what Alex had said that Marcus had been working Tyler hard. No doubt he was already at the office. As she walked out the door to head to the hospital, Melanie told herself that it may well be evening before Tyler would have a chance to get back to her. After all, the message he'd sent had come in after eleven the night before.

"How is he this morning?" Melanie asked the nurse at the station. Beth had given them permission to update her as they'd fallen into a bit of a ritual with spending time with him. Melanie came in the morning then once Beth had gotten Caden off to school and Dan's mother was there to watch her little girl, she came up for a few hours. Then Dan brought Caden up in the afternoon when he was done school. In the evening, Alex or some of the other guys from BlackThorpe would go to visit him.

The nurse's brows drew together. "He seems withdrawn more than usual."

Melanie hated to hear it but had figured it was only a matter of time. When she pushed open the door to his room, she saw that he was lying with his eyes closed. She wasn't going to assume he was asleep. She knew all about pretending sleep in order to avoid having to talk to people.

She moved to the side of the bed and sank down on the chair there. Reaching out to take his hand, she said, "Morning, Justin."

His chest rose and fell as he took a shuddering breath before opening his eyes. The heartbreak Melanie saw there had her tightening her grasp on his hand. She knew that today wasn't going to be a day for words. At least not from him.

When his eyes slid shut again, Melanie stared at her friend. The hard edges of his face seemed even more pronounced as he lay there. And when a tear trickled down his cheek and dropped onto the pillow, Melanie leaned forward and laid her hand on his cheek.

"Oh, Justin." Seeing this man's pain was heartbreaking. Then she remembered the day Tyler had seen her heartache and prayed for her. Could she do the same for Justin? Would he find the same peace she had? Did she even know how to pray in a situation like this?

Keeping one hand on his cheek and the other grasping one of his, Melanie bent her head. She prayed silently for a few minutes, but the feeling that he needed to hear her words rose inside her. Softly, she began to say the words aloud, feeling his fingers wrap around hers as she did.

She didn't think too much about the words that came out. If it came to her mind, she said it. Over the past few days, the words of Tyler and the pastor about bad things happening had replayed in her mind on an endless loop. Even Justin's words about seeking God's will had been part of the litany. When it came right down to it, their words were the ones that made sense and gave her any measure of peace in this horrible situation.

The only time doubts rose in her mind came when she allowed herself to think about the fact that she was no longer guaranteed protection from bad things happening to her in the way she thought she had been. Aside from that first day, Justin hadn't touched on that again. It was as if he'd processed it and figured out how to deal with it. She needed to know how he'd done that, but this was the time for his healing. Hers would come later.

"Thank you." Justin's gruff words at the end of her prayer had Melanie lifting her head to look at him.

Relief spread through her when she saw that some of the tension had eased from his face though his eyes still shone with his heartbreak. "Praying is kind of a new thing for me. I wasn't sure..."

"I hear ya." The corners of his mouth lifted and his gaze lost focus. "I felt the same way when I started to pray out loud. Alana always tells me that God knows the prayers of our hearts whether we're eloquent or stumbling over our words."

"I'm relieved to hear that because I think I'm still stumbling around," Melanie said as she sat back from him but left her hand resting on his.

"Want to tell me what's up with your eyes?" Justin asked.

Melanie looked down at the bed. She'd rehearsed what she'd say to people who'd ask when she'd decided this morning to leave her contacts out. But Justin was different. He was a friend. "Are you ready for a long story?"

Justin nodded. "I figured it might be. I could use the distraction, to be honest."

By the time Melanie made it to the Wellness Center just after eleven, her emotional state had shifted to a more positive place. Telling Justin her story had been freeing and now gave her the courage to share it with Tyler. And if things changed between them because of it, at least she'd know. Slowly, she was picking a path through the rubble that had been left behind when the foundation she'd built her life on had shattered.

"Good morning." Heather greeted her with a smile when she walked into the office. "How is Justin this morning? Any news on Alana?"

"Nothing on Alana," Melanie said. "But Justin seemed a bit better today."

"I can't imagine what he must be going through," Heather said. "The not knowing has to be the hardest."

Melanie remembered her parents saying the same thing about the time she'd been gone. "All we can do is pray that she'll be released soon."

Heather nodded. "And you're doing okay?"

Melanie gave her a small smile. "I'll be fine. Compared to what Justin is going through…it's put things in perspective for me."

"Well, you can relax for a bit. You don't have any appointments until one."

She chuckled at that. "Relax? I still have plenty of other stuff that I need to catch up on. And on that note, I'd better get to it."

Once she was seated at her desk, Melanie took a moment to draw in a deep breath and let it out. She needed to shift her focus from Justin to her work at the Center.

She'd only been working about twenty minutes when Heather appeared in the doorway, a worried look on her face. "Uh…just got a call saying there's something happening down in the garden. They thought you'd want to check it out."

Melanie propped her chin on her hand. "What's going on?"

"No details. They just said you'd probably need to deal with it."

"Okay." Never an end to problems these days. Melanie pushed back from her desk and grabbed her phone. She quickly looked at the display to see if she'd missed anything, but the screen was as blank as it had been the last time she checked. Another distraction might be good.

When she got downstairs, she saw Molly standing at the entrance to the garden. The older woman gave her a small smile when she saw her. "Sorry to interrupt your work, but it seemed important you deal with this situation."

"That's alright, Molly. Where is the problem? And *what* is the problem? Heather didn't say."

"They're in the back corner by the falls. Not sure what the problem is, just had one of the residents come tell me that there was someone back there that was refusing to talk to anyone but you."

Melanie nodded. Though she didn't interact with each of the residents on a personal level during their stay, she did meet them all when they arrived at the Center and sometimes she went on to spend time with them if they requested it. Usually, that meant they showed up at her office door, but it wasn't unheard of for her to go to them if needed.

Hoping she was in the right frame of mind to deal with the situation, she said a quick prayer for wisdom as she made her way to one of the more secluded parts of the garden. It was somewhat surprising how quickly praying had become her response when facing something she wasn't sure how to handle.

She followed the rounded path that led to the back corner, the serenity of the setting calming the edges of her frazzled nerves. When she rounded the last corner, her steps slowed as she took in the scene before her.

A small round table set for two.

Two chairs.

And Tyler standing behind it all.

21

WHEN MELANIE CAME into view, Tyler held his breath, waiting to see her reaction. She looked so good. As usual, she wore one of her pantsuits, but it was her face that had his attention. He wanted to go to her and take her into his arms, but he waited.

"Tyler?" She moved the last few feet until she stood on the other side of the table from him.

He noticed immediately that she wasn't wearing her brown contacts. Her blue eyes met his, and he saw all kinds of emotion in them. "I thought we needed to talk."

She glanced at the table then over her shoulder. "You had some help with this."

"I did. Quite a few people helped make this happen. Heather. Molly. Ryan. Your brother."

"Alex?"

"Yes. I asked him if it would be okay if we each took a little time off today. He was all for it." Tyler moved to stand behind one of the chairs. "Would you like to sit down?"

Melanie nodded and stepped toward the chair he held for her. She hesitated for a moment and more than anything, Tyler wanted to touch her. *Not yet.* He caught a whiff of her perfume as she sank into the chair in front of him.

He quickly rounded the table and took the other seat. "Heather helped me get some food from the deli, so I hope you'll like it."

A small smile played at the corners of Melanie's mouth. "To be honest, I think eating is about the last thing I can do right now."

Tyler nodded. "So can I just dive right in and ask about your eyes?"

Without hesitation, Melanie nodded. She appeared to take a deep breath as her gaze dropped briefly to the table. When she looked back up, he saw fear on her face and wanted to instantly reassure her, but he waited.

"You know the story I told you about Jenni?"

Tyler nodded, a sick feeling suddenly flooding his body. Even before she continued on, things began to fall into place like the pieces of a puzzle.

"That's my story too. I was one of the twelve." She swallowed hard and lifted a hand to touch her hair. "I color my hair and wear colored contacts so I'm no longer what they are looking for. It was just one of the ways I protect myself."

"Along with the weapons and the self-defense training," Tyler added.

"Yes." She sank back into the chair, her hands in her lap.

"Why didn't you ever tell me?"

"My thought at the time was that I didn't want my past impacting what I might have with you. You know the details of what happened to Jenni. That's what happened to me too. I just didn't want to...taint things with you." She gave a small shrug. "Of course, I was totally ignoring the fact that my past was already impacting every aspect of my life."

"You have to know that what happened to you wouldn't change how I thought of you. Of us." Tyler leaned forward, resting his elbows on the table. "When you were so upset that night at the hospital...can you explain that to me? Was it because Justin got hurt?"

Melanie tilted her head. "Do you think I have feelings for Justin?"

Though he hadn't wanted to, Tyler hesitated.

"I don't. Well, not in the same way I have feelings for you. Justin is a good friend, but that's all he is. Yes, I was upset about him being hurt and Alana being abducted. I was also extremely tired that night. I'd taken two sleeping pills to help me sleep, so my ability to cope was at an all-time low." She paused, her gaze dropping for a moment before meeting his again. "What really hit me hard was the realization that all the measures I'd put into place to protect myself were useless. If someone like Justin couldn't manage to protect himself let alone Alana, what hope did I have? Everything I'd built my life on was gone. I was scared."

As Tyler took in her words, understanding came too. The obsession he'd noticed and commented on to Ryan had been about this. About keeping her body in such good shape so she could protect herself. It was an obsession like he'd suspected, but he'd been way off base on the reason for it.

"I'm sorry," Tyler said, knowing the words weren't sufficient to express the remorse he felt for not having stepped up during the past four days.

Melanie's brows drew together. "For what? None of what happened to me was your fault."

Tyler stared at her, feeling his failure deep in his heart. "I should have been there for you. I should have stayed in contact to make sure you were okay." He took a deep breath. The effort he'd made for her today suddenly seemed like nothing. When he should have stepped up, he'd stepped back. He hoped with all his heart that this wasn't too little, too late. "I'm so sorry."

"It's been a rough couple of days. Being there for Justin has helped me to focus on something besides my own issues, but that can't go on forever." Melanie looked down at her hands and let out a sigh. "I'm going to need help. In the past, I went for counseling, but in the back of my mind was always the thought that no one but me knew that the only way to live my life was to learn how to keep myself safe."

Tyler could see the confusion on her face as he searched for the right words to say. "How are you feeling right now?"

"A little lost." She crossed her arms, hugging herself. "I'm trying to trust God. To believe in His will, but it's hard. I don't want to believe that what happened was His will for me. That makes it really hard for me to trust Him. I don't know what to do."

"It is hard to trust God's will when bad things happen. I struggled with that too." Tyler ran a hand through his hair, praying for the right words. "At first, it was a little easier to accept given that I could have ended up even more seriously injured or dead in the accident, but then when Kelly left me, that made me question everything again."

"How did you work it out?"

"Every day I wake up realizing that all of that has brought me to this point in my life and made me who I am today." Tyler paused. "And more recently I've come to realize that if even just one of those things hadn't happened, I would never have ended up here. With you. Hoping you'll give me a second chance. I would go through it all over again just to know that it would bring you into my life. Into my heart."

Melanie's lips parted as her beautiful blue eyes sparkled with moisture. She lifted a hand and pressed her fingertips to her lips. "Do you really mean that?"

Tyler got to his feet and came around to Melanie's chair. He held out his hand and waited for her to take it. When she did, he drew her to her feet then led the way from the table to a small sitting area tucked in amongst the greenery and not far from the waterfall.

Once they were seated, Tyler took both her hands in his and looked into her eyes. "Yes, I really mean it. Will you give me another chance? I know I don't deserve it, but I want the chance to show you that I'll be beside you through whatever is to come. Good or bad."

Melanie stared at him, her gaze serious. It wasn't quite the reaction he'd been hoping for. A sick feeling slowly seeped into Tyler's gut. She wasn't going to give him that chance, and he had no one but himself to blame.

Her brows drew together. "I think maybe I need a little time."

Tyler straightened but kept her hands in his. She hadn't pulled away. She hadn't outright said no. Yet.

"If you need time, I'm willing to wait." The words just about choked Tyler, but he knew they were what she needed to hear.

"I'm sorry, Tyler." Her gaze dropped as her grip tightened on his hands. "You went to all this trouble..."

"Don't apologize. You have nothing to be sorry for." Tyler paused and waited until she lifted her gaze to his again. "You do what you need to. Just know that I'm there for you."

She nodded, and Tyler saw her eyes flood with moisture. "I'm sorry."

Pulling her hands from his, Melanie got up and walked away from him, taking his heart with her.

Melanie willed herself to keep all emotion from her face as she made her way back to her office. Voices were clamoring in her head to be heard but right then, all she wanted was to hide away.

She walked into her office and, without looking at Heather, said, "I'm not to be disturbed."

With shaking hands, she closed the door and locked it before going to her chair and sinking down into it. She bent her head, gripping handfuls of her hair. What had she been thinking? Tyler had apologized and asked for a second chance. Why hadn't her response been *yes*? Why was she sitting here alone in her office feeling like her chest was held in an ever-tightening grip?

Her heart was aching with what she'd just done. Had this been her last chance at love? Tyler had said he'd wait, but would he? Would he really wait for an emotionally screwed up, scared-of-the-world woman?

He will wait. The soft, calm voice broke through the emotional clamor in her head. *He said he'd wait. Trust him.*

So now she was supposed to trust Tyler *and* God? It felt like too much. After years of relying on herself, the idea of trusting others with her emotions—her life—was overwhelming. But she'd told Tyler she was going to get help, so she would.

Though they had good counselors at the Center, Melanie knew she needed someone not as involved in her life to help her. Taking a deep breath, she turned to her computer and typed a name into her search bar.

The next morning, Melanie turned off her alarm and pushed to a sitting position. Today was going to be different. Justin had gone home the previous afternoon so she wasn't going to the hospital like she had been other mornings. Instead, she had an appointment at nine o'clock with a psychiatrist.

A tremor of unease tightened her gut, but she ignored it. If she wanted to live a full life, she needed to do this. If she wanted to have a life with Tyler in it, she needed to do this. If she wanted to be free of the fear that had dictated so much of her life for the past fourteen years, she had to do this. She *had* to do this.

She swung her feet over the edge of the bed and picked up her phone. Out of habit, she checked the display and froze when she saw two text messages waiting for her.

"Be strong and of good courage, do not fear nor be afraid of them; for the Lord your God, He is the One who goes with you. He will not leave you nor forsake you." Deut. 31:6

Praying for you.

Tyler. Warmth spread through her as she got to her feet. He said he'd be with her, and apparently this was his way of doing that since she'd shut down any other option.

She needed to respond, but she wasn't sure what to say so finally settled on a simple *Thank you.*

He didn't reply, but the next morning when she got up, two more texts waited for her.

"Have I not commanded you? Be strong and of good courage; do not be afraid, nor be dismayed, for the Lord your God is with you wherever you go." Josh. 1:9

Praying for you.

After sending back another *Thank you*, Melanie made her way to the bathroom to prepare for her appointment with the psychiatrist. At least her nerves over the appointment weren't like they'd been the first time.

Given the ongoing situation with Justin and Alana, in addition to her own emotional state, she'd agreed to meet each day with the psychiatrist for the first week. It had been a difficult initial session. All her defensive mechanisms had kept trying to kick into place, the ones she'd used the first time she'd gone through counseling. Thankfully, the psychiatrist was also a Christian so was open to her discussing her struggles with trusting God as well as everything else.

The hardest part of each day was turning out to be going to work. Heather had never brought up what had happened with Tyler, but her subdued demeanor was difficult to ignore. Melanie wondered if the woman thought she was being selfish or stupid or both. Maybe one day she'd talk to her more about what was going on, but first she had to figure it out for herself.

Day three brought more texts from Tyler.

"Whenever I am afraid, I will trust in You. In God I have put my trust; I will not fear. What can flesh do to me?" Psalm 56:3-4

Praying for you.

Though she knew Tyler had sent the verses to encourage her, they'd had the added effect of sending her to her Bible. She'd found herself looking up the verses he'd sent her and reading through the chapters they'd come from. Inasmuch as those verses were no doubt meant to connect her to God, they were her lifeline to Tyler as well.

"Yea, though I walk through the valley of the shadow of death, I will fear no evil; For You are with me; Your rod and Your staff, they comfort me." Psalm 23: 4
Praying for you.

"Peace I leave with you, My peace I give to you; not as the world gives do I give to you. Let not your heart be troubled, neither let it be afraid."
Praying for you.

Melanie settled onto the cushions of her favorite spot and closed her eyes. The sounds of the nearby waterfall soothed her. It had been a long couple of weeks.

"Care to share your space?"

She cracked her eyes open enough to see her sister slump onto the seat opposite her. Adrianne sprawled back, her exhaustion evident in her long sigh.

"How're the plans?"

Adrianne rubbed her face with her hands. "Plans for the banquet are fine. Trying to incorporate the crazy security Marcus wants is another thing altogether."

No one blamed him, especially since the situation with Justin and Alana was *still* ongoing. No word from the kidnapper. No sighting of Alana or the man suspected of kidnapping her. Marcus was treating this as if it was tied to all the other attacks. But when push came to shove, it really didn't matter what the connections might be when Alana was still missing.

If Justin had been a silent, imposing figure before falling in love, he was even more so now as he waited for news on

Alana. Melanie tried to touch base with him each day, but it was hard to know what to say anymore. He was living his own personal hell all the while wondering what sort of situation Alana was in. Next to his concern for Alana was his concern for Caden. Than had been spending time with the two of them to help with communication since Justin's sign language was still not fluent enough to help Caden through this difficult time.

"Are you going with Tyler?" Adrianne asked.

Melanie closed her eyes and curled onto her side. "No, but I guess I'll be seeing him there."

The verses had continued to show up each day, but aside from that, they'd had no communication. Countless times she'd questioned why she'd felt the need for space. She *missed* him. Not just their budding relationship, but their friendship. But there was no denying that being able to focus on the therapy without having to worry about recapping it to Tyler had been good. She'd tell him about it one day. Hopefully soon because she was ready to explore life with him.

One of the things she'd discovered through therapy was that in letting go of the tight focus on keeping herself primed for a fight she could fully enjoy more areas of her life. No longer did she exercise to make sure she could take on a bad guy. She did it because she enjoyed it. And if she didn't feel like doing it one or two nights, she didn't. In the past, skipping those parts of her routine would have had her panicking about losing her edge.

And food... She didn't feel the absolute need to restrict herself from eating the foods which were a little less healthy anymore. There was no way she'd ever completely abandon the healthy eating habits she'd developed over the years, but there wouldn't be the focus on it that there had once been. The next time she went with Tyler to a Timberwolves' game she hoped to get him to take her to that restaurant where they'd gone with Ryan and Gabe. And she was going to order the chicken pot pie without a thought to how healthy or unhealthy it was. Then, at the game afterward, she'd share an order of nachos with him.

The thought of going out with Tyler like that made her smile. She hoped they'd get back to that point sooner rather than later. Maybe the night of the banquet would be a good place to start that journey back.

Melanie reached up to touch her hair, tugging a bit on the strand right by her ear. It had been just one more step in the long process to finding her way to the life she wanted. The life that wasn't bound up by fear but was defined by love and trust. Oh, she still had a ways to go, but the hardest step—the first one—was now behind her.

Her gaze swept the large room from her vantage point on the second-floor balcony. They'd had to change venues in order to accommodate Marcus's security measures and they'd been lucky to be able to get such a beautiful place at short notice. Small white lights were draped or hung from every available surface. The perimeter of the room was filled with large round tables that would soon hold the guests of the evening while they ate the delicious meal Adrianne had planned for them.

The Center of the room was slowly filling with people mingling, drinks in their hands. But the person she wanted to see above all others was still not there. Had he changed his mind about coming since they hadn't been in contact?

"I will be so glad when this night is over."

Melanie glanced over to see Adrianne join her at the railing. Her sister looked stunning in an emerald colored evening gown. The jeweled halter-style neckline left her shoulders bare. She'd chosen to wear her hair up which accented the long drop earrings she wore. But even the flawlessly applied makeup could do nothing to hide her exhaustion and the worry that each member of BlackThorpe carried around with them daily now.

"You've done a great job as usual," Melanie assured her sister as she slipped an arm around her shoulders. "Even with everything Marcus threw at you, you made it work. Not sure anyone else could have done it like you did."

Adrianne didn't say anything, just kept flicking her gaze between the growing crowd below and the small tablet she held in her hand. Yeah, this banquet lacked the ease of ones in the past, but as long as it ended without anything going wrong, they'd all breathe a sigh of relief.

Spotting the arrival of their parents, Melanie decided she'd go down and keep them distracted until Tyler showed up.

"Melanie, darling," her mother said with a smile as she drew her close for a kiss. "You look absolutely divine. I'm so happy to see you back with your original hair color. And your eyes. So beautiful."

"Thanks, Mom." Melanie turned and lifted a hand toward the room. "Isn't it just gorgeous? Adrianne has outdone herself this year."

"Yes. She's done a wonderful job," her father said, pride evident in his voice. "That's our Adrianne."

"It is very elegant and the lights are lovely," her mother added. "It's spectacular."

Melanie sighed. Why her mother found it easier to dish out compliments when Adrianne *wasn't* around made no sense to her. Before she could comment, her mother spotted friends of theirs, and the next thing Melanie knew, she was standing there watching her parents walk away.

Once again, she looked across the room, spotting the tall figures of Alex and Marcus as they stood together talking with a group of people. She wondered how Marcus tolerated events like this since he was never one to really socialize— even with people he knew. A smile curved her lips as she looked toward the entrance and recognized Hank and Shauna as they stepped into the room.

Even from this distance, Melanie could see the delight on Shauna's face as she took in the décor of the ballroom. Unable to keep from smiling herself, Melanie took a couple of steps in their direction, but then jerked to a stop when

Shauna turned to speak to the people behind them. The *couple* behind them.

Tyler stood there, a statuesque brunette at his side, her hand looped through his arm as they talked with Shauna and Hank. Melanie remained frozen in place, trying to get her brain to kick into gear. The noise in the room faded away under the sound of her blood pulsing through her head. Then confusion settled in.

He'd told her he'd wait for her. Hadn't he? It had been the one thing she'd clung to as she'd gone through the difficult task of staring down her past. Had it all been a lie? She lifted a hand to touch her hair. All the certainty she'd had earlier rushed out, and all she wanted to do was turn around and find an exit and leave.

But...she was sure he *had* said he'd wait for her. There had been a verse from him that morning just as there had been every day since she'd last seen him. She took a deep breath and let it out. This was about trust. Could she trust his word and believe that regardless of how things looked at that moment, he really was still waiting for her?

Melanie turned away for a moment. She needed to calm down and having them in her line of sight was *not* helping. *Trust.* It was what she struggled with the most, but it was also what she wanted the most. Her heart and mind were in agreement with the desire to trust Tyler. There could be no love without trust, so she would choose to trust him because she loved him.

Turning back around, Melanie had to search for where they'd gone. As the time neared for the start of the evening, the crowd continued to grow, making it more difficult to find people. It took a couple of minutes, but finally she spotted them talking with Ryan.

She took a deep breath and began to move through the crowd to reach them. Tyler had his back to her as he stood next to the woman he'd accompanied. Ryan was the first one to spot her. His mouth dropped slightly as his eyes widened then a smile spread across his face.

Tyler glanced over his shoulder at her before looking back at Ryan but then he turned again, this time with his whole body. Melanie stood still as his eyes swept her from head to toe before returning to meet her gaze. She took the time to look at him as well. He wore his black tuxedo like it had been made for him. His curls looked like he'd had them trimmed again, but they still hung in loose disarray around his face in the way she loved.

"You look..." Tyler paused as he took a step closer and reached out to take her hand. "You look breathtaking. I mean, you were always beautiful...just now, knowing what this represents...breathtaking."

"Thank you." The emotion that rushed through Melanie threatened to spill over. Her fingers tightened on his. "For everything."

Tyler moved closer and Melanie had to tip her head back to meet his gaze.

"I would do anything for you, sweetheart. Anything." He reached up and touched her cheek. "Your happiness is my happiness."

"My happiness includes you in my life," Melanie said with one hundred percent certainty.

"That's my happiness too." The smile that spread across Tyler's face took her breath away. "I've missed you."

Even though they were in a crowd of people, it was if her world had narrowed to just the two of them.

"I've missed you too." Melanie placed her hand on his sleeve, gripping his arm as she decided to take the ultimate step of trust. Trust that what motivated Tyler's promises to her was love. Trust that this was God's will for their lives to be intertwined. "I love you, Tyler."

For the first time ever, it seemed she'd rendered Tyler speechless. He stared down at her, shock on his face. Maybe this hadn't been the best place to tell him, but life was too short. What was going on with Justin and Alana had proved that. Why not share what was in her heart?

"I know it's not really the place—"

"It's perfect." Tyler lifted his hands to cup her face. "You just surprised me. I thought for sure I'd be the one to say it first."

"You don't have—" Tyler's thumb pressed against her lips kept her from continuing on.

"I love you too, Melanie." He moved his thumb as he leaned down to brush his lips to hers.

"Ah...my baby."

Melanie felt Tyler's smile against her lips. He pulled back but slid an arm around her waist. "We'll continue this later when we don't have my mother for an audience."

As he tucked her against his side, Melanie smiled at Shauna where she stood, her hands clasped beneath her chin, emotion filling her eyes.

"Well, handsome, it looks like you're going to be my date for the remainder of the evening." The voice had a refined British accent and reminded Melanie there was a stranger in their midst. "But first, Tyler darling, introduce us, please."

When she got her first look up close of the woman beside Tyler, Melanie realized that she was older than she'd originally thought.

"Eleanor, this is Melanie Thorpe, the woman I love," Tyler said as he glanced down at her with a smile. "Melanie, Eleanor is Hank's cousin. She came with them to attend this fundraiser."

Melanie took the hand the woman held out and returned the firm shake. "It's a pleasure to meet you."

"The pleasure is all mine," Eleanor said with a warm smile then she slid her hand through Ryan's arm and looked up at him. "And now, young man, entertain me."

Tyler spent the evening as close to Melanie as he could. After finally being with her again after way too many days apart, he wasn't ready to be separated from her even for a few minutes. He'd had a lot of time to consider how the counseling might change Melanie. He'd even had a few moments late at night when it was just him and his thoughts and he'd wondered if she might come to the realization that she could do much better than him.

But now she was here, different in many ways but in all the ways that mattered, she was the same woman who'd captured his heart. The dark blue dress looked perfect with her light blonde hair and blue eyes. It wasn't a poufy dress and fit her figure without being too tight. Whatever the design was, he thought it looked terrific on her. He couldn't wipe the smile off his face as the evening progressed. Melanie sat with them at their table until it was time for her to give her presentation to the people gathered there.

Knowing what all she'd been through over the course of the past few weeks, pride filled Tyler as she stood behind the podium and confidently spoke about the BlackThorpe Wellness Center's latest project. The PTSD service dogs. There was plenty of applause as a couple of the residents shared their stories and experiences with their dogs. Tyler hoped that it would result in even more financial support for the program.

He was grateful for the presence of programs like that for those that needed them. For whatever reason, he'd escaped the long-term struggle with PTSD. He'd had some moments right after the accident, but it had certainly not been on the scale that others had experienced. Tyler had no idea why he'd been spared that struggle, but he was grateful, and it made him even more determined to help others who hadn't been as fortunate.

The only thing casting a pall over the evening was the absence of Justin and Alana. Tyler knew there had been a discussion about canceling the banquet altogether, but in the end, Justin had been the one to encourage them to continue on with it.

As he watched Melanie make her way back to him once her part of the program was done, Tyler wondered what he would do if something like that ever happened to her. His heart clenched at the thought and he prayed he'd never have to find out.

Once back at the table, Melanie sat down in her chair next to his and looked up at him with a smile. "How did it sound?"

"Perfect." He slid his arm around her shoulders. "Having the dogs here with their owners was a great idea. Puts a face on the need and how well the program is working."

Melanie nodded. "That's what we were hoping for."

They sat close as the program continued and then after it was finished, Melanie took him and his family to meet Adrianne, Alex, and Marcus. Tyler didn't miss the looks the twin siblings shared with each other and then their little sister when they saw them holding hands.

"Melanie?"

Tyler looked over to see that a middle-aged couple had joined them. The woman's brows were drawn together as she looked at them and then at where Adrianne and Alex stood side by side. It took a moment, but he suddenly realized that these were Melanie's parents. And from the looks of things, they had no idea about the two of them.

"Hi, Mom. Dad." Her hand tightened its grasp on his. "I'd like you to meet my boyfriend, Tyler Harris." She looked up at him and smiled. "Tyler, these are my parents, Dennis and Pamela Thorpe."

Tyler held his hand out first to her mother then her father. Both shook his hand without hesitation though he could see the curiosity on both their faces. "It's a pleasure to meet you."

"So, darling," Pamela Thorpe began, her gaze going from him to her daughter. "How long has this been going on?"

Melanie gave a one-shouldered shrug. "A couple of months."

"A couple of..." Finely plucked brows drew together again.

Before she could say anything further, Tyler gestured toward his mom and Hank. "These are my parents, Shauna and Hank Wakeford."

As he watched greetings be exchanged, Tyler wondered if Melanie was going to get grief for not talking to them about their relationship sooner. The fact that they were standing there with *his* parents made it pretty clear that they had known about the relationship before the Thorpes did.

"I think I'm ready to call it a day," his mom said a short time later. "I'm still on London time so it's very late for me."

"Me, as well," Eleanor was quick to add.

They had rooms at the hotel where the banquet was. Since Eleanor had traveled with them this time, it had made sense to stay at a hotel instead of his place. Hank would have offered to get him a room as well, but they knew he preferred the comforts of home when they were close at hand.

"See you tomorrow, Momma," Tyler said as he bent to press a kiss to her cheek. "Sleep well."

"You, too, sweetheart. Love you." His mom gave Melanie a kiss as well before turning to the Thorpes. "It was wonderful to meet you. I hope we'll see you again soon."

Pamela's eyes widened briefly at that comment, and her gaze shot to Melanie before looking back at his mom. "That would be lovely."

Before Pamela could say anything more to Melanie, Alex drew his parents' attention to someone else he wanted them to meet. Somewhere in all the introductions, Adrianne had slipped away, and Ryan and Marcus headed off as well, leaving them alone.

"Well, that was fun," Melanie said with a grin, her blue eyes—he still had to get used to them—sparkling.

"I gather you still hadn't mentioned us to your parents," Tyler said as he slid an arm around her waist and began to weave them through the crowd to the exit.

"No," Melanie said with a sigh. "I don't mind them knowing. I was just trying to spare myself the focus of my mom's determination to marry us off."

As they left the ballroom, Tyler looked around then asked, "Is there a restaurant or bar in this place?"

Melanie nodded. "There's both on the main floor."

It wasn't long before they were seated in a booth—both on the same side—and lamenting the lack of comfortable clothing.

Tyler let out a long sigh of relief to finally be away from the crowds of people. He usually didn't mind them, but tonight, after everything that had happened, he just wanted to be alone with Melanie. Reaching out, he ran his fingers through the ends of her hair.

"Just so you know," he began as he rubbed the silky strands between his fingertips, "you're as beautiful to me this way as you were the other."

She blinked rapidly a couple of times. "Thanks."

"Did that worry you?" Tyler let his thumb brush across his cheek. "That my type was cute brunettes with brown eyes?"

He was a bit surprised when she hesitated, her gaze sliding away from his for a moment.

"Hey, what I feel for you goes way beyond your outward appearance. The things I love most about you are inside you." His fingers slipped under her chin, turning her to face him. "I know a lot has changed for you over the past couple of weeks, but here's something that hasn't—how very much I love you."

Melanie leaned forward and pressed a kiss to his lips then whispered, "Thank you for loving me. And thank you for helping me see that trust is not just possible but necessary for love to flourish. I love you, too."

EPILOGUE

"*Popular Questions*?" Melanie asked as she read the paper she'd pulled from the bowl. "What kind of category is that?"

Rena shrugged with a cheeky grin from where she was curled up next to Jeff on the couch. They were hosting the monthly gathering which Melanie was attending with Tyler for the seventh time. She'd quickly come to love his friends and claim them as her own. Even Betsy St. John.

Tonight, they'd had a barbeque to celebrate the beautiful spring day, but now they were gathered inside for some weird version of charades. Someone had made up the categories and then instead of guys versus girls like they did most the time, they'd paired them up guy and girl. If someone had a significant other, they were together and the others were paired up with whoever was left.

"Are you ready for this?" Melanie asked Tyler as he picked a paper from the bowl marked *Popular Questions* and then came to stand next to her. She took a moment to admire the way the man looked that night. White button down shirt. Faded blue jeans. His hair a tumble of curls that always made her itch to run her fingers through it. Thankfully, she was allowed to do that now. But what she liked most was the look in his eyes whenever his gaze met hers.

"I'm like a Boy Scout. Always ready," Tyler said with a grin as he looked down at the paper in his hand.

"I think that's always prepared, bro," Ryan remarked wryly.

Tyler waved his hand at him. "Same difference."

He turned to Melanie "Ready?" When she nodded, he held up four fingers.

"Four words."

Tyler nodded and held up his index finger.

"First word."

Another nod. He tugged his ear then pulled out a dollar from his pocket.

"Sounds like....dollar?"

He shook his head and held the dollar up with both hands.

"Money?"

Another shake.

"Bill?"

Nod.

"Sounds like bill." Melanie paused. "Dill? Jill? Kill? Mill? Nill? Pill?"

She was mentally flipping through the alphabet, getting frustrated as he kept shaking his head. "Sill? Till? Will?"

Vigorous nod.

"Will? The first word is will?"

Another nod and then he held up two fingers.

"Second word." She watched as he pointed to her. "Me?"

He shook his head and held up four fingers.

"Fourth word? What happened to the second word?" Melanie asked in confusion.

Again Tyler put up four fingers and then pointed to her.

"Okay. Fourth word is me?"

Tyler nodded and went back to two fingers, this time pointing to himself.

"Man?"

He shook his head, pointed to her and then to him.

Melanie stared at him for a moment then tapped her fingertips to her chest. "Me. You?"

Tyler smiled as he nodded.

"Will you..." Melanie paused. "Me?"

As the expression on Tyler's face turned from teasing to serious, shivers raced up and down her spine. She looked around, the expectant expressions on the faces of their friends did nothing to slow the pounding of her heart.

When she turned back to Tyler, he reached out and took her hand. Gripping it tightly, he slowly went down on one knee and dug in his pocket.

"Will you marry me?" Melanie whispered the question as Tyler looked up at her.

"Yes. Will you marry me?" His blue eyes showed his love for her as he waited for her answer.

Everything they'd been through in the months following the BlackThorpe fundraising banquet—the ups and downs, the good and the bad—all of it faded away in that moment. Tyler wanted to spend the rest of his life with her. And she knew without a shadow of doubt that there was no one else she wanted to be with.

"Yes." She blinked back tears. "Yes, I will."

Still holding her hand, Tyler pulled himself back up to stand in front of her. She knew that wasn't an easy move for him, but as soon as he was steady, she wrapped her arms around his neck and kissed him. "Always and forever...yes."

Tyler kissed her and then took her left hand. "I love you, sweetheart."

Melanie watched as he slid a beautiful diamond ring on her finger then lifted her hand to kiss it. He drew her into his arms again, holding her close. In that moment, Melanie knew that even though she hadn't completely embraced her past just yet, knowing that all of it had led to this point, she couldn't regret it.

As their friends gathered around them to offer congratulations, Melanie felt a sense of peace and rightness in being there with them for this important moment in her and Tyler's lives. Their support had been staunch once they'd heard Melanie's story.

Thank you, God, for bringing us here. For bringing me Tyler and helping me learn to love and trust.

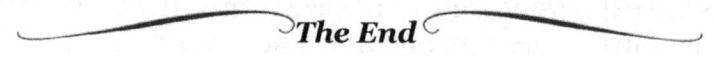

The End

OTHER TITLES BY

Kimberly Rae Jordan

Marrying Kate

Faith, Hope & Love

Home Is Where the Heart Is (*Home to Collingsworth: 1*)
Home Away From Home (*Home to Collingsworth: 2*)
Love Makes a House a Home (*Home to Collingsworth: 3*)
The Long Road Home (*Home to Collingsworth: 4*)
Her Heart, His Home (*Home to Collingsworth: 5*)
Coming Home (*Home to Collingsworth: 6*)

This Time With Love (*The McKinleys: 1*)
Forever My Love (*The McKinleys: 2*)
When There is Love (*The McKinleys: 3*)

For news on new releases and sales
sign up for Kimberly's newsletter

http://eepurl.com/WFhYr

Please visit Kimberly Rae Jordan on the web!
Website: www.kimberlyraejordan.com
Facebook: www.facebook.com/AuthorKimberlyRaeJordan
Twitter: twitter.com/KimberlyRJordan

Made in the USA
Las Vegas, NV
02 January 2022